DEFICIENT

MICHAEL SOLIS

DEFICIENT

bhc)
press™

Livonia, Michigan

DEFICIENT

Published by BHC Press

Library of Congress Control Number:
2022941268

ISBN: 978-1-64397-349-4 (Hardcover)
ISBN: 978-1-64397-350-0 (Softcover)
ISBN: 978-1-64397-351-7 (Ebook)

For information, write:
BHC Press
885 Penniman #5505
Plymouth, MI 48170

Visit the publisher:
www.bhcpress.com

For Tara

Accelerated Ability Status, Official Classifications, and Colloquial Names

COMMON ABILITIES

ABILITY STATUS	OFFICIAL CLASSIFICATION	COLLOQUIAL NAME
S	Enhanced Strength	Atlases
R	Rapid Movement	Racers
L	Levitation & Flight	Sky Gliders
Tp	Telepathy	Know-it-Alls
Tk	Telekinesis	Mind Movers
I	Invisibility	Unseens

RARE ABILITIES

ABILITY STATUS	OFFICIAL CLASSIFICATION	COLLOQUIAL NAME
M	Multi-accelerated	Legions
F	Freely Accelerated	Ferals

ANOMALIES

ABILITY STATUS	OFFICIAL CLASSIFICATION	COLLOQUIAL NAME
Class D	Deficiently Accelerated	Deficients

DEFICIENT

CHAPTER ONE
HYENAS AND COWARDS

L ife never goes the way you want it to when you're a Deficient. It's a lesson I learned long ago—seven years ago, to be exact.

Now, at fifteen, it's one I'm reminded of every morning on the way to the academy.

My forehead cools as I rest it against the smooth glass of the shuttle bus window. I don't bother paying attention to the hovering vehicles outside or the bright blue lights of the highway. Instead, I watch raindrops race to the bottom of the foggy window.

Some drops are bigger than others. They gobble up the smaller ones as they slide down, but the big ones pay the price for their size. After absorbing so many of the tiny droplets, they grow too large to sustain themselves. They succumb to gravity, falling from the window to their deaths on the illuminated highway below.

Splat!

My thoughts snap back to my surroundings, and my eyes dart to the biggest droplet of all—a gooey glob of saliva that's splashed near the upper corner on the inside of my window.

I grit my teeth. *Idiots.*

The fourth-year Atlases sitting across the aisle cackle away.

"You missed, moron!" one says.

"I won't next time," the second replies.

My skin prickles with goose bumps—a familiar sign of fight or flight. But fleeing isn't possible, and fighting won't help. The evolutionary theorists should have come up with a third option for a Deficient who's backed into a corner. With their enhanced strength, Atlases can do whatever they want with someone like me.

"Aren't you gonna stand up for yourself, defective loser?" the third one asks.

I fail to answer the question—a trick that usually buys me some time, though it tends to generate immediate resentment.

"Say something, defect!"

"He's so stupid he can't even talk," says the first. Ironic, since his brain is dimmer than a black hole.

Knowing I can only remain silent for so long, I let out a deep sigh before turning away from the window to stare at them.

"*Something*," I mutter.

Their eyebrows narrow, and their words transform into snarls. They remind me of a pack of rabid dogs.

"This Deficient fecker thinks he's smart."

The second Atlas inhales and releases another wad of phlegm that spurts out so fast I can't dodge it. It hits me hard on the cheek, forcing me to turn toward the window once again.

Splat! Splat! Splat! Splat!

I raise my arm to block the onslaught of spit. It ends after a few seconds. The Atlases laugh and give each other high fives.

I wipe at the warm, sticky moisture on my face with the sleeve of my academy jacket. The contrast between the gooey yellow mucous and black fabric makes my stomach churn.

I want to hurl every curse I know at the Atlases, but I bite my tongue. Provoking them was a stupid mistake. Acting on my emotions never ends well.

Two years until I'm out of Achewon. It feels like forever, but it will come eventually. Counting down the hours left in the day usually helps—a reminder that time is, in fact, passing—though it's a little early in the morning to start doing that.

The shuttle bus comes to a stop. The Atlases get up and laugh their way down the aisle. Quieter kids look away as they rush past my seat. None are willing to stand up in my defense, let alone look me in the eye. They scamper to the exit, panicking as if the shuttle bus has suddenly gone ablaze.

They're hyenas and cowards, all of them.

Once all the students have passed, I slide my backpack over my shoulder and make for the door. The shuttle bus driver looks out the window instead of rewarding me with a goodbye or wishing me a great day like he does the other students. I don't mind. I've had seven years to get used to not being acknowledged.

The shuttle bus lifts into the air and starts to accelerate before I can dismount. *Thanks, Mr. Shuttle Bus Driver.* I jump. My legs wobble when I touch the ground, but my landings seem to be getting better.

I take in the dampness of the November air before I see it—the place I hate more than any other on this planet.

Achewon Egalitarian Academy.

I shudder. Seven hours down. Only seventeen more to go.

CHAPTER TWO
BRACING FOR ARMAGEDDON

Achewon Egalitarian Academy is a massive white structure nestled next to the tranquil, silvery expanse of the Achewon Lake. The building looks like two snow-covered mountains that blend smoothly into the gray, stone walkway below. Its façade has a crosshatching of glass windows that glow golden in the early morning hour.

Above the entrance is the academy's glitzy motto. The illuminated letters sparkle as if they're made of crystal. *Opening doors and expanding horizons, regardless of ability.*

If only my brain could vomit. *How do I manage to spend six days a week here?*

The chattering of voices above pulls my attention to the hazy clouds. A group of gossiping Sky Gliders flies overhead and lands *en pointe* on the wet walkway. They carry on with their conversation as though defying gravity means absolutely nothing.

They make it look so easy. I'd give anything to fly or even hover. I think I'd enjoy hovering very much.

I'm forced off the walkway when a group of stampeding Atlases nearly tramples me beneath their black boots.

"Stupid arseholes," I mutter under my breath. They think they can do whatever they want with their enhanced strength.

An Atlas decouples from the group and steps in front of me. A chill courses through my veins when I realize who it is.

If all Atlases are arseholes, then Landon Waters is the arsiest of the lot. Once, back in primary school, he threw me across the courtyard using his newly acquired strength. My last memory before passing out was the green grass drawing closer to my face. I ended up with a concussion.

He's enjoyed tormenting me ever since.

"Did you just say something, defect reject?" Landon asks.

I scratch my head. "I don't think so, unless I was talking to myself again."

"Funny. Me and my friends heard you call us stupid arseholes."

My friends and I. Resisting the urge to correct him out loud is hard.

"That would be a death sentence, Landon. I know I'm a Deficient, but I'm not a complete idiot."

"Could have fooled me. I heard what I heard, defect. Are you calling me deaf now too?"

This isn't going where I want it to go, but I'm hopeful that big words might distract small minds.

"Have you ever heard of catachresis?" I ask.

Landon rolls his eyes. "What the feck does that have to do with this?"

"Everything, really. Catachresis is when people misuse words. It's something I avoid like the plague. Stupid arsehole is an example of catachresis. I mean, how can an arsehole be stupid? Or smart? It's just a hole with a very specific function."

Much to my surprise, Landon laughs, so I laugh too. This is great. We're both laughing. Maybe he won't kill me after all.

Silly Alejandro, I think as Landon yanks my collar and lifts me into the air. His face is stone-cold. He's not laughing anymore.

"You never learn your lesson, do you? I should have knocked your Deficient teeth out a long time ago."

My heart palpitates into hyperdrive. Not only is Landon an Atlas, but he's on the academy's security track, which means he's trained in all kinds of martial arts. If he wants to kill me, he probably knows a thousand ways to do it.

A sudden boom of thunder draws my attention upward. A tsunami of charcoal clouds floods the sky, consuming the gray haze. I've never seen the transition happen so quickly. A giant scratch of white lightning cracks across the black clouds, and the thunder roars yet again. The rain that follows is an onslaught, like we're beneath a waterfall.

"*Scheisse*," Landon says. He tosses me to the side, and I plummet to the ground with a painful thud.

I'm wet and cold. My face is pressed against the stone, and my lip is moist and tastes like copper. Splattering feet shuffle past me. No one stops to ask what's wrong or to help me up. It's not the first time I wish I could disappear like an Unseen.

"Alé!"

I smile into the ground when I hear my nickname. It's not a name I hear often. In fact, there's only one person at the academy who uses it.

I push myself onto my hands and knees to see Yalamba running toward me, her gray academy skirt swishing.

In one hand, Yalamba is holding a glowing umbrella that emits a generous halo of white light. It evaporates the raindrops before they reach her head, keeping her dry. In her other hand, she has her sketchbook.

"Alejandro Aragon!" Yalamba says as soon as she's at my side. She twitches her nose at me—a natural tic. "Don't tell me you let that piece of scheisse knock you down again."

"What else was I supposed to do, Yals?"

"Stand up for yourself. Fight back. Defend your rights."

I can't help but laugh as she guides me to my feet.

"Sure, fight back against Landon." I wipe the grit from my face. "Any other death wishes you want me to make while I'm at it?"

"He's a dim-witted Atlas. Your mind can dance circles around his."

"And he can crack my head open like a chicken egg whenever he wants. I'd prefer to keep my brain inside my skull, thank you very much."

Shielding me from the rain with her glowing umbrella, Yalamba interlocks her plump arm with mine as we walk to the academy's entrance.

In the light of the spotless lobby, I notice Yalamba's braids have changed to violet, matching the new color of her eyes. The day before her hair had been a shocking pink and her eyes their normal brown. The grin on her face is wide and mischievous. I can tell she's been up to something.

"You were the one who made that storm happen, weren't you?" I ask.

Yalamba winks a purple eye and opens her sketchbook. I see a drawing of Landon and me on the walkway. Rain pours from the sky, and a bolt of lightning flashes above our heads in the picture.

"It was a quick sketch, but it served its purpose."

It's hard to suppress my smile as I think about Yalamba's ability to draw objects and scenarios into existence. She's the only Feral at the academy with that kind of talent. To the other students, she's a freak, but to me, she's magical.

"You didn't have to do that," I say.

"Should I stand by as you get beaten into a bloody puddle? That's not going on my to-do list anytime soon."

I sigh. "It's not even first module, and I've already been spat on and nearly killed. It must be Monday."

"You've got to start standing up for yourself, Alé."

"And with what accelerated ability am I supposed to do that?" It's as though she's forgotten I'm a Deficient.

"You don't have to be accelerated to defend yourself. You have so many positive qualities that people would be lucky to have."

"Like…"

"Like kindness. Loyalty. Love."

"Kindness, loyalty, and love," I repeat. "Maybe next time I should attack Landon with lollipops and bunnies. Lots and lots of bunnies."

Yalamba rolls her eyes as we approach her locker. "You know, an Atlas-eating bunny would be kind of awesome. You might have inspired my next art project."

She swipes the white identity band on her wrist across the sensor, and the door pops open. She deposits her sketchbook and pulls out a large roll of paper she needs for her first module.

"So did you submit your application yet?"

Here she goes again. Yalamba has been pestering me for weeks about the upcoming assignation ceremony. At the end of the semester, the prefecture will formally determine what career paths we'll embark on postgraduation. The decision will influence our coursework in the second half of our third year and throughout our fourth and final year, not to mention our futures. We have an opportunity to submit an application for what we'd like to do, but the final decision is up to the prefecture.

I still haven't written a single word, and there are only three more weeks until the deadline.

"I've thought about it," I say, "but I decided, for the thousandth time, that there's no point."

"Ugh, Alé! For a smart person, you can be extremely dense."

"Exactly! A dense Deficient. That is why the prefecture will never take my request seriously."

"Why leave it totally up to chance though? You don't need an ability for every job. There's still a possibility the prefecture might listen."

"*Might* is the key word. Like a 0.0000001 percent probability."

"That's still better than nothing. You're good with words, and you like to do the right thing. People like you should be working for the Truth and Justice Division. You might actually make a difference in this stupid world."

"The Truth and Justice Division needs mind readers, not Deficients."

"You need to start believing in your own damn mind, because no one else is gonna do it for you."

The academy bell beeps before I can offer a response.

"Two minutes to first module," a robotic voice says.

"Work on your application, Alé. If not for you, then for me. You owe me one for today."

Yalamba blows me a kiss and heads off to her next class. She's always been a master of getting the last word.

With her painting and drawing skills, Yalamba knows she's destined for something artsy. Even if I do apply, the prefecture will probably still condemn me to a lifetime of something dull and monotonous like ore extraction. Or worse, waste management. I'd be uber-qualified for a career in fecal sludge after all the scheisse I've put up with at the academy.

But maybe Yalamba is right. A legal profession with the Truth and Justice Division would be way better than feces. It would also be a one-way ticket out of Achewon. I'd get a fresh start in the capital. I might get to be someone else. Someone new.

I smack my forehead at my stupidity. *There you go again, Alé, getting your hopes up.* It's as though I've forgotten the simple truth that has proven itself to me, time and time again.

Hope is a veil. A thin, gossamer veil that barely covers what's behind it.

Bleak and utter disappointment.

❋ ❋ ❋

When lunchtime comes around, Yalamba and I sit by ourselves while the other third years eat in larger groups, self-segregated according to ability. Yalamba and I are fine eating alone. We've never needed anyone else.

I don't see Yalamba again until our last module, Physical Education. It is by far the worst one of all, and today is no exception. Typically, we have group martial arts or calisthenics training, but as luck would have it, today is the first day of the Achewon Dodgeball Tournament. It's an annual competition all students have to take part in, even if it's the last thing some of us want to do.

If there's anything worse than being the only Deficient at an academy of accelerated students, it's being the only Deficient in a game of dodgeball. I trudge to the back of the court and try tightening the belt of my PE jumpsuit around my scrawny waist. The black fabric is so loose it feels like I'm wearing a parachute. Is it possible to look any more ridiculous?

I'm surrounded by thousands of cheering fans. The audience is always here to root, howl, and boo whenever we play. That's because they aren't fans at all—just virtual projections programmed to respond to our performance.

A red laser shines across the center of the court, splitting it in half. The centerline automatically triggers an alarm if someone crosses over it. More lasers zap above the centerline every meter or so until they reach the ceiling.

I remain in the back while my teammates line up near the blue quarter line that cuts each side of the court in half. I smile at Yalamba, who has been assigned to the opposing team. She places her hands on her curvy hips and mouths, "I'm so over this." My eyes shift to the slots along the centerline. They open and six rubber balls rise from the floor. Their white surfaces are dotted with tiny colored lights, which are touch, motion, and heat sensors.

The referee raises her arm, and the lights at the four corners of the court shine bright red, yellow, and finally, green. A loud beep causes the crowd to cheer.

Both teams' Racers are off, zipping from the quarter lines. Ours swats two balls to our side, but she's hit before she grabs the third. The crowd goes wild in response, the fans chanting their praises in unison.

The arrogant Landon Waters is the opposing team's captain. He throws first and throws hard. Unfortunately for our Know-it-All, a boy named Simon who sits in a hoverchair, the ball flies right into his chest. The poor guy's glasses fly from his face the moment he's hit.

Landon bares his teeth at me like an angry dog, which I take to mean that I'm next. He jerks to the side in time to dodge a ball from Jeong, an Atlas and our team captain, and I'm thankful for the distraction. The audience gasps as the ball registers Landon's body heat, missing him by a hair's breadth.

Jeong orchestrates a combined throw with our Mind Mover and one of our Unseens. The Unseen throws a ball high, and our Mind Mover redirects it with his thoughts.

It's a classic and predictable move, yet it always seems to trick someone. This time, it lures the other team's Sky Glider, a heavyset boy who can fly faster than one might expect. He catches the first ball, but he isn't prepared for the one Jeong throws at him with immense speed. The hit to the boy's stomach is so powerful it flings him backward into the court's hard boundary.

The Sky Glider slides to the ground, and I hear the definitive crunch of breaking bone. He clutches at his leg and screams in agony.

Nurses rush onto the court within seconds. One of them is a Mind Mover, and before long the boy's hefty body hovers across the court and through the exit. The game resumes. Not even injuries can end dodgeball.

I take a moment to assess our losses. With three people down on our team and all six balls on Landon's side, things aren't looking good. My teammates back up to where I stand, bracing for Armageddon. Landon calls for a charge. It's no surprise he aims for me first. I manage to duck in time, but my legs turn to water when I hear the ball slam into the boundary with a resounding boom.

We now have five people left and four balls on our side. Jeong calls for a huddle. He instructs my teammates to throw the balls at Landon. I'm the only one who doesn't have to do anything, which is perfectly fine by me.

Landon is ready to dodge Jeong's throw when our Mind Mover's telekinetically charged ball comes at him. Landon spins in a quick circle and catches the ball. He flashes his perfect white smile, and the crowd goes crazy. Distracted by his inflated ego, Landon isn't paying attention when our Sky Glider throws her ball at him from above.

I bite my lip in anticipation. *Hit him. Hit him. Hit him.*

The dodgeball stops in midair, and my spirit deflates. I hear the audience cheer and realize an Unseen has made the catch.

Unfazed, Landon chucks his ball at Mixie, our Feral. To no one's surprise, the ball sails straight through her body. The crowd doesn't react at all, which means the ball doesn't register anything—motion, temperature, or touch—as it passes through her. I nearly drool at the thought of her rare fading ability.

Mixie readjusts the red dreadlocks that have fallen over her face and takes off after the ball. Once she has it, she hurls the ball with all her might. It's about to hit the other team's Know-it-All, but it curves at the last minute and falls into the embrace of their Mind Mover.

That leaves Jeong and me on our side with seven players and all six balls on Landon's.

"You're done for, Jeong," Landon says.

Jeong turns around and throws me a look of scorn. I respond with an awkward wave. My irritable captain grunts like a warthog before facing Landon.

"We were at a disadvantage from the start," Jeong says. "You don't have the Deficient on your team."

Something inside me sinks, but I stop it before it can go all the way down. Clenching my fists, I recall what Yalamba told me this morning. *Stand up for yourself. Fight back. Defend your rights.*

"Sorry, Jeong," I say, "but when did staying in the game become a bad thing?"

"You're completely useless!" Jeong exclaims.

"And your life centers on the equally useless sport of dodgeball. How stimulating."

"You'll pay for that, reject." I know I will. Atlases are vengeful pricks. Each and every one of them.

"Touch him and you lose a limb."

I'm shocked to see Yalamba standing at the centerline, big, bold, and defiant with her arms crossed.

"What are you gonna do, Yalamba?" Jeong asks. "Draw one of your little pictures?"

Yalamba's nose twitches, and she gives Jeong the fiercest glare I've ever seen.

"I might. How about one of a lioness gouging out your insides?"

Jeong hesitates and takes a step back. I wonder if he's afraid. He should be.

"You started with ten people to our team's nine," Yalamba continues. "The fact that you only have two left isn't Alé's fault. It's yours."

Jeong growls. "I didn't want him on my team to begin with."

"That doesn't matter." Yalamba's face wrinkles with anger. "Your team is about to lose 'cause you failed as captain. You're a pathetic leader."

"You're all talk, Yalamba. Why don't you try throwing a ball for once?"

"Maybe I will after you grow a pair of your own."

The referee yells that we're ten seconds away from a time violation. It's a significant threat, since such a violation is equivalent to a failing performance grade.

Landon's team doesn't waste any time, and his throwers charge. Jeong catches one ball and blocks a second. However, he isn't fast enough for Landon's ball when it takes out his shin, causing him to fall flat on his face.

The audience lets out an explosion of sound. I have the urge to celebrate as well, except this means I'm the last one left on my team.

Landon smirks at me in his glib, self-contented way. The silver arrowhead dangling from his ear glimmers from across the court.

"Well, look who's left. Something tells me it's time for defect reject target practice."

Something tells me it's time for your pimply face to get pureed by a food processor.

"Aren't you gonna throw one of those itty-bitty balls at me?" Landon asks. "You've got all six of them."

Landon is right. All the dodgeballs are on my side, waiting to be thrown. They've been motionless for a while now. Judging by the grumbles, the crowd is getting antsy about it.

"The clock is ticking!" the referee yells, her voice cracking. "Don't forget you're being evaluated on your performance!"

As if I didn't know that. Yet I remain still, contemplating why being the last surviving member of my team isn't considered "performance." The sport is called dodgeball. I dodged balls. My performance should be lauded.

Instead, the audience's groans have transformed into loud boos.

"That means throw the ball!" Landon shouts.

I roll my eyes and traipse over to the nearest ball. As I bend to pick it up, I hear Landon yell, "Nobody catch any of them!"

I try to get a firm grip on the ball, but my palms are sweaty.

"Ten seconds," the referee bellows.

I close my eyes. I try to picture myself as someone with muscles more inflated than Landon's.

Or as someone whose mind can move objects.

Or as someone who can fly at will.

"Five seconds!"

I hate dodgeball. I've always hated dodgeball. Ever since I was eight and played with my brothers against a bunch of jerks on the lake. That was the day I opened my mouth. The day I learned my lesson.

"One second!"

When I open my eyes, I take a few clumsy steps forward and throw with all the strength I can muster. It's not much. The ball flies low and lands on the other side. It bounces a few times before rolling over to Landon's feet.

Landon laughs as though he's heard the funniest joke ever. *Stupid arsehole.*

Infuriated, I pick up two more balls and throw one with each hand, a little harder this time. They still hit the floor, but with a little more oomph than before. The computerized audience moans. Everyone on the opposing team laughs except for Yalamba.

"Keep 'em coming, defect reject," Landon taunts. "Make it hurt!"

It's at moments like these that I truly wish I had an accelerated ability. If I had been an Atlas, I would have chucked the ball so hard that it broke Landon's ribs.

Landon grins and glances at the fuming Yalamba before turning his attention back to me.

"Today is your lucky day, defect reject. As captain, I realize I have to incorporate all of my team members into the game."

I can feel my blood coming to a boil. I don't have to be a Know-it-All to know what he has in mind.

Landon snaps his fingers at his team's Mind Mover, who uses his ability to pull Yalamba from the rear of the court to the centerline. Her sneakers squeak as she tries to dig her feet into the floor.

"Yalamba, I'd like you, as our team's weakest link, to be the one to finish off the defect reject," Landon says. "The win would give you some much needed self-esteem and boost your crowd ratings."

Landon touches a dodgeball to Yalamba's shoulder. "Aim well, Student Koroma."

"Are you an idiot? I'm not throwing anything at Alé!"

Landon chuckles. "Tell that to the referee after she fails you for lack of participation. I'm not the one who'll have to make up PE next semester."

Grumbling, Yalamba squeezes the ball with her artist's fingers. Her fingernails are painted their usual black. I can't make out the white dots on them from where I'm standing, but I know they're there. Yalamba has always had a thing for black dice.

She looks at me, and the anger in her eyes is unmistakable. Like me, she isn't doing well in PE since she rarely participates. Now she has the chance to improve her grade, but it's at my expense. I want her to throw the ball. I'll jump into it if I have to. If either of us can get something good out of this ridiculous situation, then we should make the most of it.

Yalamba scowls at Landon and walks to the centerline. The anxious crowd has broken into a haunting chant. "Finish him! Finish him!"

Seriously, who programmed these people?

The referee calls the ten-second warning. I can't tell what's going through Yalamba's mind as the time dwindles, but it's obvious that she's furious. She raises her left arm and squeezes her right hand into a tight fist. The seconds tick by. I flinch and prepare to get hit.

At the last second, Yalamba launches the ball though not in my direction. Instead, she spins around and chucks it at Landon. Landon is standing so close to her that he fails to dodge, and the ball hits him square in the face.

Everyone gasps, including the fake crowd. Even they've been programmed to know what it means when someone throws a ball at a teammate.

Yalamba backs away from Landon as he tumbles to the floor. He tries stifling the flow of blood that's gushing from his nostrils with no luck.

"You *perra*!" Landon shouts before spitting blood on the floor. He leaps to his feet and charges at Yalamba, but she sprints over the centerline to my side of the court, triggering the alarm.

Landon tries to follow her, but suddenly he rises into midair. The Mind Mover nurse is back, and she's taking him for treatment.

"You'll pay for this, you fecking Feral!" Landon yells as he's carried off the court. His profanities echo from the hall long after he floats through the exit.

Yalamba grabs my hand and squeezes hard. Her hand is surprisingly dry in my sweaty palm.

"I'd never hurt you, Alé," she whispers.

"I know." My voice shakes.

I don't get a chance to thank Yalamba before her hand tears free from mine. The referee, an Atlas, is squeezing Yalamba's arm.

"Who in this prefecture do you think you are?" the referee asks.

"Did someone call for an ogre? I know I didn't!" Yalamba says.

The referee's face brightens like lava, and she digs her fingers deeper into Yalamba's arm, causing her to wince.

"Another disciplinary infraction. Let's see what the headmaster has to say about this!"

The referee uses her immense strength to yank Yalamba toward the exit. Yalamba resists long enough to look back and yell, "Shame on you, Achewon, for being a bunch of mindless and complicit fools!" Then she is dragged through the door.

We don't have a referee to preside over the rest of the game, so I leave the court and sit on the sideline. No one says anything to me. They don't ask me to join when they start up a new game. I don't mind. I sit with a grin on my face as I think about my best friend—a Feral perra who threw that dodgeball better than any Atlas ever could.

CHAPTER THREE
MARINATED BUD OF UNBLOSSOMED CACTUS

I stick around the busy lobby after the last module of the day, since I normally meet Yalamba here before walking to the shuttle buses. Standing on my tiptoes, I try to get a better view of the lobby. I wish I were a foot or two taller so I could see over everyone's heads, but at my rate a growth spurt isn't going to happen anytime soon.

Yalamba is nowhere in sight. I guess she must still be speaking with the headmaster. I hope they let her out soon. I want to know what she was thinking when she decided to chuck a dodgeball at her team captain's face.

Though I'll never admit it to anyone at the academy besides Yalamba, I'm thrilled she did it. Landon has had something like this coming for a long time, and today it feels like justice was served.

The only downside is that justice rarely, if ever, comes without a price. Unfortunately, I think Yalamba is the one who has to pay it this time.

"Hey."

I spin around when I hear the voice. I'm surprised to see Mixie Trait, the Feral with the fading ability.

Mixie brushes a loose fire-colored dreadlock out of her face. She stares at me with a concerned expression, and I realize her amber eyes are the same color as the freckles on her skin.

"Have you…happened to see Yalamba?" she asks.

It's hard for me to find my words. Amicable acknowledgment from other students occurs with about the same frequency as suns explode and moons crumble into dust. Though I barely know Mixie, I do know she gets on well with Yalamba and they've shared several modules.

I clear my throat. "I was waiting for her after PE module."

Mixie lowers her head and sighs. "It's not fecking fair. I thought what she did was brave. I wanted to let her know, but—"

"The academy got in her way."

"It always does. Are you going to wait for her?"

"I think I'll swing by the office before I miss my shuttle bus."

"If you see her, let her know I was looking for her. I…was hoping to see some of her latest drawings."

"No worries. I'll make sure she gets the message. If she ever gets out, that is."

Mixie thanks me. Her arms remain stiff at her sides, like she wants to do something with them but she's not sure how. Instead, she offers me a troubled stare.

"You get a lot of scheisse around here, don't you?" Mixie asks.

So she's noticed.

"It's not fair," she adds. "Yalamba speaks so highly of you. She says you're the most genuine person in the prefecture. That means a lot, coming from someone like her. Whenever it gets hard, remember that."

An unexpected lump clogs my throat and prevents me from saying goodbye. Instead, I wave to Mixie, and she heads for the shuttle bus lot.

It's nice knowing that Yalamba has another friend she can count on, but I wonder why she rarely talks about Mixie. Or any other friends for that matter. She always makes me feel like it's just me.

Yalamba still hasn't shown up by the time the other students have cleared the building, so I decide to go to the headmaster's office to find out what's going on. I let myself in and sit in the small waiting area.

Assistant Clarkson is a large woman with breasts that look like melted watermelons. She stares at me intently as I pretend to read from my holo-screen. I can never tell if her face is naturally the color of a beetroot or if it only turns that way when she's angry. She always looks like she's about to spontaneously combust.

"What are you doing here after academy hours, Student Aragon?"

"Funny. I was about to ask you the same thing."

"I'm working." Her words come out like regurgitated globs of flan. "Administrative hours differ from student hours."

"Oh, really? I thought they were the same, you see."

Assistant Clarkson rolls her mantis eyes and lets out a heavy puff of breath. "Please tell me why you're here, Student Aragon."

"I'm waiting for Yalamba Koroma."

"Student Koroma is going to be inside for quite some time. Her parents are on their way to meet with Headmaster Slaughter."

They called her parents? Yalamba's father's black beard and angry eyes flash in my mind. This is a bigger deal than I thought.

"I'd advise you to go outside and catch your shuttle bus before it leaves." Assistant Clarkson's face is now an even deeper shade of beet.

I look to the illuminated digits above the lobby door. It's less than a minute until 16:30. Not much time to spare.

Since it's clear I won't get to see Yalamba anytime soon, I follow Assistant Clarkson's advice and bolt. I sprint, hoping that maybe, just maybe, my shuttle bus is running late for the first time in a century and will still be there to take me home.

I'm halfway to the shuttle bus when my breath leaves me and I'm airborne. My lower body tingles as my feet register the sensation of griplessness.

Is this what it feels like to be a Sky Glider?

Of course not, Alejandro, I think after plummeting face-first into the polished floor. I skid across it like a penguin on ice, back when the earth still had frozen poles.

"Nice landing, defect reject."

I recognize Landon's voice immediately, though it sounds atypically nasal. I had hoped his injury might keep him away from me for a week or two. I guess some pieces of scheisse will always float their way to the top.

Landon tugs at my jacket with his Atlas strength. While he holds me in the air, I can't help but notice the large white bandage covering his nose.

"What the feck are you looking at?" Landon's forehead wrinkles in a way it shouldn't until he's at least forty.

"A person who treats others with dignity and respect?"

Landon growls. "I don't need any of your smart-ass comments, defect reject. All I want to know is one thing. Tell me that you and your Feral friend were in on it from the start."

I have an inkling that Landon isn't going to believe me even if I tell him the truth, but I give it a try anyway.

"We couldn't have planned it. Yalamba and I were on different teams, and neither of us is a Know-it-All."

"You talked about it before PE." He tightens his grip on the fabric of my uniform until the collar is squeezing my neck. I gasp for air, but none gets to my lungs. It's impossible to breathe, let alone defend myself.

"Tell me you planned it." Landon shakes me. "Tell me!"

I try to speak, but I can't form the words. The pressure in my head rises the longer Landon holds me in the air. I wonder what color my face has turned. Maybe beetroot like Assistant Clarkson's.

I need oxygen. My face gets hotter by the second. A sudden, dense pressure fills my ears, making it difficult to hear. My eyes are open, but blackness swallows my vision.

"Blet blim blow!" someone says. Thanks to my muffled hearing, it takes me a minute to realize they'd actually said, "Let him go!"

It takes a heartbeat for Landon to release his grip. I collapse to the floor, my bony body clanking against the surface. I heave, trying to gulp as much air into my lungs as possible.

When the blackness recedes and my vision settles, I'm shocked to see Gwen Manghi. Her blond bangs are angled in a way that leaves only one amazonite-colored eye exposed. The glare she offers Landon is pure ice.

At six feet, three inches, Gwen is taller than Landon. And since she's a multi-accelerated Legion, she's also stronger. In fact, as an Atlas, Racer, Sky Glider, and Mind Mover combined, Gwen is classified as having Ability M-4. Having so many abilities is practically unheard of, and it makes her the most powerful student at the academy by a long shot.

Landon crosses his arms and scowls. "What the hell do you want, Gwen?"

"I want you to leave him alone," Gwen answers.

It takes a few seconds for Landon to retort, but when he does, it's not the response I expect.

"Make me."

Make me? Did Landon Waters just say "make me" to Gwen Manghi? Maybe he really is an idiot.

It takes less than a second for Gwen to attack. She bashes Landon with three powerful kicks. He isn't fast enough to dodge, though he blocks them with his forearms. Landon counters with a spinning back kick that Gwen catches with ease. She clutches at Landon's ankle and casually flips her long ponytail back as he struggles to keep his balance.

With the flick of her arm, Landon's entire body spins through the air. He collapses onto his back, wheezing.

"Pathetic Atlas," Gwen mutters.

I cover my mouth with both hands. Watching Landon get beaten up on two separate occasions in one day is beyond amazing.

Gwen crosses her arms and examines me. I realize I must appear at least ten thousand times more pathetic than Landon.

"Thank you," I manage to say. My voice cracks adolescently on the "ank."

Gwen scoffs, lowers her hands to her hips, and heads down the hall, hovering above the white surface without taking a single step. It makes me wish, once again, that I could hover too.

I can't help but wonder what I did to deserve her help. Gwen is like a goddess among rats at this stupid academy. My skin tingles from having been in her divine presence.

I look back at Landon, the king rat. He's still wriggling on the floor. I wonder if he has broken something else, and a part of me—albeit a minuscule, practically invisible part—wonders if he's okay. I take his movement as a sign that he'll recover on his own, so I do what Deficients do best when there's an open window. I flee.

✹ ✹ ✹

By the time I make it to the lot, the shuttle buses are long gone.

I think of my options. If I have another fan in this life besides Yalamba, it's my mother, Paquita. She has never babied me, but she has always supported me. Even though she's assigned to teach at an accelerated-only institute, no one gets away with talking badly about Deficients in her presence. My dad gets embarrassed when Mom goes on her rants, especially in public, but I like it. I feel like I can rely on my mom. Like she'll always be there when I need her.

Except when she doesn't answer my calls. I try several times on my wrist comm to no avail. Maybe she's caught up at an after-school meeting, or maybe she's already busy preparing dinner. My mother and I are usually the ones who prepare the food, since my father and brothers can't be bothered to lift a finger except to shovel something into their mouths.

I sigh at the thought of having to call my father, Los. Yalamba calls him the notorious *L-O-S*. He's a burly Atlas whose muscles have softened after too many years of sedentary office work. Like my shuttle bus driver, my dad either ignores me or grunts when I'm in his presence. If he's forced to speak to me, it's because he's ordering me to pick something up or to perform some chore that he's too lazy to do himself. He doesn't act that way with my Atlas brothers. He's more than happy to take both of them out on weekends for strength training.

He used to take us all out for training when we were little, back when there was still hope that I might become an Atlas. I did my sprints and push-ups, fully expecting to become like him one day. I *wanted* to be like him. He was a different person then. He used to smile and laugh in my presence; he'd even kiss and hug me. That all ended as soon as I was classified as a Deficient. Since that day, I've been dead to my father. And I think a part of him died that day too. Our relationship has been scheisse ever since.

But I'm still his son, and I figure I have nothing else to lose by calling him. Maybe he's having a bad day and could use me as an excuse to get out of the office.

"What is it, Diego? Rodrigo? Alejandro?"

My dad always says my brothers' names before mine. He's done it so often that the few times he actually does call me Alejandro on the first try it sounds odd.

"Sorry to call you while you're at work. I missed the shuttle bus. Is there any way you could—"

"Back up. You did what?"

"I missed the shuttle bus."

"And whose problem is that?"

"Well, it's not technically yours, if that's what you're getting at."

"I know it's not *my* problem!"

Here we go...

"So tell me. Whose problem is it?"

I expect his scorn to start oozing through my earpiece like viscous tar.

"Are you really going to make me say that it's my problem?"

"Yes, you interrupted me during my work hours."

I sigh. A big, emphatic, sometimes-I-wish-I-had-another-father kind of sigh.

"Okay, it's my problem. But I was hoping you could swing by and pick me up anyway."

"I'm working overtime. Call your mom or get a ride from someone else."

The earpiece beeps. The call ends.

My cheeks burn. I can't simply get a ride from someone else, and he knows that. People don't give rides to Deficients. Not even at the Achewon Egalitarian Academy.

I'm about to start the ten-kilometer walk home when, to my relief, my mom calls back.

"Are you about to tell me what I think you're about to tell me?" she asks before I can explain anything.

I can't help but smile. "If it's that I think you're the best, most wonderful, and most beautiful mother in the entire world, then yes."

"Spit it out, Alé."

I let out a defeated sigh. "I missed my shuttle bus again."

"Are you serious?" I can hear the disappointment in her voice. "Is it really that hard to get to the lot after your last module?"

"Not usually. Something happened today, and I couldn't get there on time."

"What do you mean by *something*?"

It's almost like she was trained to sniff out the truth. Sometimes I think she's even better at uncovering it than a Know-it-All.

"Oh, you know. I just got into a thing with an Atlas. Nothing new."

"What kind of thing?"

"I'm fine, Mom. No need to worry."

My mom goes eerily silent for a few seconds, and I know the larger conversation isn't over. "I'll be on my way soon. I'm in the middle of helping your aunt move a few things around her housing unit. You know how she likes to use my mind. We're the best of friends when she's on her knees."

In the background, I can hear my aunt yelling a chain of profanities. My mom tells her to shut up in Spanish.

"Give me half an hour," Mom says. "If you help me with dinner, we can have it ready by 19:00. I have sixty assignments to grade tonight. I probably won't get to bed until midnight."

As a Mind Mover, my mom is used to having everything right where she wants it. That includes her schedule, which she tends to share with others as a way of organizing her thoughts.

"You do realize this is the second time you've missed your shuttle bus in a month."

"What can I say? Children are imperfect by nature. Sometimes they do things like miss their shuttle buses. Or light things on fire. Or consume their parents' sacred cacti."

My mom chuckles at the reference. When I was two, I ate the bud of my dad's queen of the night cactus—a rare plant that only blossoms one day per year at midnight. Apparently, I ate the bud a few days before it was expected to blossom.

My dad threw a fit when he found out what I had done. My mom had calmed him down by reminding him that a child who lives and breathes every day is much more special than a plant that blooms once per year.

The irony isn't lost on me. That cactus wasn't the only thing that failed to blossom in my father's life. If he had known at the time that I'd turn out to be a Deficient, he would have traded me in for a spiritless succulent without the slightest qualm.

❋ ❋ ❋

When Mom comes to pick me up, she greets me with a hug—something she never fails to do. She gesticulates effusively while driving and goes on about her sister and her school day. We're about halfway home when she finally asks how my day went. She probably waited to ask because she already knows the answer.

"Slightly better than awful," I say.

"Don't be so pessimistic, Alé."

"I was being optimistic."

Mom sighs. "What happened?"

"We had to play dodgeball. Again."

"Everyone has had to play dodgeball at some point in life. That doesn't make it an inherently bad day."

I tell her about the game. I'm nearly crying with laughter by the time I get to the part where Landon curses at Yalamba with blood gushing from his broken nose.

"Good for Yalamba," Mom says. "Did she get into trouble?"

"That's what I was trying to figure out after the academy let out. I wanted to check on her to see if she was okay."

"At least you were doing something noble."

That's me. Alejandro Aragon—noble dodger of dodgeballs and the reason for Landon's extraordinary day of suffering.

"Did your shirt get ripped before or after the game?" Mom asks.

I examine my white academy shirt. There's a long tear running from the collar to my chest.

"I'm not sure."

"Was someone harassing you again, Alé?"

I'm too embarrassed to tell her what Landon did to me. I don't want to admit I'm incapable of defending myself. Everyone knows that's the case for Deficients—society's weakest links in our accelerated world—but it's not something I like acknowledging out loud.

"Don't worry about it, Mom. It's nothing I can't handle."

"I can contact the headmaster. Whoever it was shouldn't get away with treating you like this."

"Calling the headmaster would only make my situation about eleven million times worse. Trust me."

Mom bites her lower lip. As an instructress, she understands the ins and outs of inter-student conflict, so she knows I'm right.

"So, what are we making for dinner?" I change the subject.

Mom cracks a smile for the first time during the ride home.

"Your favorite. Marinated bud of unblossomed cactus."

"Funny."

I sit back and look out the window at the glowing blue high-way and the orange sun above the horizon. In the span of a day, I've been rescued by three women—Yalamba, Gwen, and now my mom. It surprises me that there are people out there who will stick up for me. I don't have any idea what's in it for them, but I'm happy they do it. Handouts are few and far between, and when they come, I accept them gladly.

My stomach grumbles. Suddenly, I'm so hungry the idea of a marinated cactus dish makes my mouth water.

CHAPTER FOUR
SUNNOT

By the time I finish my homework, it's 22:30. I go to bed, but falling asleep is impossible. Images of today keep spinning in my head. The rebellious Yalamba. The broken-nosed Landon. The beet-faced Assistant Clarkson. The stalwart Gwen. And the best dodgeball game I've ever played.

Yalamba hasn't called or messaged, so something must be wrong. It's not like her to keep me out of the loop for so long. She must be in major trouble with the headmaster.

I know Yalamba would want me to work on my prefectural application, but I can't think about my future when she's going down for defending me.

Instead, I do what I always do when I need to hash out my ideas—I crack open my journal and write. A letter seems like the best way to go. I figure it can't hurt to try, especially if it might prevent Yalamba from being expelled.

I think for a moment about what to say. It doesn't take a Know-it-All to know Yalamba meant to throw that ball at Landon. Plus, there were actual Know-it-Alls in the room who could attest to that. I tap my pen to my chin and begin my first draft:

Dear Headmaster Slaughter:

As an eyewitness to the events that occurred during the Achewon Dodgeball Tournament, I would like to speak out in the defense of Student Koroma. Technically, Student Koroma didn't do anything wrong when she threw a ball at ~~her piece of scheisse captain~~ her teammate. There is nothing in the rules and regulations of dodgeball that prevents a person from throwing a ball at his or her own teammate. Though this might not make much strategic sense, it is allowed. Therefore, how can Yalamba be held accountable for committing a violation if said violation doesn't exist?

Sincerely,
Anonymous Student

The letter is okay, but it still doesn't explain why Yalamba threw the ball at Landon's nose, of all places, when she was in such close proximity. I add another paragraph:

Injuries in dodgeball are common occurrences, and account for a significant percentage of registered injuries at Achewon Egalitarian Academy. The fact that Student Koroma threw a ball at ~~her piece of scheisse captain~~ her teammate (which is not listed as a violation under the "Global Rules and Regulations of Dodgeball") and broke said teammate's nose should not be held against her—especially since Student Koroma has never proven herself to have very good aim in the past.

I sigh. Maybe this is a lost cause, but I can't just sit around and do nothing. I have to help Yalamba. She's always been there for me.

* * *

Yalamba and I met when we were seven years old. We were in the same class in primary school. She wore her hair in two big puffs, and she was bossy—so bossy that she got in trouble for telling the instructress how to teach.

We were partnered with each other on a word-creation project that involved rolling six lettered dice and making words using the letters on the surfaces. On Yalamba's first roll, she got an *S, N,* and *U.* I ended up getting an *O, N,* and *T.* Yalamba put her letters together to spell *SUN,* while I put mine together to spell *NOT.* The combined result, *SUNNOT,* sounded so much like *snot* that we rolled around on the floor, crying with laughter. We were so out of control that our irate instructress forced us to opposite corners of the room for quiet time.

Yalamba and I stuck together as everyone around us became accelerated. We were excited to get our abilities—so much so that we created an adventure game where we'd fight imaginary monsters in the nearby woods, each of us armed with the special ability that we wanted.

Obsessed with animals in all their forms, Yalamba wanted to be a Sky Glider so she could feel like a bird. I always wanted to be a Legion with Atlas and Mind Mover abilities like my parents. My urge to become an Atlas deepened when my little brother Rigo accelerated into one at the age of four. Few things are more embarrassing than having a little sibling accelerate before you do. Since my older brother Diego was also an Atlas, I figured it was only a matter of time before I became one as well.

Weeks went by and neither of us accelerated. Yalamba and I grew increasingly anxious. We both knew a person couldn't accelerate after turning eight years old, because the brain's synapses for acceleration shut down. Once you're eight, it's over.

Yalamba's eighth birthday drew nearer, and we still hadn't developed an ability. What would our parents say? Would we be forced to leave school? Would people make fun of us for being different?

The day before her eighth birthday, Yalamba grabbed my hand like she did during the dodgeball game—the way she does when she wants to make sure I know she cares.

"We'll always have each other, Alé. Right?"

I nodded and Yalamba smiled.

We hadn't played our accelerated ability adventure game in a while. We couldn't bring ourselves to play the game when it seemed like we were close to being classified as Deficients. We sat with each other that evening in the common area outside of my housing complex, praying to the stars and hoping something profound and eternal would answer our wishes.

Fortunately for Yalamba, her wish came true later that night.

After returning home, she stayed up late to draw. She sketched a kitten. Shortly after adding the whiskers, Yalamba was surprised to hear a tiny meow from behind her. When she looked over her shoulder, she found a kitten, identical to the one she had drawn, staring up at her with big, glossy eyes.

Yalamba examined her drawing and the kitten until her mind processed what was going on. Delighted, she scooped the animal into her arms and hugged it to her chest. It was alive, it was real, and it was hers.

It was the first of many animals.

"You'll be next," Yalamba said when she called to tell me the news. "I know it!"

But as my eighth birthday neared, I still hadn't received my ability. My parents were visibly nervous. As soon as I turned eight, they brought me to an accelerated ability specialist who put me through a series of tests. For the first test, the specialist had me squeeze two metal bars together as hard as possible. They barely budged. Lights in the bars turned on as I applied pressure, and numbers flashed on the specialist's holo-screen. This was obviously the test for Ability S, enhanced strength. It was also obvious that I failed it with flying colors.

The Ability R or "rapid movement" test proved that (1) I wasn't Racer material and (2) I was slower than the average boy my age. A double hit to my rapidly waning self-esteem. For the Ability Tp test, the specialist focused on a set of cards, and I had to telepathically guess the numbers he was thinking. I was unsuccessful. The next test was a meditation exercise where I had to visualize oneness, clarity, and nothingness, and I was supposed to turn invisible. Scratch Ability I. Trying to telekinetically move even the smallest of objects proved impossible during the Ability Tk test. While jumping on a trampoline for the Ability L test for levitation and flight, my stubborn, earthbound body refused to defy the law of gravity.

The tests for Ability F, Yalamba's classification, were just as bad. I had to touch objects of varying textures for an extended period, sit in a dark room for an extended period, stare at a candle for an extended period, stand with my hand in a pitcher of water for an extended period, touch my hand to a holo-screen for an extended period, and look at the clouds for an extended period. Basically, I did a whole bunch of things for a long time until nothing happened. The specialist decided to reexamine my blood and DNA. I sat with my parents in the waiting room for another extended period as he processed the results.

After about thirty minutes, the specialist came into the waiting area. He called in my parents. He said he wanted to talk with them in private.

Why is he doing that? I wondered. The only reason he would talk to them without me is if he had bad news.

Ten minutes went by, and my parents were still talking with the specialist. My insides twisted with the anticipation. Half of me wanted to know if I had an ability, but the other half could already sense something was wrong.

My head felt hot, and my mind spun. The door opened. My dad was the first to enter the waiting area. He didn't bother looking at me as he stomped toward the exit. Instead of waiting for the automatic sliding door to open, he punched it, shattering it to bits. I was stunned. I'd never seen him do anything like that before.

My mom came out next. Her eyes were watery and her tan face reddened. She took one look at me and broke into sobs. She lowered herself to her knees and gave me a hug.

"No one is ever going to hurt my son," she said, weeping.

I looked up to see the specialist closing his door. Apparently, his work was done.

"Does this mean I don't have an ability, Mom?" I tried to swallow the lump in my throat.

Mom pulled back and stared at me with her green eyes. They weren't like my dad's or brothers' coffee-colored eyes or even my aqua blue ones.

She nodded. "That's what the specialist said."

I couldn't swallow. My face was burning. Teardrops slid down my cheeks.

"So what does that make me?"

Mom paused for a few seconds to collect her thoughts, then she smiled.

"I guess it makes you Alé."

She hugged me even tighter than before, her arms a blanket of warmth.

"Is Dad mad at me?" I asked.

"No, no. He'll be fine. I think he's angrier at himself than anything else."

I didn't know what she meant by that, and I still don't. Even after all these years my dad remains angry. I'm certain that *he* is not the one he's angry at.

Word that I was a Deficient spread around school before I saw Yalamba again. Eight-year-old Landon started calling me "defect reject" when he heard the news. The nickname stuck, and the use of it and its variations spread quickly among the other students.

Yalamba's parents told her to stop hanging out with me, since I might be a "bad influence." But Yalamba told them she wasn't going to stop being my friend just because I wasn't accelerated. In a determined fit of rage, she drew a picture of the two of us holding hands. Then she drew the same picture with us a few years older, followed by a picture of us with different hairstyles as teenagers. Finally, she drew a fourth one of us even older, past the awkward years.

They were pictures of us being friends forever. And because Yalamba had drawn them, I knew they had to come true.

Yalamba stuck with me. She stayed with me even during the years I was homeschooled by my mother, because there weren't any schools nearby that accepted Deficients. When I applied and got into the Ache-won Egalitarian Academy—the only secondary institution in a three-hour radius that accepted all students regardless of ability status—I thought I had it made. I hoped my life would magically get better.

My mother knew otherwise. She was the only person besides Yalamba who congratulated me for getting in, but she did so with tears in her eyes.

"I'm so proud of you, Alé. Don't get me wrong. I just don't want you to get hurt."

"Why would I get hurt, Mom? It's an egalitarian academy."

She chuckled and ran her fingers through my hair. "You've always had sunshine in your heart, my dear son, despite everything. Don't forget I'm an instructress by training. I know how cruel kids can be."

"I won't make friends with the mean ones. I have Yalamba."

"I know you do. But if you come across people who aren't like Yalamba, don't lower yourself to their standards. You're better than that."

I decided to take my mom's advice. I wouldn't lower my standards to anyone else's. It turned out that no one would lower theirs to my level either.

✱ ✱ ✱

The beeping of my wrist comm forces my mind back to real time. I've been daydreaming again, allowing my thoughts to drift to the past in an attempt to make sense of the present.

At this hour, it can only be Yalamba.

Normally her calls make me happy, excited even. But my stomach churns and my hands shake at the thought of what might have happened with the headmaster. Yalamba seems to pick up on my concern. She tells me to calm down and that she's biking over. It's pouring outside from a nighttime storm, but that won't stop her.

Yalamba doesn't get to my housing unit until well after midnight. My parents are already fast asleep. I tiptoe through the narrow corridor of my home until I reach the door. When it slides open, I see Yalamba. She's completely drenched, and her dark purple braids are plastered against her face. She gives me a soggy hug.

"Why didn't you use your umbrella?" I ask.

"I forgot it in my locker. Besides, it's just water."

Yalamba swings her academy backpack from her shoulder and unzips it. Gently, she sticks her hand inside and pulls out a tiny black rabbit with spiky white ears.

"Luckily, this little guy is dry," Yalamba says, "and that's all that matters."

"Another bunny?"

"Meet Lucy. I doodled him into existence during my meeting with the headmaster."

"*Him?*"

Yalamba nods. "I thought Lucy was a girl at first, but he turned out to be male. Who would have thought? Sometimes drawings surprise you."

Yalamba presses Lucy's tiny nose against her face. "I can't change your name now, can I? That might confuse you."

"She—I mean, he is really cute."

Yalamba laughs. "Looks can be deceiving. If all goes according to plan, he'll be able to bite off an Atlas's finger with one chomp."

Could this be the Atlas-eating bunny Yalamba had talked about?

I bring Yalamba to my room and give her a towel and bathrobe so she can dry off and change. She sets Lucy on the paneled floor. The bunny hops around with its nose twitching as it sniffs.

Yalamba flops onto my sleeping mat with an exhausted sigh. She covers her face with her hands and laughs. And laughs. And laughs.

"What happened?" I ask.

She's still laughing. Tears slide from the corners of her eyes.

"Those *cabrones* suspended me! How could they do that after what Landon did in PE?"

Cabrones was right. They couldn't suspend Yalamba. They had no right.

"What did Headmaster Slaughter say?"

"That I deserved to be suspended, because I purposely attacked Landon."

"Did you purposely attack Landon?"

"Yes! And I'd do it again!"

I sigh. "Lack of remorse isn't going to help, you know."

"Maybe you're right, but people like Landon can't get away with their behavior. If they aren't set straight, then nothing in this cesspool of a society will ever change."

"You've got to think about your future too, Yalamba. A suspension you can get past, but what if you had gotten expelled?"

"If I get expelled from the Achewon Egalitarian Academy for trying to make the world a more just place, then so be it. I wouldn't want to be a part of this system anyway."

Yalamba is so riled up she's practically sparking.

"I sort of felt this pulse of energy go through me when I did it," she says. "Some force that was telling me to be the karmic channel that would give Landon what was coming. Only after I threw the ball at his face did I start to think, and my first thought was *feck yeah*."

I sigh again. Yalamba will never change.

"I have an idea. I started writing a letter that I'm going to send anonymously to Headmaster Slaughter. I think it could help get your suspension revoked."

Yalamba sits up and looks at me, shocked. "You're writing a letter for me?"

I nod. "I need more time, but I should have it ready by tomorrow."

Yalamba's stare doesn't break from mine, and her violet eyes go glossy.

"You don't have to do that, Alé."

"I know, but I want to. You're my best friend."

Yalamba's head drops to her chest and stays there. I wait a few seconds, but she doesn't move. I'm not sure why she looks so sad.

"What's wrong, Yals? Was it something I said?"

"Nothing is wrong. It's just…well… I don't really know how to say this."

Yalamba is one of the most outspoken people I know. If she doesn't know how to say something, it must be complicated.

"Can I whisper it to you?" she asks.

I'm confused. No one in my family is awake. *What is she worried about?*

Yalamba doesn't wait for a response. She takes a deep breath and leans in. Her wet hair feels slippery against my face and neck. She still smells of fresh rain.

"Close your eyes," Yalamba whispers into my ear.

I obey, though I'm not sure why. Then I feel her soft, warm lips press against mine.

I pull back immediately.

"What are you doing?"

"Shh. It's okay, Alé."

I gulp. My heart is thudding so fast that it might rip through my chest. Her lips touch mine again. They move in a way I never imagined they would, as if they're trying to convince mine to do the same.

I'm frozen. Caught in a blizzard. Trapped in a block of ice.

The kiss lasts for what feels like an eternity. I don't understand it. I don't want to open my eyes or move my lips. I don't know what to do to with my arms, which are rigid and locked at the elbows. My hands keep me supported on the mat, but I can feel them sliding down my blanket.

Yalamba pulls away. The girl I see isn't the one I knew a few seconds before. For the first time in my memory, Yalamba is staring at me like I'm a total stranger.

I want to say something, but my throat is so dry I can't formulate the words.

"You don't have to be scared," Yalamba says. "It's just me."

"I think that's the point."

"What? You didn't like it?"

"I…I don't know if I liked it or not. I think I'm shocked."

"Shocked? Is it honestly a surprise that I…"

Her words decrescendo into nothingness, and her nose twitches. She starts up again. "Is it honestly a surprise that I might like you as more than a friend?"

"What?" My voice is barely audible.

"I think I like you, Alé. There. I finally said it."

I hear Yalamba clearly, but it doesn't make the situation any less bizarre.

"It's just, well…you're sort of like my sister, aren't you?"

Yalamba's eyes widen, and she covers her mouth with her hand.

"What?" I ask. "Isn't it true?"

She grunts and turns away. "This wasn't how it was supposed to go."

I don't understand. How was it supposed to go? Does Yalamba really think I'm going to kiss her back after how long we've been friends—practically siblings?

"Does knowing how I feel make you the slightest bit happy?" Yalamba demands.

"I…I don't know. More like confused."

Lucy is back from his hopping expedition and nudges his head against Yalamba's thigh.

"You mean to tell me that you've never felt something special between us? Never once have you thought that maybe, just maybe, it might feel right to—"

"Something special, yes. Just a different kind of special."

Yalamba shakes her head. "Are you serious?"

"I told you. You're like my sister."

"I see."

She gathers up Lucy, gently tucking the bunny beneath her arm. Then she springs up from my sleeping mat and takes off.

"Yals, where are you going?"

I scramble to my feet and follow her to the door of the housing unit. She opens it, welcoming in a gust of cool wind.

"You can't go out there alone. Let me come with you."

Yalamba stops to look at me one last time.

"Alé, I'm storming off in a mortified rage. I'd prefer that you didn't follow."

"But why? I'm fine with being friends if you are."

Yalamba stares at me with what might be the saddest eyes I've ever seen.

"Well, I'm not."

I feel like I've been gutted. I don't know what to say, so I stand there with my mouth hanging open. I want to stop her but know I can't. Instead, I watch as Yalamba mounts her bike and rides into the storm.

And just like that, she's gone.

Back in my room, I collapse onto my sleeping mat and attempt to process what just happened. I had never imagined the possibility that Yalamba, or anyone for that matter, could like me. Let alone kiss me.

Yalamba has changed absolutely everything. It feels like I've lost something I'll never get back. How am I ever going to look at her the same way again? Will she ever look at me the way she used to? Like a friend? Have I just lost my best friend?

I roll over and my hand brushes across Yalamba's sketchbook. It's an old one, judging by the cover that's been turned into an abstract piece of doodles, shapes, and designs.

Yalamba has never kept anything from me, or at least that's what I'd thought. Her sketchbook is where she pours all her thoughts and emotions. Just as the words in my journals have always been hers to read, the drawings in her sketchbooks have always been mine to view.

I hesitate for a second, then flip through the pages. While most of the drawings are animals and people, some of them are more abstract. Those kinds of sketches never manifest, since they're too bizarre to take physical form in the present and future.

I turn to the last page. I gulp when I see it, marveling at the breathtaking detail. The shadows, crosshatches, and highlights have been so masterfully applied that the people practically leap from the two-dimensional surface.

A curvy girl in a bathrobe is leaning over and kissing a skinny boy with dark, choppy hair. The boy's eyes are closed, and his shoulders are slightly raised. He looks like he's just taken a deep breath that he doesn't want to release.

I close the sketchbook and shut my eyes. I spend the rest of the night tossing and turning, thinking about Yalamba, our kiss, and how impossible this will all be without her.

CHAPTER FIVE
MISSING SOMETHING VITAL

I wake up the next morning to a black sky. I feel like I've barely slept. I can feel the dark circles lurking like pits beneath my eyes. I need sleep, but the more I force it, the less likely it is to happen.

As soon as the sun rises, I send Yalamba a message. She doesn't answer. After breakfast, I try calling her. Again, no answer.

This has never happened to me before, at least not with Yalamba. Normally it only takes her a few seconds to respond. The silence is palpable and purposeful. She's ignoring me, pretending I don't exist. Yalamba has always been the single person at the academy who wanted me to exist. The only one who made me feel like I deserved to be alive.

It's a situation I never thought I'd have to grapple with, but here it is, hacking away at my soul.

I guess I can't blame her. Yalamba told me she liked me, and I didn't reciprocate. I wish I could have responded differently. I wish it could have felt right for me, like it did for her.

If thoughts are dust, then my brain has become a giant bin. I have so much to get out, but I don't know how to do it. Instinctively, I grab my journal and open it to a blank page, but my pen feels heavy—like a broadsword in my fingers. Words refuse to come, and the prospect of reflecting makes me nauseous. I want to kick myself when I think about all the stupid things I said to Yalamba last night. Why couldn't I have just kissed her back like a normal person?

Because you aren't normal, silly Alé. I thought Yalamba knew that, but she kissed me anyway. How could she do that? Most people can barely stand the thought of touching a Deficient, let alone kissing one. Having a relationship with a Deficient is unheard of. Technically, it's not even legal for Deficients to reproduce. The hope is that eventually we'll disappear.

When I was little, it made me sad to know I'd never be able to love someone or have a family. I've had enough time to get used to it though. Why on earth would I risk bringing another Deficient into this world? I wouldn't want to inflict that sort of pain on anyone.

Yet here I am, hurting the one person I'd give anything to have back.

I toss my journal aside and press my palms to my face. Warm tears slip through the cracks between my fingers.

Writing won't help. Instead of taking away the clutter, it only adds more.

❋ ❋ ❋

The next two weeks plod along slowly. With no one to socialize with at the academy, I have no choice but to focus on my modules and dodge the spit wads that come my way.

It feels like a long time. I hope it's long enough for Yalamba to reconsider our friendship. She still hasn't reached out to me, and I can't help but wonder if she ever will.

The day Yalamba is meant to come back to the academy after her suspension I'm not woken up by my alarm, but by an emergency alert from my wrist comm. The startling buzz shakes my arm and fills me with a sense of dread. The only way to stop it is by reading the alert, so I wave a finger over the flashing red light and project the message in the dark room.

Security Alert: Two Achewon citizens have been found dead in housing complex C17. Cause of death: homicide. The matter is being investigated by Achewon security. We request all citizens to monitor their movements. If you have any information, report immediately to Prefectural Security.

Homicides aren't particularly uncommon, even in Achewon. Conflicts between people with accelerated abilities can quickly go bad. We get updates on them every week from Prefectural Security, but there's never been a case so close to home before. Complex C17 is right around the corner from where I live.

I fish around for more information until I find live coverage of a prefectural reporter communicating from the housing unit.

"The deaths of two beloved citizens sadden us all," the reporter says. "Karlyle and Kassandra Kerrain were found lifeless in their housing unit late last night. Both had multiple stab wounds. While the matter is being investigated, it appears there was a violent altercation between the two, as there is no biological evidence of a third party having been present. A message written on the wall of the housing unit in what looks to be blood is also being investigated."

The projection from my wrist comm zooms in on the message. *DEATH TO FERALS.*

I can hardly believe what I'm hearing and seeing. I actually know these people. Kassandra and Karlyle are—or were—the aunt and uncle of Kaylee Kerrain, a Feral who's in my year at the academy. Kaylee is a quiet girl with the not-so-useful ability to change her skin color. Being a Feral hasn't helped her social life, nor has the fact that she's been eerily quiet ever since her parents died in a vehicle accident. I was only six at the time, and I remember not knowing what to say to her when she returned to school. It was the first time I conceived the concept of death and its blatant finality.

Kaylee's aunt and uncle have taken care of her ever since. Things always seemed fine between Kassandra and Karlyle whenever I saw them, but apparently that was an illusion.

Then there's the threat written in blood. *Death to Ferals.* Deficients aside, Ferals are seen as the weirdest and least desired of the ability types. Their abilities are often seen as random and unhelpful compared to other ability groups. Most Ferals can do things like change colors, elongate their limbs, or grow their hair and fingernails on command. A rarer few have particularly bizarre abilities like Yalamba's. But despite all that, who would write such a thing about Ferals? Surely not the Kerrains. They were Ferals themselves.

Something isn't right. I want to talk about it with Yalamba as I get ready for the academy, especially since she has taken modules with Kaylee. But it's no use. I know she won't respond.

When I'm finally at the academy, Yalamba doesn't meet me at our usual spots—my locker before first module or in the cafeteria for lunch. I pass her once in the hallway, but she keeps her gaze fixed on the floor. Not even Lucy, tucked under Yalamba's arm, twitches its nose in my direction.

Yalamba is clearly avoiding me, which is something she has never done before. It makes me feel empty—like I'm missing something vital, maybe a long intestine or an arm.

It's not that I haven't been ignored before. I couldn't give a scheisse about the other people who ignore me at the Academy, but with Yalamba it's different. She's the only friend I've ever had—the only one who has ever bothered to get to know me.

It leaves me stuck with no one but myself, and it's frustrating. If Yalamba and I still have something in common, it's that I'm not excited about hanging out with me either.

I have no choice. I can't sit around any longer waiting for something to change. I need to know what's going on in Yalamba's mind. Since I'm not a Know-it-All, I'll have to talk to her. That's the only way I'll find out if there's anything I can do to fix our friendship.

I decide to confront Yalamba at the end of the day. Since she's been moved out of my PE module, I can't track her down after the bell beeps. I figure she'll need to stop by her locker to grab her art supplies and latest sketchbook before catching her shuttle bus.

When I turn the corner of the hallway, I catch Yalamba approaching her locker from the other side. She hasn't even lifted her identity band to the door's sensor before I call her name.

I stand next to Yalamba. This is the closest we've been since the night she kissed me. I'm surprised to see that her irises have gone as black as onyx. Her hair is just as dark with no trace of her purple highlights. Rose thorn tattoos curl their way up the skin of her neck. I know if I look through her latest sketchbook, I'll find a dark-eyed and tattooed self-portrait that looks more like a vampire than anything else.

Lucy, fluffy and cozy in Yalamba's arms, turns toward a group of passing students. Its whiskers twitch. It makes a series of noises that sounds like a mix of hisses and growls.

"Calm down, Lucy," Yalamba says.

"What's up with her?"

"*Him.*" The word hits like a punch to my stomach. "He doesn't like Atlases—males in particular."

My eyes drift to the students who had passed. Two of them are male Atlases.

Yalamba doesn't make eye contact with me. She keeps her focus on Lucy, cooing and petting his head to calm him down.

"What's wrong, Yalamba?" My pitch is higher than I want it to be.

Yalamba rearranges the loose braids of raven hair on both sides of her face, tucking them behind her ears.

"Nothing is wrong. Nothing at all."

I don't have to be a Know-it-All to know she's lying to my face.

"Then why haven't you responded to any of my messages?"

Yalamba takes a deep breath and sighs. "Seriously? You have to ask?"

I can feel the corners of my mouth losing control. The muscles spasm up and down as I fight to hide my sadness.

I turn away. I don't want Yalamba to see me like this, but I know I can't fool her. She's known me long enough to know exactly how I'm feeling.

"Please don't, Alé."

"I'm not." But I am, and I feel ridiculous.

"Hurting you is the last thing I want to do, but I'm hurting too. I need time."

"Time for what?"

"To let the feelings go. You know how I feel about you. I need time before things can go back to how you want them to be."

But why? Why can't she just be the same girl who drew fluffy animals, spelled out words like SUNNOT, and stood up for the rights of all students, even the Deficient? That girl wouldn't leave a guy in the dust with no one in the world to turn to—would she?

Yalamba doesn't say anything else. I know she won't be talking to me again anytime soon.

"I guess I should go," I say.

Yalamba nods, and I know I've lost.

My face is hot and tingly, and I think my lungs might be collapsing. Or maybe I've forgotten how to breathe.

There's nothing left for me to do but walk away from the only friend who has ever accepted me.

A tear runs down my cheek as I part ways with Yalamba. More tears want to fall, but I don't let them, not in front of everyone. I make for the bathroom, but I'm so flustered my left foot fumbles over my right. I collapse to my hands and knees.

Everything goes silent. I don't want to get up. I keep my eyes closed, sensing everything going on around me. I hear giggles. Someone calls me a stupid Deficient. My wrists hurt, my knees throb, and the floor is grimy from everyone's footsteps. This place smells like dirt. I want to scream, but what good will that do? I bite my tongue instead.

Eventually, I push myself up from the floor. I brush at my clothes and keep moving. There's no looking back or to my sides. Only forward. Always forward.

I come to a halt a few seconds later when I hear the shattering of glass followed by a raspy scream—Yalamba's scream. It's a sound that sends me back to a dark wooded world of imagined monsters and abilities. But this time, Yalamba isn't pretending.

I turn around to see what's wrong, but so has everyone else in the hallway. Since many of them are taller than me, I can't see Yalamba.

They don't have the right to block me from her. She's my best friend, and I want to know what has happened to her before any of them do. I'm the one who should be there, telling her not to worry.

One of the perks of being a Deficient is that it's easy to squeeze through crowds of accelerated people. There's a myth that touching a Deficient will increase the likelihood of having a child born Deficient. It doesn't make any scientific sense, but enough people still believe it. When I press through the crowd, the other students back away. A few recoil and gasp as I brush against them. Before long, a pathway opens. I walk through without having to bump a single elbow.

As I approach Yalamba's locker, my foot slides out from under me. My arms swing back in large circles, and I'm falling for the second time in less than a minute. A personal record. I land flat on my butt and in something wet and tepid. When I lift my hands from the floor, they're bright red. I look down to find I'm sitting in a crimson puddle.

My eyes drift from the puddle to the base of Yalamba's locker. I nearly vomit when I see the bloodied head of what looks like a decapitated rabbit. Its black eyes are wide open like it's just spotted a ferocious carnivore, and its ears are matted and stiff. The glass shards surrounding it suggest that it had been in a blood-filled jar that had fallen from the locker. The blood has splattered everywhere, leaving red stains and spots all over the floor.

I close my eyes and bite my tongue to stop myself from gagging. My stomach twists as I sit in the lukewarm rabbit's blood.

When I open my eyes, I see something else that makes me retch. There is a note written in blood on the inside of Yalamba's locker door. It reads: *DIE FERAL.*

I push myself away from the puddle and stand up on quivering legs. I try to find Yalamba, but I can't see her anywhere. She must have run away. She hates blood, and the fact that it's rabbit's blood probably made it a thousand times worse.

I have no idea where she could have gone. All I can hear is the echo of her scream.

The moist, red splotches that stain my clothes are growing cooler. Some of the blood has already dried into crusty maroon patches on my skin.

I push through the crowd of students and run to the bathroom. Inside, Simon Polk is washing his hands at the sink. His hoverchair is angled to the side, and he's twisting his upper body so he can place his hands under the faucet.

The sight suddenly makes my own problems seem much more trivial.

Simon eyes me in the mirror through his thick-framed glasses. A Know-it-All prodigy, he's capable of clearly distinguishing the thoughts of a roomful of people simultaneously. Most Know-it-Alls can only focus on the thoughts of a single person at a time. He stares at me for several seconds with his light blue eyes before rotating his hoverchair to face me.

"That's blood, isn't it?" he asks.

"From a rabbit."

Long, drawn-out seconds pass. I feel naked in Simon's presence. I can only imagine what kinds of synapses are triggering in his brilliant mind. Most Know-it-Alls wouldn't dare leap into the thoughts of a Deficient. They think a Deficient's thoughts can contaminate theirs. But Simon—a classified genius who is on both the academy's astrophysics and chemistry tracks—isn't most Know-it-Alls.

"You don't have to be enlightened to comprehend that a myth is a myth," Simon says, "yet many people will never understand."

It's strange knowing that someone has broken into your skull and snatched away your thoughts without you feeling the slightest thing.

"I know you weren't responsible if that makes you feel any better," Simon says.

"What?" I'm confused.

"I said I know you didn't do it."

"That's what I thought I heard. What would make you think I did something like that in the first place?"

Simon turns his head to the bathroom mirror. I follow his gaze to my reflection. Blood is everywhere. My clothes. My hands. My face. I'm a hideous sight.

"You're red-handed. Literally."

"I was only trying to find out what happened."

"I know you were. You're a good friend to Yalamba, but the masses tend to jump to conclusions, especially when they can't read minds."

"But you're reading mine right now."

"I am, and it doesn't frighten me. Should you need me to vouch for your innocence in the future, just ask."

"Vouch for my innocence? I didn't do anything!"

Simon nods and hovers past me out of the bathroom, rejoining the war zone that is Achewon Egalitarian Academy.

I place my hands under the faucet and splash water onto my face. I watch, almost hypnotized, as the clear hits the red, causing the dried blood to brighten. There's so much of it. Little spots splash all over the white sink. I try to rub them away with my fingers, but they have blood on them too. I only end up making more of a mess.

Something catches my eye in the rectangular bathroom mirror beyond my horrific reflection. Someone is there. I nearly choke on my gasp when I realize who it is.

Landon is back, and he's angrier than ever.

CHAPTER SIX
SOMETIMES YOU'VE GOT TO BREAK THE RULES
IF YOU WANT TO WIN THE GAME

A war drum beats in my head, the pulse an ominous bellow.

Bum. Bum. Bum. Bum.

The space around Landon goes blurry, like splotchy watercolors bleeding into one another, yet everything about him remains crisp and clear. His black eyebrows are etched in a sharp V, and he's gritting his teeth. The nose bandage is gone, but even after two weeks, purple patches still lurk beneath his eyes.

Bum. Bum. Bum. Bum.

My flight response kicks in immediately. I dart toward the exit, but Landon slides in my way to keep me from escaping.

Bum. Bum. Bum. Bum.

There's no way I'm getting out of this alive.

"The defect reject." Landon's umber eyes narrow. "You enjoyed that bloodbath back there, didn't you?"

Of course. How did I not think of it as soon as I saw the bloody mess at Yalamba's locker? Landon is the one who did that to her.

"Can't say that I did. It was quite a stunt you pulled."

Landon laughs. "Who me? Why would I do something like that to your crazy Feral friend?"

The dodgeball game comes to mind, but it's best not to bring that up.

"I can't help but notice something's changed," Landon says. "Lately, it seems like things have been different between you two."

Why on earth has Landon—the self-centered, egotistical *culo* that he is—bothered to notice the rift between Yalamba and me?

"What?" Landon asks. "You didn't think I'd figure out what happened after you two locked lips at your place?"

My jaw drops. I can't believe what I'm hearing. Yalamba never would have told that to anyone, least of all Landon. Did he force something out of her?

Landon glances at the bathroom's entrance, which is blocked by a wall of light blue tiles.

"Get over here." He motions with his fingers. "Now!"

A head pokes out from behind the wall. I recognize the student as Kazuki Tanaka, a second-year Legion with Know-it-All and Unseen abilities. I've seen him around the academy before, but we've never spoken.

When Kazuki steps from behind the wall, only his head, neck, and shoulders are visible. He's using his ability to conceal the rest.

"I'm going to need my robe back, *por favor*," Kazuki says. He must be fourteen, but his chirpy voice sounds like a seven-year-old's.

Landon tosses him a wrinkled piece of black fabric. "Good call. No one wants to see that."

With a casual motion, Kazuki slips the robe over his head and torso. As he ties it around his narrow waist, his skinny arms and legs become visible. Once finished, he pushes the clunky frames of his transparent glasses up his nose and offers an awkward smile.

Scheisse. At some point, Landon had acquired a few more intelligence points than I had given him credit for. If he had wanted something from Yalamba's mind, he'd found a way of securing it through Kazuki.

"We're gonna play a little game," Landon says.

"Oh, wow, a game?" Kazuki squints repeatedly. "I love games!"

"Good. If you didn't, I'd be stuffing your head into one of those toilets."

"Hmm…not really in the mood for that. But don't worry. I never lose. My dad says it's because I use my abilities to cheat, but that doesn't make sense since he can read my mind too."

"Shut the feck up and tell me what *he's* thinking." Landon points at me.

"All righty then. What do I get if I win?"

"You get the privilege of not having your face smashed in or your head dunked in a toilet."

"That's it?"

"What did you think you were gonna get?"

"I dunno. Maybe some of your prefectural stipend? I could use a stylish new robe or a new pair of glasses."

"Stipend, my arse. Use your ability and use it now."

"He's a bossy one," Kazuki says to me, "but I'll play anyway. I'm ready to win."

How Kazuki can remain so perky in Landon's presence is a mystery. He reminds me of a small child who's blissfully unaware of the dangers surrounding him.

Kazuki brushes at his robe and shifts his black eyes toward me. Like most people, Kazuki doesn't make direct eye contact with me. Instead of staring into my forehead or over me, he focuses on the space between us, blinking away at something invisible yet highly absorbing.

"Question one, defect reject," Landon says. "Don't you ever get tired of it?"

Tired of what? You won't get much out of me if your questions don't make sense.

"Tired of what?" Kazuki asks. "You won't get much out of him if your questions don't make sense."

Damn you, Kazuki!

"Damn me, Kazuki!" Kazuki parrots.

Landon clenches his teeth. "Then I'll specify. Don't you ever get tired of being a pathetic, little weakling?"

Why, in fact, I do, Landon. It's so kind of you to ask.

"Why, in fact, he does, Landon. It's so kind of you to ask," Kazuki says.

Who does this little second-year Legion think he is, invading my thoughts and giving them to Landon for free? I want to strangle Kazuki. I'm not used to having my mind read, so I have no idea how to censor myself in front of him.

"He wants to strangle me," Kazuki says matter-of-factly.

"I would too if you were reading my mind, so stay out," Landon says. "Next question, defect. Why do you stick around here? Why do you think you deserve to be at the Academy when you clearly aren't wanted?"

That was two questions.

"That was two questions," Kazuki says.

"Does it look like I give a scheisse?"

"Does it look like he gives a scheisse?" Kazuki repeats.

Landon's angry eyes lock onto Kazuki's. "Don't repeat what *I* say, you idiot! What kind of Know-it-All are you?"

"Okay, sir. Sorry about that. Sometimes I get confused. For that last question, he was thinking that he belongs here because this is an egalitarian academy."

Landon hocks up a mouthful of saliva and spits a wad of it next to my boots.

"Egalitarian academy, my culo. Everyone knows it's an egalitarian institute in name only. Why do you think you're the only Deficient here? Wouldn't there be more of you if it were truly egalitarian?"

Not all Deficients have a parent like my mother. Someone who wants their Deficient child to succeed.

"He has a supportive mother who encouraged him to come," Kazuki says. "Wow! He has a nearly perfect grade point average. Except for PE module, he has all Class 1 grades."

"I don't believe that for a second," Landon says.

"You don't have to. But you'd lose the game, since that's what he's thinking."

Landon's eyes drill into mine. For the first time, the antagonism wanes, if only for a moment. It's as though he's trying to see into me, the way a Know-it-All like Kazuki can. Like maybe he's trying to figure me out for once instead of attacking.

The moment doesn't last long. Landon crosses his muscular arms and shakes his head.

"Always surprising me, defect reject. All this time I thought you were mentally incapacitated."

That's because your mind has been stuck in a vegetative state since birth.

Kazuki brings his hands to his mouth and laughs. He stops the second Landon shoots him a scornful glare.

"What did he think?"

"I shouldn't tell you." Kazuki peeps from behind his fingers. "It'll probably make you cranky."

"A little late for that." Landon snatches Kazuki by his robe and lifts him into the air.

"Landon, put him down!" I say.

"Don't even think about telling me what to do, defect." Landon looks at Kazuki. "You'll tell me what he thought right now."

"Okay, Mr. Bossy, but don't kill the messenger. He said your questions are basic even to someone who's mentally incapacitated."

An interesting interpretation of my thoughts.

Growling, Landon turns to me with hatred swirling in his spiteful eyes. "Let's get to the point then. Did your Feral friend purposely throw that ball at my face during the dodgeball game?"

I cover my ears with my hands, anything to protect my head, my thoughts. *I won't tell Landon anything about Yalamba. I won't betray her. I'll die first.*

"What's he thinking?"

"He's blocking his thoughts," Kazuki says. "He'd rather die before telling you anything about Yalamba."

The corners of Landon's mouth rise into a sinister grin. "Then maybe we should see how true he is to his word."

Landon grabs at my bloodied uniform and pulls me toward him. Once again, the war drum booms in my mind. *Bum. Bum. Bum. Bum.*

"Did she do it on purpose?" Landon asks between gritted teeth.

I try to block the event from my mind. *I don't know, I don't know, I don't know.*

"He doesn't know, he doesn't know, he doesn't know," Kazuki says.

"Tell me!" Landon lifts me into the air and shakes me so hard that my neck whips back and forth.

Yes is the last word I want to think, yet it's the only word that comes to mind. And each time it does, I know I'm betraying my best friend.

"No," Kazuki says.

"What?" Landon asks.

What is right. What Kazuki said wasn't what I was thinking at all.

"He thought 'no.'" Kazuki presses his fingers against his temples. "He's thinking that Yalamba didn't do it on purpose. She was scared and sort of freaked out."

"Yalamba, scared?" Landon asks.

Kazuki shrugs. "I only deliver messages, not explanations."

Landon looks to me. "I don't believe you."

I don't believe me either.

"He thinks you should," Kazuki adds.

"You little freak." Landon grabs more tightly at my collar. "I know you were in on it. Don't deny it."

"I wasn't," I finally say.

"Then admit it. *She* was!"

She threw a fecking ball at your face, you piece of scheisse. Of course, she was in on it!

Kazuki bursts out laughing.

"What?" Landon asks. "What did you hear, Know-it-All?"

"Why does everyone call me a Know-it-All? I'm a Legion, people. And have I won yet? I'm getting bored."

"Weaklings," Landon says, grunting. "I've had enough of both of you."

Landon sets us down and drags us toward the stalls. After all these years of getting picked on by Landon and the other Atlases, I've never actually been dunked in a toilet. I guess it's because no one could stand the thought of touching me for that long, fearing my germs might contaminate them.

Apparently, Landon doesn't believe the myth. If he does, it doesn't bother him.

There's an explosion of sound when Landon puts his hand in front of the sensor of the nearest stall. Suddenly, he lets go of my shirt and flies backward over the sinks. The mirror he crashes into cracks into a web of broken glass and triangular shards fall to the floor.

I gasp when I see Gwen Manghi standing inside the stall. She looks like a model as she poses with her hands on her hips. Her statuesque form looms over us.

"Didn't your mother teach you how to knock?" Gwen asks.

Landon snarls from the floor. "What the hell are you doing in the boys' bathroom, streetwalker?"

Oh no, he didn't…

Gwen marches from the stall and slams her black boot into Landon's stomach. He lets out a terrible moan.

"Binaries bore me," she says, "and so do you."

Landon writhes as he levitates from the floor. His body follows the trajectory of Gwen's amazonite eyes. When her eyes dart to the side, he slams against the bathroom wall. This happens two more times before the tiles crack.

"Stop it!" Landon croaks.

"Maybe I will," Gwen says nonchalantly, eyeing her manicure. "It depends on how well you meet my list of demands."

"What list?" Landon is wincing from the pain. *Whoa, is he fighting back tears?*

"First, I'd like you to apologize for calling me a streetwalker."

"But you're a—"

Gwen squeezes her hand into a fist. Landon clutches at his neck and his eyes widen. Choking sounds splutter from his throat.

"That didn't sound like it was going to be much of an apology, did it?" Gwen asks.

Landon groans and kicks his legs. After a few seconds, Gwen finally lets up so he can speak.

"I'm sorry! I'm sorry!" Landon gasps. "You're not a streetwalker! Just a fecking bitch on the entertainment track!"

Gwen shrugs. "I'll take that as a compliment. Second, I'd like you to report committing an ability infraction to the headmaster's office."

"What?" Landon's voice cracks.

"You heard me. You used a fellow student's powers to your benefit through coercion. That's a violation of academy rules. I want you to turn yourself in."

"Sure, Gwen. While I'm at it, I'll tell them you were taking a piss in the male bathroom."

"Tell them it was a massive scheisse. I'm sure they'll appreciate the detail."

"You're a disgusting perra."

"And you're a vile creep who should be fed to the sharks in a distant water prefecture."

Finally, Landon makes the wise choice to remain silent. From the way he bites his lower lip, I can tell it's killing him.

"My eyes are on you, Atlas," Gwen says. "If I don't see you in that office reporting your infraction, then guess what?"

Gwen raises her hand, as if threatening to choke Landon again.

"Okay, okay! I'll do it."

"Is he telling the truth?" Gwen asks Kazuki.

Kazuki nods. His mouth hangs open as if his jaw no longer functions in Gwen's presence.

"Good." Gwen focuses on Landon again. "Last but not least, I want you to apologize to Alé."

"What?" Landon exclaims.

What is right. Did Gwen just say what I think she said? Alé? As in me, Alejandro Aragon? Gwen Manghi knows my name?

"You heard me loud and clear, you pathetic excuse for a human," Gwen says. "Apologize."

"No way!" Landon yells. "I'll never apologize to a Deficient."

Gwen clenches her fist and strangles Landon yet again. He kicks at the wall, cracking it further. When Gwen releases her hold, he coughs and heaves for air.

"Okay! Okay! I'm sorry, Deficient! I'm sorry!"

"That's better. Remember this, Landon. If this disgusting perra sees you come after Alé again, I'll chase your prissy little culo down until you're nothing but a splattering of flesh and bone beneath my boots. Got it?"

Landon grits his teeth but says nothing.

"I didn't hear you," Gwen says, her tone threatening.

"Understood," he mutters.

"Good."

Gwen lowers her arm, and Landon drops to the floor in a pathetic heap. He groans in pain while rolling from side to side. The fight has left him for now at least.

"You make my eyes bleed," Gwen says to him.

And with that, she exits.

I feel like I've just witnessed something fantastical, like a nine-headed Hydra or a glittery, rainbow-colored unicorn. I stare after Gwen, wondering why she saved me from Landon for a second time. Maybe I'll never know.

The sound of Landon's hacking brings me back to reality. Kazuki and I look to one another before sprinting out of the bathroom.

"This isn't the end!" Landon yells after us, still coughing. "You'll pay for this!"

I don't know if he says anything else, since Kazuki and I are down the hall so fast someone might think we're Racers.

Kazuki and I are huffing and puffing by the time we make it to the shuttle bus lot. We've arrived too late though. All the shuttle buses have already departed.

"You really think they're all gone?" Kazuki asks.

Of course, he's read my mind.

"Unfortunately. This is the third time I've missed my shuttle bus in a month. I'm becoming an expert at it."

"Three times in one month? That's pretty bad."

I nod. "So what'll you do, Kazuki?"

"When there's a problem, there's always a solution. That's what my dad says."

Kazuki presses at his wrist comm and speaks into it.

"Hi, Mom. I missed my shuttle bus. Can you please pick me up from the academy?"

Within seconds a sensor light on the wrist comm glows bright green.

"She's on her way." Kazuki grins.

"I've never seen a sensor like that on a wrist comm before."

"My dad is an inventor with the Prefectural Innovation Lab. He made this for me because my parents think I ask too many questions. It's easier to communicate with colors. Green is for yes, red is for no, and blue is for stop bothering me."

"That's very—blunt."

"Tell me about it. But it's okay. I have more inventions."

Kazuki reaches into his backpack and pulls out another contraption—a silver ball that fits into the palm of his hand. He throws it as hard as he can, and the ball spins and swirls in the air before flying back to his hand.

"My dad designed this prototype for me for whenever I get bored. It's pretty good, but he should probably invent something to repair all the windows I've broken."

Kazuki's father sounds amazingly clever, not to mention patient. Very, very patient. I lower my head as I imagine my dad sitting behind his desk at the Household Modernization and Resizing Unit. I can picture the vein of his forehead throbbing the second he realizes I'm calling for another ride. My mom will be just as annoyed about having to pick me up from the academy yet again.

"Your parents seriously wouldn't come to get you?" Kazuki asks.

"I don't know. You've got to stop doing that."

"Doing what?"

"Reading my mind before I speak. It's kind of annoying."

Kazuki's face goes bright red. His dark eyes focus on the space in front of me.

"I'm sorry. My mom always says I've got to stop communicating with people's minds. It's hard for me. I've always had trouble differentiating between what people are thinking and what they're saying. You know?"

I don't know. I've never had the privilege of being telepathic.

"Can't you just look at someone's mouth to know when they're speaking?"

"I guess. I don't really like looking at people when they talk. It makes me feel squeamish inside."

I hadn't noticed that Kazuki's habit of not looking at people directly applied to everybody instead of just me. I'd also never met an accelerated student whose ability inhibits them in some way. It's an idea I have trouble wrapping my unaccelerated mind around, but I find it fascinating.

"You don't have many friends, do you?" Kazuki asks.

"To the point much?"

"I guess I've only ever seen you with Yalamba."

"Yeah, just Yalamba." *Once upon a time...*

"I don't really have friends either. Just me. And I'm an only child, no less."

"Siblings are overrated."

"That's what everyone says, but I still wonder what it would be like. At least you have Yalamba. Or had her...before the whole rift thing."

I give Kazuki a death stare to indicate that he's in the red zone.

He apologizes, and there's a prolonged silence as Kazuki and I stare at the pavement of the shuttle bus lot.

"I wonder who did that to her locker," he says.

There's not all that much wondering to be had. Clearly Landon has something against Yalamba and Ferals in general. If anyone was going to put a rabbit's head in her locker and leave her a death threat written in animal's blood, it was him.

"I don't know if you can point your finger at Landon right away," Kazuki says. "He doesn't like Yalamba, especially after what she did, but he's really got something against you since you're a defect—"

Kazuki catches himself before completing the phrase.

"I mean...Deficiently Accelerated."

He lowers his head.

"Sorry. That other phrase isn't nice."

"You don't have to apologize. I am what I am."

"But I'd never read your mind before. I didn't know how it felt."

Another stretch of silence follows as we refuse to look at one another.

"You didn't have to do that back there, Kazuki."

"Do what?"

Does he really have to ask? Can't he read my mind?

"I'm trying not to," Kazuki says.

I let out a defeated sigh.

"What? Was it something I said?"

"Yes!"

"Sorry..."

Kazuki's chin falls to his chest. With his small size and shaggy black hair, he looks like a scolded toddler.

Maybe I've been too harsh. I'm not like Landon. I don't get any pleasure out of hurting people's feelings. Not Yalamba's after she told me she liked me, and not Kazuki's, especially when he clearly means no harm and has risked a lot to help me out.

"I'm sorry, Kazuki. I'm not mad at you for using your ability. You didn't have to use it to help me though. I know you were making things up."

Kazuki grins and pokes at the bridge of his clear glasses.

"Maybe I am a cheater after all. Sometimes you've got to break the rules if you want to win the game."

I can't tell if Kazuki is nuts or a genius. Maybe he's both.

"How about we make a deal?" I ask.

"Yeah?"

"Let's try looking at each other from now on when we talk."

Kazuki nods. "I think I can manage that."

"Good."

Kazuki and I look straight into each other's eyes. After about five seconds of staring, we can't take it any longer and turn away.

"Okay, that was kind of weird," I say.

"Maybe we should start with small increments. Today we look at each other for five seconds. Tomorrow, we do ten."

Is he being serious? Does he want to keep associating with me?

"I mean, only if you want to," Kazuki says.

"Oh no, it's not that. It's just… Well, I—"

"Oh! You thought I wouldn't want to hang out with you because you're a def—"

Kazuki stops himself once again.

"I mean…because you're Deficiently Accelerated."

"I guess I'm surprised. As you said, I don't have many friends."

"Neither do I. I wonder why that is."

Maybe it's because you read people's minds incessantly.

"I heard that," Kazuki says.

"Proving my point exactly."

"It's who I am, Alé. I can't stop being my authentic self!"

Alé. It still sounds strange hearing someone besides Yalamba say my name.

"Alé, Alé, Alé, Alé, Alé, Alé, Alé, Al—"

"What are you doing?"

"I'm saying your name over and over. Alé, Alé, Alé, Alé, Alé, Alé—"

"Yeah, I noticed that. Why?"

Kazuki shrugs. "Because people don't say it enough."

The little mind reader has a point.

"You know what?" Kazuki asks. "I'm glad Landon dragged me to the bathroom and forced me to read your thoughts. It was fun."

"I'm glad to be the source of your entertainment."

"You know what I mean. You're not afraid to think certain things, even when you're around intimidating people. It's refreshing."

My eyes shift to a small, white pod vehicle hovering into the shuttle bus lot from the highway. It pulls up to where we're standing, and the tinted window slides down. I can see the pale and expressionless face of Kazuki's mother inside.

"Looks like Mama Tanaka is here," Kazuki says. His dark eyes scan me from head to toe. "She won't be thrilled about the blood on your clothes, but I'm sure we can find a towel or something. Give me a second."

"You don't have to—"

Ignoring me, Kazuki scuttles to the vehicle. He and his mother stare at one another for an awkward amount of time.

It's always strange seeing Know-it-Alls communicate with each other. Their arms and hands move, though their mouths don't budge, as their thoughts bounce back and forth between their minds.

After a few seconds, Kazuki's mom peers over her single-lens sunglasses in my direction. Once she completes her inspection, she covers her eyes and acknowledges her son.

When Kazuki lowers his head, I know he has lost. The tips of his boots drag along the walkway as he returns.

"I'm sorry, Alé. Maybe it's better if we try another time. My mom says she doesn't want to get the pod dirty."

"No worries. You go, and I'll find my way home." I always do.

Kazuki gives me a sad, almost longing look that seems to suggest there's something more behind the rejection. He waves before folding himself into the passenger seat of the vehicle. Kazuki's head remains lowered as the vehicle's black window slides up. I watch the pod hover through the shuttle bus lot and zoom out of sight.

Though I can't read minds like Know-it-Alls can, I think I know exactly what transpired between Kazuki and his mother during those moments of silent communication.

I don't bother calling my parents this time. Instead, I walk. It takes me nearly two hours to get home by foot, but I don't mind. I have one good piece of news for anyone who's interested in learning how my day has gone. It doesn't matter that I fell into a puddle of rabbit's blood or that I nearly got my head dunked into a toilet by Landon or that Yalamba still doesn't want to talk to me.

No. None of that seems to matter when I might have made my second friend ever.

CHAPTER SEVEN
SICK, DEMENTED, TWISTED LITTLE MONSTER

T he long walk home gives me time to think.

I mentally replay what happened in the bathroom. I can't understand why Landon would have gone so far out of his way to get such an obvious answer from me. Anyone with eyes could have told him Yalamba had thrown that dodgeball at him on purpose. Why did he need me to confirm it for him? And why did he want to know if I'd had anything to do with it? If my existence was so worthless to him, then why should he care about what I did or didn't do?

Then there was Kazuki. I'd thought he was betraying me with every thought he read until he'd started lying in my defense. And Gwen—the beautiful, golden-haired Legion that other students fear because of her spectrum of awesome abilities. She's decided to use her abilities in my favor two times now for no apparent reason.

I want to wipe my nose with my sleeve, but my uniform is still covered in the dried rabbit's blood I had practically been swimming in at the academy. Just thinking about it makes me want to puke. Why would a person do something so disgusting? And why would they leave a message as dark and hateful as *"DIE FERAL"* inside my best friend's locker?

The words remind me of the ones left in the Kerrains' home at the scene of their murders. Could the person who was behind what happened at Yalamba's locker also be responsible for what went down at the Kerrains'?

It doesn't take a Know-it-All to figure out Landon had something to do with the rabbit's blood. I'm prepared to bet a whole year of prefectural stipends on it. Could he be demented enough to have targeted the Kerrains as well?

My hamstrings are like iron cords by the time I reach home. I check my wrist comm for messages, but Yalamba hasn't reached out. I want to see if she's okay, but she asked for space. Calling will only push her farther away.

My dad still isn't home from work when I return to the housing unit. My brothers are in their rooms. Judging by the smells of the anchovy stock, garlic, onions, and beans, my mom has gotten a head start on her bean paste soup. With everyone in my family occupied, it's easy for me to sneak into the bathroom. I hop into the shower with my crusty clothes on to get the blood off me. It rushes across the tiles in bright red streams. The longer I scrub and shampoo, the more blood I seem to find. When the water turns from red to pink to clear, I know my work is done.

I change into a night-robe and make my way to the kitchen. My dad has just gotten home, and he's sweaty and deflated after a long day of bureaucracy and computing. My family and I eat dinner together like normal, seated on the floor around our low table. No one talks. Instead, my father and brothers distract themselves with whatever is glowing on their holo-screens. My mother eats quickly. Judging by her furrowed brow, I guess she has exams to grade.

Diego, my older brother, has the same beefy build as my dad. He doesn't look at me when he eats. The only time he acknowledges me at the dinner table is when he gives me a dead arm as he gets up to leave, which is extremely painful since he's an Atlas. Rigo, my little brother, is a smaller version of Diego but with more bronze to his skin. He's picked up on Diego's example and pretends like I don't exist. He hasn't started hitting me yet, at least.

After excusing myself, I return to my room to continue working on an essay for my history module. I write a few pages about the globe's political restructuring after the Great Catastrophe—a period of mass death and destruction following the eruption of an enormous supervolcano in the western hemisphere. I'm still sorting out a few historical facts about the impact of climate change and the years between the dissolution of nation-states and the launch of the Supreme Chancellorship, the world's present governing body, when I rest my head on my desk and close my eyes. I tell myself that I'll reopen them after I count to ten. But ten seconds turns into twenty, twenty seconds into thirty, and then I lose count.

Suddenly I'm floating on top of a bunch of clear, bouncy bubbles. Lying on top of them, I feel as light as a feather.

Then, one by one, the bubbles burst. I don't hear them pop, but my body sinks as they disappear. They keep bursting until I'm floating on just a few. Then they're all gone, and I'm falling through a clear blue sky.

Why I thought lying on a bed of bubbles was a good idea, I'll never know. I guess sometimes you don't recognize bad ideas in dreams until all your bubbles pop.

I wake up to the beeping of my holo-screen. My heart races. I haven't heard that beeping sound in a while, but it comes as a welcome relief. I know it has to be Yalamba. She's the only person who ever calls.

The illuminated digits above my door show that it's just past two in the morning. I rub my eyes and get up from my desk to examine the holo-screen. The name *Memuna Koroma* flashes on it. *Odd. Is Yalamba using her mother's device to contact me?* My hand trembles as I run my fingers through the light to accept the call.

Instead of Yalamba, I see her mom's face staring back at me. Her brown eyes are puffy and rimmed with dark circles as if she's been crying, and her hair isn't as neatly kept as usual.

Already I have the sense that something is wrong.

"Can you…can you see me?" she asks in an unsteady voice.

"Yes, Ms. Koroma. Is everything all right?"

Ms. Koroma closes her mouth and her head drops.

"No…it's not."

I gulp. What does she mean?

Ms. Koroma would only be this sad if something happened to one of her daughters. I wonder if the incident at the academy upset Yalamba more than I realized. Maybe I should have called to check if she was okay.

The picture on the holo-screen shifts and Kamal Koroma, Yalamba's father, appears. "Listen you little Deficient! Tell me what you did to my daughter right now!"

"I…I don't know what you're talking about."

"I don't give a flying piece of scheisse if you know what I'm talking about! Yalamba never came home from school. We've been looking for her all night. You're the only person she hangs out with outside of the academy. So where the hell is she?"

His black hair is disheveled, like he's been yanking at it, and he looks bug-eyed and crazy.

"Calm down, Kamal," Ms. Koroma says. "Maybe he has something he wants to say. Al—"

She stops, unable to utter the rest of my name.

"Do you have something you want to tell us?" she eventually asks.

"I don't know, Mr. and Ms. Koroma. To be honest, Yalamba hasn't spoken with me in a while."

"And why's that?" Mr. Koroma demands.

"It's personal. I can't really say."

"You're obsessed with her, aren't you, you little rodent?" Mr. Koroma says. "You told her you liked her, and she broke your heart. Is that it?"

I shake my head. "No. That's not it at all—"

"And then you did something to her!" Mr. Koroma's energy causes the holo-screen's image to shake. "Tell me now, you little Deficient! Tell me what you did to my daughter!"

"Kamal!" Ms. Koroma shouts. She stares at her husband with a mixture of terror and sorrow. It's as if in that moment the situation has finally become real.

"Do you have any idea where Yalamba is right now?" Ms. Koroma is barely holding herself together.

I shake my head. "I wish I knew."

Ms. Koroma closes her eyes and takes a deep breath. "Do you have any idea where she could be?"

"Someone did something to her locker today," I blurt out.

"What?" Ms. Koroma asks.

"Someone put a dead rabbit's head inside her locker," I say hesitantly. "There was blood everywhere. Whoever did it left a message that said: *DIE FERAL*."

Ms. Koroma gasps and places her hand over her mouth. I wonder if she's thinking, as I had, about the message left at the Kerrains' housing unit.

"No one knows who did it," I add.

"I'll tell you who did it!" Mr. Koroma shoulders his wife out of the image. "You're a sick, demented, twisted little monster!"

"But I didn't—"

"We're calling the prefectural authorities. If you plan on running, then you'd better start now. We're coming for you."

"But I—"

My holo-screen goes blank. They've hung up.

And that's that. Yalamba's parents woke me up in the middle of the night to tell me that my best friend is missing less than twenty-four hours after someone left her a death threat. Of course, I'm the first to be blamed. It doesn't matter that Yalamba and I have been best friends for years. I'm a Deficient.

What the feck is going on? Where did Yalamba go? Why am I automatically at fault?

Red-handed, the masses will think. Just as Simon predicted.

CHAPTER EIGHT
THE HEADMASTERLY INQUISITION

I don't know how anyone could sleep after that. I try venting in my journal, but words don't help at all. What power could they possibly have? It's not like they can undo anything the Koromas said.

I lie down and force my eyes shut, but it doesn't count as sleep. I wait for what feels like years before the color outside my window changes from black to navy blue. Going to the academy is the last thing I want to do, especially if Mr. Koroma plans on following through with his threat. But I need to know what happened to Yalamba.

She's got to be okay. There's no other option. Things will go back to normal. She'll be waiting for me at the academy just like every other day.

Stupid Alejandro, I think the moment my wrist comm vibrates. I don't even have to look at it to know what it's going to say.

Missing Person Alert. Yalamba Kadija Koroma, sixteen years of age, was last seen at the Achewon Egalitarian Academy. Respond immediately to this message should you have any information regarding her location.

Her face appears next. Her big eyes, long eyelashes, full cheeks, and black and violet braids. Her gaze conveys that she knows who she is, what she wants, and that no one will stand in her way. She's the same girl I'd known since childhood. *Why did I mess it all up?*

There's a knock on my door and my mom enters. She's already dressed in her tan instructress uniform. She lowers herself to my sleeping mat and wraps her arms around me.

"I saw the alert. I'm so sorry, Alé."

I don't know what to say. I want to cry, but I'm completely numb. I can't even feel the hug I know my mom is giving me.

"She has to be somewhere. They'll find her. It hasn't even been a full day."

"Someone targeted her." My voice sounds distant to my ears. "They did something terrible to her locker. Left a message…"

"What kind of message?"

I tell my mother about the blood, the rabbit, and the words. *DIE FERAL.*

"Kids can be absurdly cruel to one another," she says, "but I never imagined cruelty could descend to this level of hatred."

"Neither did I."

Mom runs her fingers through my hair.

"You look tired, Alé. Did you get any sleep?"

"Not really." I can't bring myself to tell her about the Koromas' accusation. I guess she'll find out eventually if Yalamba's father has his way.

"Are you sure you want to go to the academy today? I'm surprised they haven't closed."

As much as I loathe the academy, not going isn't an option. I have to be there. What if Yalamba suddenly turns up?

Hope. Again, the veil. That stupid, idiotic veil. Yet it's all I have. Giving up hope means giving up on my friend. I can't do that. Not now. Not ever.

"I'll go. I've got to be there in case Yalamba turns up."

"I understand. I'll make you some breakfast. Go shower and change. The water will take the sleep from your eyes."

At breakfast, my dad and brothers are already sitting on the floor, eating their morning porridge. Their eyes are lost in their glowing holo-screens. No one offers me as much as a look, even though they've all received the alert.

They know Yalamba. They've seen her countless times. She's my best friend. Yet her disappearance means nothing to them.

"Have a seat, Alé." Mom hands me a warm bowl of porridge. She clears her throat and raises her voice to the others. "It might be considerate of us to ask Alé how he's doing after the alert."

Diego spits a mouthful of porridge into his bowl. "You mean about the Feral?"

My body tenses, and my face flushes with heat. *Her name is Yalamba.*

"Yalamba is missing," Mom says. "If anyone hears anything, please let us know right away."

"The prefectural authorities will sort it out," Dad says with a grunt. "That's their job."

"The way they've done with the Kerrains?" I ask. "The authorities don't have a clue what they're doing."

My father raises his gaze from his holo-screen and glares from beneath his dark and furry brows.

"She's just a girl. How hard can she be to find? She probably ran off with someone and got lost."

"The Kerrains are dead," I add. "The message at their home was similar to the one Yalamba received. Ferals are being targeted."

"The Kerrains were lunatics. They were never right in the head."

"Can you keep it down?" Diego says. "I'm watching something over here."

Diego's eyes are still fixed on his holo-screen. The privileged arsehole only thinks about himself. He's always been that way. The fecker doesn't understand what it means to be hated, and he never will.

I leave my bowl of porridge on the table, untouched. There's no way I can eat anything. Not with what has happened. Not with these people.

While riding the shuttle bus, I think about the time my mom forced my brothers to bring me with them to play dodgeball at Achewon Lake. Halfway through the game, one of the kids on the other team refused to go out after I hit him. I called him out on it since he had clearly broken the rules.

Wrong move. Before I knew it, he and his larger friends had surrounded me. I had assumed my teammates would back me up, but when I turned to see where they were, they had all backed away to the sidelines. Even Diego and Rigo—two Atlases with incredible strength.

I've gotten hit since then, but nothing has ever compared to what I felt that day. I remember trying to protect my face as boots bashed into my head and stomach. One of the kicks to my chest felt like someone had caused my lungs to collapse. A cracked rib, I later learned.

"Fecking Deficient!" they had shouted. "You don't deserve to live!"

My brothers could have stopped them. Instead, they stood there and let it happen. I didn't know what hurt more—getting beaten up by a gang of strangers or realizing I meant less than nothing to my own flesh and blood.

My muscles are still tense by the time I arrive at the academy. I shift my focus back to what I need to do.

You'll find her, I tell myself. *You'll find her, you'll find her, you'll find her.*

But that's not what happens. I show up to her locker before first module. And wait. And wait. And wait. No Yalamba.

I give up with a minute before the bell beeps. As I walk down the halls, I can't help but notice the side-eyes from the other students. Some cup their hands over their mouths as they whisper to one another, as if that will hide the fact they're gossiping.

The behavior persists throughout the day. By the time lunch comes around, it seems like the entire body of third-year students has stopped what they're doing to give me a collective death stare.

They are an eerie, silent audience that I have no desire to entertain. I back away from the cafeteria, one cautious step at a time. I sprint to the place where I have the best chance of being alone.

I only make it halfway down the hall before a chirpy voice calls my name. I turn around to find Kazuki running as fast as he can, his arms pumping.

"Wait up, Alé!" he says, panting. "Where do you think you're going?"

"I have no idea."

Kazuki cocks his head to the side like a little bird. "Don't lie to me, mister. I know you're going to the bathroom."

There he goes again, reading my mind without permission. Yesterday it might have been endearing, but today I'm not in the mood.

"Then why did you ask?" I demand.

"I...I don't know. I guess I was trying to break the ice."

"Don't you have a module to attend?"

"I finished telepathy lab early and thought I'd find you. Little did I know I'd see you running down the hall in your strange sort of way."

In my strange sort of way?

"Do you have something you want to tell me before I go to the bathroom in my 'strange sort of way?'"

"Yes, I do. I've been hearing things. Not good things. I wanted to let you know that...well... I don't think you did it."

"Did what?"

"You know."

"No, I don't know, or I wouldn't be asking. What are you talking about?"

Kazuki scratches his head. "What I mean is...I don't think you did the thing everyone thinks you did."

"Which would be?"

"You know, the whole kidnapping Yalamba thing."

"What?" My eyes go so wide I feel like they might burst from their sockets.

"No need to get shouty. I'm just the messenger."

"Yeah, a messenger who's delivering a ridiculous message."

"Sorry, I don't mean to make you angry. That's what I'm hearing, and from a lot of people too. Everyone got the alert about Yalamba's disappearance, and the Know-it-Alls have heard that her parents have filed a report with the academy and prefectural authorities."

"And somehow, I'm to blame, despite the total lack of evidence?"

"Well…a lot of people did see you covered in blood."

Red-handed.

"Because I slipped and fell in it. That doesn't mean Yalamba is gone or that I had anything to do with it."

"The Know-it-Alls also picked up on the rift between you and Yalamba. Some think you might have something against Yalamba now—maybe all Ferals. Deficients are the only ones lower than Ferals in the ability hierarchy. Since you're the only Deficient here, you're the obvious suspect."

Simon had predicted that I might be blamed for the rabbit incident, but this has descended into a level of idiocy that I couldn't have anticipated.

"How would they know about the rift in the first place? The only people who knew were Yalamba, Landon, me, and…you."

Kazuki's face flashes as pink as the rising sun. "They could have gotten it from any of us. I hope it wasn't me, I really do, but you never know who might snatch your thoughts or when. Our minds are shooting in a thousand different directions at any given time. I'd say they might have even gotten it from you, except…"

"Except what?"

Kazuki clears his throat. "Most Know-it-Alls won't risk reading your mind. You know that."

I dig my fingers into my scalp and try not to scream. Of course, I didn't merit a mind reading, the disgusting Deficient that I am.

I've always loathed Atlases, but now I have a particular desire to strangle all the Know-it-Alls at the academy.

"Whoa, Alé, there's a whole lot of anger coming from you right now. You've got to stop being so negative."

"I'm not being negative!" I ignore the echo of my words in the empty hall.

Kazuki crosses his arms and looks me straight in the eyes. He remains that way for a few seconds, chewing at his lower lip. After a few more seconds, he thumps his foot against the ground, undoubtedly trying to distract himself from the discomfort.

"Fine. Maybe I am being a little negative." I work to control my tone. "But I have every right to be. My best friend is missing, and there's a rumor going around that I'm the reason why."

Kazuki lowers his head and twists the tip of his boot on the floor. "The thing is, they don't just think you kidnapped her. They think you—"

"What?"

Kazuki slices his finger across his throat. My entire body shivers.

"They think you…killed her."

My brain goes blank. The possibility that Yalamba might be dead had never crossed my mind.

"It was the message. *DIE FERAL*," Kazuki adds. "It's a lot like the one at the Kerrains' home. It's fishy. People aren't going to assume it's a coincidence… They might think that Yalamba was the one who turned you down and now you have a personal vendetta against all Ferals. If you already killed two Ferals, what's one more?"

In this moment, I realize how much I hate the Achewon Egalitarian Academy. It doesn't have a single redeeming quality. I want to set it on fire. I want it *destroyed*. I don't care if a single person rises from the rubble. They've given me nothing but trouble over the years. This place was supposed to offer equal education to all, regardless of ability, but they *don't*.

"Calm down, Alé. I really don't like hearing what you're thinking right now."

"Then stay out of my mind! Just because you have your stupid telepathic ability, it doesn't mean you have to read my thoughts all the time."

I close my eyes and take a deep breath. That was harsh, but I can't take it back now. What's said is said. And when it comes to Know-it-Alls, what's thought is thought.

This will all blow over eventually. Yalamba will come back. We'll be friends again. We'll suffer through dodgeball together in PE module, and we'll hang out after school. She will show me her drawings, and I will read her my journal entries. It will all go back to the way it has always been.

I open my eyes. I guess I shouldn't be surprised to see that Kazuki is no longer here. He must have reached his limit with me, just as I had with him.

＊ ＊ ＊

I tell myself the day can't get any worse, but then I have compumetrics. We have an exam today, and I'm not prepared for it. I bite my nails as I wait for the instructress to initiate the test on my holo-screen. Unable to focus, I stand no chance of figuring out the codes. I guess I'll have to suck up the Class 5 failing grade I'm sure to get.

Only a few minutes into the exam, the module's door slides open and two Prefectural Security officers step inside. They're dressed in their uniforms—blue bodysuits with large belts and pointed shoulder pads. One is tall and has silver hair. The other is stockier and sports a mustache that looks like it has swallowed his upper lip.

The other students go silent as the officers scan the room. Eventually, they find me.

"Student Alejandro Aragon," the taller one says, "your immediate presence is requested at the headmaster's office."

I wonder why the headmaster has made such an official, shoulder-padded fanfare to retrieve me. Couldn't the office make a simple announcement like they normally do when a student is called from a module?

"Now!" the silver-haired officer demands.

I stand up and twenty-three sets of eyes focus on me and me alone. The attention makes my movements feel even more cumbersome than normal.

The eyes follow me as I step toward the prefectural officers. The mustached one stands in front of me, and his silver-haired partner positions himself behind me. Once we're in the hallway, they modify their formation so they're flanking me on both sides.

The officers are silent the entire way over to the headmaster's office. It feels like they're marching me to my execution.

Stand up for yourself. Fight back. Defend your rights. I can still hear her voice, as clear as ever. I just have to channel it.

The headmaster's meeting room has a large seating area with a low table made of black marble. Headmaster Slaughter is already seated at the far end. He is unmistakable in his official black robe and the ornate frame that arches over his head and shoulders. Everything about his youthful appearance is piercing—from his gray eyes to his platinum-dyed facial hair, which contrasts starkly with the darkness of his flawless skin.

"Good afternoon, Student Aragon," Headmaster Slaughter says. "Please have a seat."

The deep hum of his voice raises the hair on my arms.

Sitting at the table are six prefectural officers wearing glass helmets. Judging by their ostentatious blue robes, they must be Truth and Justice officers—highly trained officials who monitor legal proceedings in the prefecture.

In other words, they're here to read my mind.

Across from the officers are Yalamba's parents. Ms. Koroma makes brief eye contact with me. Heavy shadows lurk beneath her eyes. Mr. Koroma's face crumples like a piece of paper the second he spots me. He springs up from the floor and points in my direction.

"That's him! That's the one who knows what happened to my daughter!"

"Calm yourself, Mr. Koroma," Headmaster Slaughter says in his even, measured tone. "The meeting has not yet started."

"How can I calm down when we have a monster in our midst?" Spit flies from Mr. Koroma's mouth.

"Please, Mr. Koroma. If you are unable to control yourself during the proceedings, then I will not allow you to observe. I would suggest that you calm down and have a seat."

Mr. Koroma grunts but returns to his seat. People tend to obey when the headmaster makes a request.

And thus begins the headmasterly inquisition.

The meeting starts with the ringing of a small tranquility bell. It's meant to put us all at ease, but for me it does the opposite. My stomach flutters, and I want to vomit.

"We are gathered here today to investigate a complaint from the Koroma family regarding the absence of their daughter, Student Yalamba Koroma," the headmaster says, his voice impassive. "Student Koroma did not arrive home yesterday following the academy's final module. It is reported that she took her shuttle bus and disembarked at her normal stop, but according to her family, she never entered the housing unit."

Ms. Koroma sobs lightly when she hears the words, and she buries her face into her husband's shoulder.

"We have tried every means possible to contact Student Koroma, including identity band tracking," the headmaster continues. "As of yet, Student Koroma has not responded. According to data we have received from the prefecture's identification offices, the location device on Student Koroma's identity band was deactivated yesterday at 16:53. This means she had a fully functioning identity band until she got off the shuttle bus. Given what we know, we will proceed under the assumption that Student Koroma is indeed missing. What we need to find out is why. Perhaps she was apprehended by force, or perhaps it was a deliberate personal decision to leave."

"Deliberate personal decision, my culo!" Mr. Koroma points at me once again. "Interrogate him! What are we wasting our time for?"

"Mr. Koroma," Headmaster Slaughter says sternly. "One more outburst will result in your immediate removal from this meeting. Do you understand?"

Mr. Koroma crosses his arms with a loud harrumph. His wife places a hand on his shoulder and tells the headmaster that her husband understands.

"Then let us carry on," Headmaster Slaughter says. "The purpose of this gathering is to understand more about this situation from those closest with Student Koroma. That is why we have called you here today, Student Aragon."

Does the headmaster expect me to believe him? This situation looks and feels more like a trial.

"To my left are prefectural officers from the Truth and Justice Division of Prefectural Security," says the headmaster. "They are here to record our words and thoughts and to ensure the honesty and integrity of this interaction. Student Aragon, please understand that any deviation from the truth, be it minuscule or profound, is grounds for punishment at the discretion of the academy and prefectural leadership. It may also result in your removal from this institution."

I know I hate the Achewon Egalitarian Academy, but that doesn't mean I want to get kicked out after putting up with it for two painful years. Then I'd be stuck in Achewon forever.

"I understand," I say tentatively.

Headmaster Slaughter nods. "Let us begin. Student Aragon, when was the last time you saw Student Koroma?"

The tiny fibers inside of the six Truth and Justice officers' glass helmets light up with multi-colored sparks. They trace the frequency of the officers' thoughts as they read my mind. Every second that goes by is prime material—a thought for the taking that is automatically recorded.

"I…I was outside of her locker," I say. "I wanted to say hello. Things between us haven't been very good for a while, but I wanted to see if there was something I could do to make them better. We talked for a bit by her locker, but the conversation didn't go anywhere. I decided to walk away, but I tripped and fell. I got up, and then I heard Yalamba scream. I turned around to make sure she was okay, and there was a commotion around her locker. I pushed through the students and slipped and fell a second time. There was blood everywhere. When I looked closer, I saw the rabbit's head. There wasn't a body anywhere or anything. The rabbit looked like it had been dead for a while."

"Do you recall anything else about the scene at Student Koroma's locker?" Headmaster Slaughter asks.

"Yes. There was a message written in blood on the mirror. *DIE FERAL.*"

"Do you have any idea who wrote the message?"

I shake my head. "None at all." *But I have my theories.*

A Truth and Justice officer, who has vibrant purple lips, shoots her hand into the air. "Recommendation to question Student Aragon about any potential suspects he has in mind regarding the rabbit incident."

That was quick.

"Recommendation approved," Headmaster Slaughter states.

I know there's no point in hiding my thoughts. The Truth and Justice officers will hear them anyway.

"I think…it might have been Student Landon Waters."

"And why do you say that?" Headmaster Slaughter asks.

I clear my throat. As much as I dislike Landon, it still feels weird being the one to rat him out.

"There was a dodgeball game a couple of weeks ago that ended with Yalamba throwing a ball at Landon's face. It broke his nose. He left the game screaming that Yalamba would pay for what she did."

"Tensions were undoubtedly high between them," says the headmaster. "I even received an anonymous request to pardon Student Koroma, which unfortunately, I could not do."

He got my letter after all.

"How do you think Student Waters acquired entrance to Student Koroma's locker?" the headmaster asks.

I haven't thought this part through yet. "I'm not sure. If he didn't have her identity band, then I don't know how he could have gotten in. Maybe she left the door open accidentally."

Headmaster Slaughter says nothing to refute the theory, which makes me wonder if it might be true.

"Student Aragon, you mentioned that 'things' between Student Koroma and you hadn't been 'very good' for some time. Could you please expand on this?"

A bead of sweat drips down my temple. This is the last thing I want to discuss.

I look to the Truth and Justice officers and realize, yet again, that I have no choice. I take a deep breath and fess up. I tell them about Yalamba's visit, what she admitted to me and what I said in return. I leave out the parts about Yalamba's picture and us kissing. I can't bring myself to talk about those things out loud.

But the Truth and Justice officers do it for me. They read my mind and recount everything that happened, including the kisses, when there is absolutely no need.

"I don't believe it for a second!" The vein in Mr. Koroma's forehead swells to the point of bursting. "He's lying. My daughter would never... She could never!"

"Mr. Koroma," Headmaster Slaughter says severely. "I am afraid you have overstepped your bounds one too many times during the course of this meeting. I am going to have to ask you to leave."

"You can't kick me out! My daughter is missing!"

"Please, Headmaster Slaughter." Ms. Koroma's eyes flood with tears. "We want to find our daughter. Please let my husband stay. We only have one question we want to ask."

She turns to me as tears slide down her cheeks. "Do you know where she is?"

I shake my head. "I don't have a clue."

I don't know what it is exactly, but something about answering that question finally makes it all seem real to me. Yalamba is *gone*. If we don't do something soon—if I don't do something soon—she might never come back.

Ms. Koroma's lips quiver, and she presses her face into her hands, weeping.

The headmaster's expression remains as serious as before, but he doesn't make Yalamba's father leave.

Stand up for yourself. Fight back. Defend your rights. Yalamba's voice is practically singing inside my head, and I can't ignore her words.

"I didn't do anything wrong here," I said, "and I've answered all your questions. Can't the Truth and Justice officers affirm that?"

The headmaster says nothing. The Truth and Justice officers say nothing. They look to one another, as if searching for the answer in each other's eyes.

"We are unable to adhere to such a request," the officer with the purple lips finally says. "We may only conduct the investigation, not interfere with its results."

"The truth isn't an interference. The truth is exactly what it sounds like. The truth. It would settle everything."

"Student Aragon, we cannot state any information that may bias the investigation. No further queries will be received on this matter. Our procedure is final."

They've basically told me to shut the feck up. I try my best not to think *incompetent arseholes*, but I can't help it.

"What about the footage?" I blurt out.

A heaviness descends as all eyes in the room turn toward me.

"What footage, Student Aragon?" asks Headmaster Slaughter.

What does he think I'm talking about? Footage that will prove Landon did this to Yalamba and clear my name.

"Security footage," I say. "I don't know how it works, but I assume there must be devices set up to record the activities in the hallways."

Headmaster Slaughter coughs and adjusts the collar of his uniform. "Of course, we have such measures in place to ensure the safety and security of all students and staff. However, these measures are managed by the prefecture, which must provide authorization to the academy to use any recordings obtained."

"I know I'm not a prefectural officer and don't know much about these things, but shouldn't the prefecture have shared the footage with you before you started questioning students?" I ask. "I had nothing to do with Yalamba's disappearance. You could interview me a million times, and you'll get the same answers over and over. But the footage will tell you what you need to know right away."

Mr. Koroma is grinding his teeth, and it looks like he might erupt. Ms. Koroma places her arm over him to keep him quiet.

"He has a point," Ms. Koroma says. "If you've recorded something, we need to see the evidence."

One of the Truth and Justice officers raises a hand to intervene.

"The Truth and Justice Division has received and reviewed the footage. It is currently under analysis."

"Analysis?" Mr. Koroma asks between clenched teeth. "What's there to analyze? If there's something to see, then we need to see it now. This is my daughter we're talking about!"

The Truth and Justice officers glance at one another, undoubtedly passing internal communications with their minds.

"Very well," says the officer with her annoyingly purple mouth. "The Truth and Justice Division is able to grant the request. Allow us a few moments. We remind you that prefectural footage is strictly confidential and must not be discussed outside of this room."

Finally! We're making progress.

"Student Aragon must leave though," the officer adds.

"What?" I shout.

"We must follow prefectural protocol, Student Aragon."

"But you know I didn't do it! I have a right to view the footage as much as anyone else."

"You are not family of the missing person."

Like hell I'm not family to Yalamba.

"You brought me here to accuse me, and you won't let me view the one piece of information that might lay this all to rest?"

"We are doing everything in our power to advance this investigation, Student Aragon," says Headmaster Slaughter. "Trust us with this process."

My brain is overwhelmed, and my heartbeat is thumping loudly. I can't think of a reply to the headmaster's last statement. That's probably a good thing, otherwise the officers would hear exactly what I think about the academy.

"What if the family grants permission for him to view the footage?" Ms. Koroma asks.

The request catches me by surprise. Why would Yalamba's mom speak up in my defense?

"The prefecture is able to accommodate such a request, provided it does not compromise the investigation," says an officer.

"Will it compromise the investigation?" asks Ms. Koroma.

Again, the officers look to one another before answering. "Not to our knowledge."

To think that this was the division Yalamba had wanted me to list on my prefectural application.

"Then he has our permission to watch it," Ms. Koroma says. "You can read his thoughts as he does."

Of course. There's always an ulterior motive.

"Then it is settled," says Headmaster Slaughter. "Perhaps the footage will raise ideas among those who are present here today and clarify the pathway forward."

The purple-lipped officer's fingers move across her holo-screen. The lights dim and the footage is projected. The image is enlarged and crisp.

I watch the scene of the still and quiet hall with a mixture of fear and anticipation. I want to see Landon's muscular body appear on the screen, so I can prove he was the one who left the bloody death threat in Yalamba's locker.

I gasp when someone finally appears on the screen. The person is wrapped in a cloak, undoubtedly for protection from the cameras, and is carrying a small bag. They crouch down and make several jerky arm movements before standing back up. They extend their arms forward.

Too far forward. Without opening the door, their hands penetrate the locker, sinking through the metal door to insert the contents of the bag inside.

The person's head and shoulders follow, passing through the locker door and disappearing from sight.

Shortly after, the culprit bolts from Yalamba's locker and out of range of the camera's view.

My hands cover my open mouth. I've been wrong this entire time. Suddenly, I know who the rabbit slayer is, and it's the last person I would have expected.

There's only one Feral who can fade through dodgeballs, and, it seems, locked doors.

Yalamba's kidnapper is none other than Mixie Trait.

CHAPTER NINE
THE KAZUKI PLAN

The image disappears and the Truth and Justice officers remove their helmets. The inquisition is over.

"I believe that will be enough for one day." The headmaster rises from the floor as the lights brighten. "The meeting is adjourned."

"What do you mean, *adjourned*?" Mr. Koroma asks.

"We are finished," the headmaster says. "There is nothing left to cover."

"We just started!"

"Headmaster Slaughter, do you know who that was?" I ask, ignoring Mr. Koroma's protest.

"All conclusions will be drawn by the Truth and Justice officers as part of their investigation. Now, please exit the room. We have to proceed in a timely manner."

"But, Headmaster Slaughter—"

"Please exit at once, Student Aragon," the headmaster commands. He shoots a displeased glance at the two Prefectural Security officers. They jump to their feet and take their places at my sides. I stand up reluctantly. The officers walk me to the door without a word.

Fortunately, the officers don't feel the need to accompany me from the conference room to my next module, which judging by the waning hallway traffic, is about to start any minute.

I sprint like a Racer toward the telepathic module wing. I don't know what module Kazuki has next, but I need to intercept him before he gets there.

The bell hasn't yet beeped by the time I make it to the Know-it-Alls' wing. As soon as I arrive, clusters of silent Know-it-Alls stop what they're doing and look in my direction. I guess they won't be nose-diving into my brain all at once—being a Deficient has that perk, at least—but you never know.

"I'm looking for Kazuki Tanaka. Where is he?"

No one responds. They stand there like stone statues and stare at me through their clunky glasses—a trademark of the Know-it-Alls.

I catch Simon Polk drawing toward me in his hoverchair. He doesn't seem as perplexed by my presence as the others. Why should he be? He probably saw all of this coming.

"It seems like they've gone tongue-tied," Simon says.

"Like everyone else at the academy. Everything you said about me being blamed came true. I should have believed you when you told me."

"As long as the prefectural authorities know you're innocent, that's all that matters. The masses will catch up in time."

"Thanks, Simon. Sorry to ask, but would you happen to know where Kazuki Tanaka is by chance?"

"The second years usually have Telepathic Defense module now, so he should be—"

"Here."

I spin around to find Kazuki standing behind me.

"Kazuki!" I shout with relief. "We need to talk!"

I thank Simon again and pull Kazuki down the hall away from the telepathic module wing. I need to speak with him in private.

"Alé, what are you doing?" Kazuki plants his feet, so we both come to a halt. "I'm gonna be late for my module."

Kazuki winces as the academy bell beeps.

"Correction. I *am* late for my module."

"It doesn't matter," I tell him. "There's something really important going on."

I look back at the telepathic module wing. Even though it's now clear, I think and speak as softly as I can.

"Okay, Kazuki. First off, I was a total arse to you before and I'm sorry. A lot has been going on lately, and it has been wearing on me. I'm not always in a good mood in the best of times, and this is not the best of times."

"That's okay, Alé. You've got some deep-seated anger issues, and you have a great deal of difficulty trusting others, as a result of a series of abandonments and betrayals. Plus, it isn't every day you're accused of murdering your best friend."

The mini psychological evaluation catches me off guard. "Since when did you become my therapist?"

"I'm not one yet, but my mother is. I read all of her books."

My mind doesn't know what to do with this information, so I put it to the side and move on. "I'm only going to think this once, so you have to pay attention. All right?"

"Sounds good to me. Think away."

I take a deep breath, close my eyes, and remember everything that happened today. Getting pulled out of my module by the Prefectural Security officers. The meeting with Headmaster Slaughter. The incompetent Truth and Justice officers. Yalamba's pissed-off father. Yalamba's mother requesting for me to stay. And the footage that proved Mixie had left the death threat in Yalamba's locker.

When I'm done, Kazuki brings his hands to his mouth and gasps.

"Mixie?" He squints several times. "I never would have guessed. Isn't she Yalamba's friend? And a Feral? Why would a Feral want another Feral to die?"

"I have no idea. This is where you come in."

I grab Kazuki's shoulders and stare at him intently. Using only my thoughts, I make sure he understands how much I need his help to track down Yalamba's kidnapper and bring an end to all of this.

Kazuki looks directly at me, establishing unbroken eye contact for the first time since our fight. He doesn't even squint.

"It doesn't seem like you're giving me much of a choice, Mr. Bossy."

So you'll do it?

Kazuki lowers his head as he contemplates. I wish I could read his mind.

Yalamba's life is in danger, Kazuki. Do I have to remind you?

He looks back at me, and the direct eye contact reassures me. "I'm in, Alé."

A smile stretches across my face. *Can this be true? Is Kazuki really going to help me, even though I have been mean to him?*

"I'm really going to help you, even though you've been mean to me. Forgiveness is a part of life. Plus, I'm glad you asked. Seeking outside help is a major step toward overcoming your internal wounds."

Kazuki, not now.

"All right, all right. I'm sorry."

Finally! I have someone who will help. But there's still a catch. A big catch.

I haven't given a single thought as to how this can possibly work.

"Leave it to me," Kazuki says. "I've got you covered."

"What do you mean?"

"You'll find out soon enough."

"What? I need to know!"

Kazuki chuckles. "You don't need to do anything except trust me. You're in good hands. Kazuki hands."

Kazuki wiggles his fingers, and as he does, they disappear one by one.

"A couple of abilities and bit of technology can go a long way," he says. "What we need is a bug. If we could plant one in the headmaster's office, we'd be able to hear and watch any discussions they have about the investigation in real time."

Kazuki, you're a genius!

"I'm more comfortable with above average, in case you're wondering."

Fine by me. So tell me, Mr. Above Average, how are we going to get hold of a bug? Do you have one?

"One? Ha! I have like twenty. My dad is an inventor with the prefecture, remember? He lets me play with all his prototypes. I just have to swing by my locker to see what I've got. I'm sure I can dig something out of there. I can plant it now, but then I've really got to get back to my module. Telepathic Defense is one of my faves."

I want to laugh at Kazuki's combination of quirkiness and efficiency, but my mind isn't settled enough to do so. I can't believe what I'm asking him to do. The consequences, should he be caught, are severe enough to merit expulsion.

Kazuki is a smart guy. He's aware of the risks, yet he's going to do this for Yalamba anyway. A girl he barely knows.

Thank you, Kazuki. A trillion times over.

Kazuki winks. "Anything for a friend, Alé."

He then heads off to prepare himself for the biggest challenge of his accelerated life. I hope with all my heart that he'll make it back unscathed.

CHAPTER TEN
MIND YOU, MY MIND IS NOT MINE

I don't bother reporting to Sexual and Reproductive Health, my last module of the day. Sneaking out of a session about sexually transmitted diseases wouldn't be easy, and I want to see what Kazuki is up to.

Instead, I head to the bathroom and shut myself in one of the stalls. It's the only place I can think of where I'll get some privacy. I'm not sure how long it will take for Kazuki to set up the bug, but I don't want to miss a thing.

My stomach is in knots, and I dread the worst. What if Kazuki gets trapped in the headmaster's office? What if someone bumps into him and figures out he's there? He'll be expelled, and so will I once a Know-it-All is brought in to figure out who his accomplice was.

I cover my face with my hands. There's a million ways this could go wrong. How selfish am I to place this kind of burden on Kazuki? How could Kazuki, in his right mind, have possibly accepted?

If I've learned anything about Kazuki over the past two days, it's that he doesn't really have a "right mind" in the traditional sense. He has a hard time making eye contact with others. He can't always keep track of what people say or think since he often treats thoughts and spoken words like they're the same thing. He's too quirky for the Know-it-Alls and too forthright for the Unseens. Despite having two abilities, he doesn't fit in.

It's a weird realization to come to, especially when I've spent so much time thinking I was the only one in Achewon who wasn't welcome.

There's a lot to like about Kazuki. If people opened their eyes, they'd see he's one of the most fearless people at the academy. He doesn't listen to that voice inside that tells him not to take risks or to scream when he's scared or to run from danger. He takes action and puts his heart into everything he does.

In this case, he's doing me a favor and assuming all the risk. There's nothing for him to gain, yet he's decided to put himself on the line for Yalamba, a Feral he's never spoken with, and for me, a Deficient.

My wrist comm vibrates, and I know it must be him.

I'm going in, it reads.

I take a deep breath, like I'm trying to inhale all the air in the world. *Trust him*, I think.

Kazuki sends me a code that links to my holo-screen, and all of a sudden, I'm right there with him. The bug is up and running, and he's moving through the halls. The walls and tiles are surprisingly clear. The bug's lens automatically zooms in and out, focusing on anything that moves. With my earpieces in, I can hear everything, even the sound of Kazuki's breath.

"Good luck, Kazuki," I whisper to the screen.

Kazuki is standing just outside the main office when the bug focuses in on a group of people. I gasp when I realize who they are. The same Prefectural Security officers who brought me to the headmaster are flanking Mixie Trait now. The skin of her face and neck is splotchy, and she's staring down at her hands.

My heart is palpitating, and my stomach is doing flips. It's amazing that I can see all of this in such crisp detail. How has no one realized that Kazuki is right there with them?

The door to the office slides open. The first officer leads the way, followed by Mixie and the other officer. The bug is moving again. It's so close to the second officer that all I can see is his back. Kazuki must shuffle to the side, because I see Assistant Clarkson, looking as beet-faced and curmudgeonly as ever.

"The headmaster is ready to see you," Assistant Clarkson says.

Finally, I allow myself to breathe. Kazuki is in.

The cluster follows Assistant Clarkson to the headmaster's meeting room. It's just as it was when I was there earlier. Headmaster Slaughter sits at the head of the long table and the Truth and Justice officers are seated at the side. Their helmets are already sparking. Yalamba's parents are still there too. I guess they insisted on observing any remaining interviews.

The Prefectural Security officers and Mixie take their seats. Kazuki must have set himself up in the corner of the room. I can see Mixie's profile and the faces of Truth and Justice officers. I can only see the back of the headmaster's ornate shoulder frame, but that's fine. Kazuki chose a good spot.

Mixie's face is so white. She looks like she's about to throw up on the table. She keeps her head lowered and doesn't make eye contact with anyone. The headmaster announces the purpose of the meeting like he did for my meeting. When he gets to the part about Mixie facing expulsion if she doesn't tell the truth, she places her face in her palms and starts to sob.

If she's trying to convince anyone she isn't guilty, she's not off to the greatest start.

"Student Trait," the headmaster says, "we need to know if you have any knowledge of what occurred at Student Koroma's locker."

Mixie doesn't respond. She crosses her arms over her chest and rocks back and forth.

"I do not enjoy repeating myself, Student Trait. I will ask you one more time. Are you aware of what happened yesterday at Student Koroma's locker?"

Again, Mixie doesn't answer. Tears continue to stream down her face. The Truth and Justice officers remain focused, processing the text on their holo-screens.

The questions that follow are met only with sobs. I hope the Truth and Justice officers are picking up on everything they need, because Mixie is keeping it all to herself.

"Let's get to the point. Show the security footage," Mr. Koroma says.

The headmaster cooperates and shows the footage of the person approaching Yalamba's locker. Though you can't tell it's Mixie simply by looking, the person clearly slips something through the locker door in a way only Mixie can do.

"We do not know of any other students with the ability to pass through solid objects," the headmaster says.

The Truth and Justice officers' helmets spark more brightly, and Mixie slams her hands onto the table.

"You might think it's me, but it wasn't," she says. "I could never do something like that to Yalamba. Never!"

"Unfortunately, the evidence appears to say otherwise," the headmaster responds. "We have tracked your identity band coordinates at the time of this footage, and it places you in this exact location, in front of—and even inside of—Student Koroma's locker."

I cover my mouth. It was Mixie after all.

"You're wrong!" she blurts out. "The physical body isn't everything. There are other factors to consider."

Headmaster Slaughter says, "We are the agents in charge of our physical bodies, Student Trait. We must take accountability for our actions."

"That's not true," says Mixie. "Sometimes it doesn't feel like we have any agency at all."

I'm beyond confused. They've shown Mixie the footage, and they pinpointed her location. Yet she still isn't fessing up.

Mr. Koroma stands up from the table and points his finger at Mixie, just as he had done to me.

"If that was you at Yalamba's locker, then you're the one who left the death threat!"

An interesting turn. Maybe Mr. Koroma doesn't think I'm to blame anymore.

"I would never write such a thing. I admire Yalamba more than you can possibly know. Besides, we're both Ferals. We're practically family!" Mixie says.

"Yalamba only has one family, and you'll never be part of it!" Mr. Koroma yells. "Now tell us what you did!"

"No! I don't care what you say—you'll never understand!"

Mixie clutches at her red dreadlocks with shaky hands and mumbles, "Mind you, my mind is not mine. Mind you, my mind is not mine." She says it over and over.

Mixie sounds like she's gone off the deep end.

The headmaster tries establishing order. He instructs Mr. Koroma to leave. Being the most stubborn man on the planet, Mr. Koroma refuses. Soon Yalamba's mom is on her feet, trying to calm her husband and the situation.

The combination of it all—the rabbit, Mr. Koroma's words, Mixie's refusal to admit anything—fills me with dread. Something doesn't feel right. Things aren't adding up.

I hope the headmaster will ask who Mixie believes is responsible, but there isn't time for additional questions. The purple-lipped Truth and Justice Officer's helmet sparks red, and she stands from her seat.

"An alert has been detected," she says.

Within seconds, the other officers' helmets are glowing red too.

The woman scans the room until her eyes land on the corner. Kazuki's corner. She asks the other officers if they detect something. Two nod. The officers close their eyes. I imagine they must be trying to mentally hear what they cannot see.

Get the feck out of there, Kazuki!

But it's too late. The officer with the purple mouth makes eye contact with the bug, which zooms in on her expression. I feel like she's staring through it into my soul.

"Intruder," she says.

My heart rattles in my chest like a snare drum. I don't know what to do. I stand. I sit. I stand. I need to walk. I need to breathe. I can't stay in the stall. I need to get out of here.

I don't want to watch. I don't want to know how this will end, but I have no choice. I owe it to Kazuki.

Suddenly, there's nothing left to watch. The holo-screen goes blank, and the sound fades. The bug is dead.

Holy scheisse, what have I done?

CHAPTER ELEVEN
ACHEWON GREEN

My thoughts are a blur, but it doesn't matter. My legs do my thinking for me.

For once, I'm early to my shuttle bus. Leaving doesn't feel right. My heart is telling me to stay and help Kazuki, but deep down, I know there's nothing I can do. I won't be able to see Kazuki, and I don't have an ability to stop the officers. Seeing me again will only raise their suspicions even more. If they capture Kazuki, I won't be able to live with myself. I won't let him take the fall alone, not when he risked everything for me.

You don't need to do anything except trust me. You're in good hands. Kazuki hands.

Kazuki had asked me to trust him, so trust him I will. He can make it through this. If I don't believe in him, who will?

As I ride on the shuttle bus, I bite my nails until the whites are gone and the tips of my nail beds sting. At the very least, no one is bothering me. I guess it's one of the perks of being a murder suspect. People don't mess with you when they think you might be capable of killing them.

A few seconds after I hop off the shuttle bus, there's a vibration from my wrist comm. I'm surprised to see Gwen Manghi's name. She's never called me before.

"Hello?" I answer, hesitantly.

"Alé! What's up?"

I flinch at the chirpy male voice. "Is this...Kazuki?"

"Yes, sir. Who else would it be?"

"For feck's sake, Kazuki! You're alive! They didn't catch you?"

"Not so sure about that, but I'll update you later."

"What do you mean? Why are you calling from Gwen's wrist comm?"

"Mine is in my locker. I took it off so no one would see me. Plus, I'm sort of holding on for dear life."

That sounds dire. "Are you okay? Can I help?"

"Don't worry, I'll explain later. Can you meet us at the Achewon Green?"

I have so many questions. How is Gwen mixed up in this? Why the Achewon Green? And what happened with the Truth and Justice officers?

"Just get here," Kazuki says. "We'll get you back to your place before you turn into a pumpkin."

I don't have much of a choice, it seems. I've got to get to the Achewon Green.

When I tell my mom I'm planning on hanging out with a friend, she nearly drops the glass bowl she's just filled with grapes.

"What did you say?" She doesn't bother to hide her shock.

"I said I'd like to meet up with a friend. We're working on a biology article for the academy journal. We need to meet at the Achewon Green."

"Since when do you write for the academy journal?"

"This is my first week," I lie cautiously. "I've got lots of time on my hands these days with the disappearance and all."

My mom looks abashed at my subtle reference to Yalamba. "Of course, it's okay, Alé. It's just...well... Who is it?"

"Kazuki Tanaka. He's multi-accelerated. An M-2."

"A Legion. Which abilities?"

"Know-it-All and Unseen."

"Unique combination."

She wants to know how I met Kazuki, what kind of person he is, and what he likes to do for fun. I feel like I'm being questioned about my first significant other as I describe his quirks and qualities. My brothers never had to undergo interrogations before forging their friendships. Why do I have to justify mine?

When Mom asks if Kazuki is trustworthy, her voice softens. I can tell this question is important to her. I want to say yes, but with thoughts of Mixie in my head, I'm not sure who's trustworthy anymore. I tell her Kazuki seems genuine—more genuine than anyone I've met in a long time.

Satisfied after her minor inquisition, my mother brings me to the Achewon Green. I kiss her on the cheek before leaving the vehicle.

I walk around the Achewon Green's perimeter until I spot Kazuki and his shaggy hair. He's standing on the opposite side of the circular water fountain, throwing his sensor ball. It's weird not seeing him in his academy uniform. Instead, he's wearing a trendy, lilac-colored robe—the kind of casual clothing Unseens tend to wear. He must have gotten changed at his housing unit between his spy work at the academy and his arrival at the garden.

I greet Kazuki with a hand slap and fist bump. The act feels strange since I've never done it, but it's what boys often do when greeting each other in the prefecture.

I can't help but notice Kazuki has a small clump of white rice on his chin. He must be reading my thoughts, but he doesn't seem to mind. Instead of wiping away the rice, he pinches at it and plops it into his mouth.

"What happened back there?" I ask.

"I'll tell you in a bit." Kazuki continues chewing. "First, let's go inside. We have food!"

I nod and let Kazuki guide me through the garden. I haven't been here in a long time, but the place is as stunningly beautiful as it was the last time I saw it. Trees are everywhere. The dense, branchy creations form a massive, arched canopy of thousands of green leaves. The garden floor is soft and spongy under my feet.

Soon we're in the center of the eastern garden. It's a giant, grassy circle full of flowers of all types and colors—royal reds, fiery oranges, sun-bursting yellows, snow whites, bluish purples, and passionate fuchsias. Their smells are intense, some so sweet they make me dizzy.

At the center of the garden is an enormous tree that must be at least one thousand years old given the size of its massive, cavernous trunk. There's a deep crevice in the front that's big enough to enter and looks like it leads to a secret world. The roots are larger than people, and they weave up and down through the ground in a masterful display of natural embroidery. The top branches must be at least sixty feet high, spanning from one side of the circular garden to the other.

When I lower my gaze from the tree, I see Kazuki sitting down next to a young woman in a red sari dress and matching shawl.

I do a double take when I realize who it is.

"Gwen?" I ask.

"Good to see you too, Alé," Gwen says.

My face goes warm. Did Gwen Manghi really say it was good to see me?

"Have some *kimbap*," she adds. "You're too skinny."

Gwen tosses me an aluminum-wrapped roll of kimbap. I miss, of course, and it falls to the ground.

I haven't eaten anything all day and realize I'm starving, but I'm so surprised she's speaking to me that I don't know what to do.

"Don't be surprised," Kazuki says. "You're the reason why we're here in the first place."

"What do you mean?" I ask.

"You haven't told him yet?" Gwen asks.

"I was sort of hoping to keep it a surprise." Kazuki resumes munching on his own roll of kimbap.

A surprise? I'm not in the mood for surprises, unless that surprise happens to be my best friend.

"Uh oh, he's in a mood," Kazuki says.

"I'm not in a mood."

"Then who keeps thinking negative thoughts?" asks Kazuki.

If he were anyone else, I might strangle him. "Can you please stop reading my mind for a second and tell me what's going on? And yes, I am now in a mood!"

"Don't worry, Alé," Gwen says. "I'll bash his face in if he does it again."

"She's lying." Kazuki smiles coyly.

"Wipe that grin off your face, little man," Gwen says. "I would most certainly knock you out."

"That's not what I heard you thinking a few seconds ago," Kazuki teases.

Gwen's face brightens to the shade of one of the garden's pink hibiscus flowers—I've never seen her blush before. She crosses her arms and turns away with an ox-like snort.

"Please." I lower my voice. "I saw everything up until the Truth and Justice officers found you. Then the bug went out. What happened after that?"

Kazuki scrambles to his feet. Even when he's standing, he's not much taller than Gwen is when she's sitting. He nods and clears his throat. I unwrap the crunchy tinfoil surrounding my kimbap and toss a thick piece into my mouth. The soft seaweed bursts with flavors of sesame oil, yellow radish, and cooked vegetables. My mouth waters as I chew on the squishy goodness.

"It all started off fine. I was in my little corner of the headmaster's meeting room, and the bug was working. I was as comfortable as I could be with my butt on the cold floor."

"Oh, really?" Gwen raises a single eyebrow.

"Yes, really. As you may recall, Unseens have to get naked to disappear completely."

Gwen doesn't say anything, but the corners of her mouth lift in a rare grin.

"Gwen!" Kazuki's tone is accusatory. "Shame on you!"

"Shame on me for what?"

"For thinking sexy thoughts."

Gwen presses her fist into her palm. "Now I'm thinking violent ones."

Kazuki! I think. *You're getting off topic.*

"It's her fault!" Kazuki says.

"What's my fault?" Gwen asks.

"Nothing," I snap. "No one here is at fault for anything whatsoever, except for not getting to the fecking point!"

Gwen and Kazuki stare at me with unblinking expressions. It's so quiet I can hear the birds chirping in the tree above.

"I…I think we can do that, sir," Kazuki whispers.

"Good. Where were we?" I say.

"The meeting with Mixie. She was having a rough time. She wasn't answering the headmaster's questions, and Yalamba's dad was out of control."

I ask, "Did you read her mind?"

Kazuki nods. "When she first sat down, all I could hear her thinking was, 'Oh no, oh no, oh no.' After the headmaster showed her the footage of Yalamba's locker, Mixie denied responsibility. Her mind was all over the place, but she seemed convinced that she was innocent."

"But she was caught on tape, and her location was identified," I say.

"That's the mystery. Near the end of the questioning, she kept thinking, *Mind you, my mind is not mine!* That was all I heard before they found me. I nearly peed my pants, except I didn't have any pants on."

I sigh at the image of Kazuki creating a pee puddle in the headmaster's meeting room.

"They say you either resort to flight or fight when you're scared," Kazuki adds. "I've never been so afraid in my life."

"I would have fought." Gwen picks up another roll of kimbap and tosses it to me. I catch it, but I'm not in the mood to open it.

"We aren't all perpetually angry Legions with four abilities and an unrelenting desire to destroy things," Kazuki says.

"True." Gwen shrugs.

"That is why I got my butt out of there, running like a Racer. Luckily, the sensor wasn't locked, so I was able to open the door. Unfortunately, opening the door proved to everyone else that the Truth and Justice officers were right. One officer yelled, 'There's an Unseen in our midst!' I thought I could get away without a problem, but the Prefectural Security officers put on thermal visors to track my energy and movements. Clever men. I'll have to talk to my dad about finding a way to go invisible without being detected thermally."

"Cue the perpetually angry Legion with four abilities and an unrelenting desire to destroy things," Gwen says. "May I take it from here?"

"As long as you keep it clean." Kazuki gobbles up another piece of kimbap.

Gwen clears her throat and takes over. "Last module had just ended, and I was getting a drink from the water fountain. That was when one of the idiot officers bumped into me."

"Oh no, he didn't," Kazuki says.

"I chased him down the hall. He was so distracted he didn't see my throw coming."

"What did you throw?" I ask.

"My dancing heel." Gwen taps at the silver shoe on her foot. "It only took one try. It knocked him out on impact."

My jaw drops. Gwen threw a shoe at a Prefectural Security officer's head. That kind of thing was absolutely insane and beyond illegal.

"Meanwhile," Kazuki says, "I tried to shake off the remaining officer by weaving through the other students in the hall and triggering the sensor of the stairwell's sliding door. I squeezed through the crack as soon as it was large enough for me to fit."

"What about the officer?" I ask.

"He wasn't so lucky," Gwen says. "He didn't make it to the door before it closed. He kept waving his hand over the sensor, but he had to wait several seconds for the door to slide open again. Once he got through, he chased Kazuki up the stairs."

"Where were you planning on going?" I ask Kazuki.

"I wasn't planning," Kazuki says. "I went up and up until I made it to a small, hatched door built into the ceiling. There were a few iron rungs along the wall, so I climbed up them to access the door.

"And the officer?" I ask.

"He caught up to me as I was opening the hatch. I was nearly through when he grabbed my ankle. His grip was strong—bone-crushingly so. I knew he had to be an Atlas."

I can't believe what I'm hearing. Kazuki had been caught by a Prefectural Security officer! I had compromised his life—his future.

"Don't have a heart attack, Alé," Kazuki says. "The story has a happy ending."

"Yes," Gwen says. "Kazuki fell in love with the officer, and they lived happily ever after."

I can't help but laugh at Gwen's joke—the first one I've ever heard her make.

"Not *that* kind of happy," Kazuki says. "When the officer grabbed me, I lost focus and went partly visible. I think the sight of me naked shocked him. His grip lightened for a second, so I kicked him in the face. He finally let go, and I climbed up to the academy's roof. I ran to the edge and looked at the drop down. I knew I couldn't survive that kind of a fall—at least not in one piece."

I'm biting my nails again. Even though I know Kazuki is okay, I still don't like where this is going.

"That's when I heard the officer laughing. I spun around and there he was. His silver hair gleamed beneath the sunlight. He wanted to know if I really thought I could get past the prefectural authorities. I said 'yes,' so he charged at me like a bull."

"You were still on the edge of the roof?"

"Yes. There was nowhere else to go."

"So, what happened?" I ask.

Kazuki looks to Gwen, his face beaming with a smile. "She did."

"And my other shoe," Gwen says in her usual monotone.

"It was awesome!" Kazuki says. "Her aim was perfect. She hit him in the head, and he squeaked like a lab mouse."

"There wasn't much time," Gwen says. "Kazuki and I only spoke for a few seconds before he told me he was hearing voices."

"Actual voices," Kazuki adds. "Not the crazy kind."

"You mean the headmaster and the Truth and Justice officers?" I ask.

Kazuki nods. "Yeah, I couldn't make out their words, but I could hear them coming."

"Did they see you?" I ask.

"No way," Kazuki says. "Gwen took me for a ride before they climbed up the ladder. I jumped onto her back, and we flew into the sky."

"You skipped an important detail," Gwen says.

"What do you mean?" Kazuki asks.

Gwen pinches at the fabric of her dress and raises an eyebrow.

"Oh, right," Kazuki says. "Gwen tore off a piece of the officer's uniform and made me wrap it around my waist."

"She did what?" I ask.

Gwen smirks. "I don't want anyone's junk rubbing against me when I'm offering them a ride, thank you very much."

I shake my head. How these two managed to get away with knocking out two Prefectural Security officers, stripping one of his clothes, and fleeing the academy is beyond me.

"It was close," Gwen says. "As we were flying away, I felt something tug at my foot—most likely the headmaster's telekinetic energy. I looked back, but he was a speck in the distance."

"We were lucky," Kazuki says. "We flew away early enough that he couldn't make out any details."

"Are you sure?" I ask.

"Pretty sure," Kazuki says. "He didn't think anything of us. Even though we were up so high, I could still hear some of his thoughts. He never made the identification."

"What if he traces your identity bands and finds out you were the ones who left academy property?"

"I took mine off and hid it before this whole thing began." Kazuki shows me his bare wrist.

It was yet another violation of prefectural rules, but he'd done it for me and Yalamba.

"The headmaster would have to go through every student's coordinates to find out where I was," Gwen adds. "If he does that, more power to him. I'll just tell him I was flying and minding my own business. Not much he can do about that."

"Where does this leave us now?" I ask.

"That's what we were hoping you'd tell us," Kazuki says.

Me? What could two Legions possibly want from me? Gwen and Kazuki have more power in their pinky fingers than I have in my entire body, yet for some reason they're looking to me for answers.

"You're a natural leader, Alé," Kazuki says.

My cheeks and forehead feel warm, and I know I'm blushing.

"I don't know about that," I say. "We figured out a lot today. Thanks for going in there, Kazuki. You didn't have to do that, but I'm really glad you did."

Kazuki swats away the compliment. "It's all right. I'm happy to help."

"And thanks, Gwen, for taking such a big risk," I say.

Gwen scoffs. "Risk? Give me a break. That was child's play."

The comment makes me smile. "Mixie pretty much denied everything," I say.

Kazuki nods. "Yeah. She denied it even after seeing the footage. But she wasn't just saying she was innocent, she was thinking it too. She seemed genuinely convinced that she didn't do it."

"How can that be?" I ask.

Kazuki shrugs. "I don't know. That's what her mind said. I also got the feeling that Mixie is kind of obsessed with Yalamba."

That doesn't come as a surprise to me. I remember thinking something similar the day Mixie was searching for Yalamba after the dodgeball game. Why else would an accelerated person initiate a conversation with a Deficient if they weren't desperate or infatuated?

"Maybe Mixie isn't fully to blame," Gwen says.

"What?" Kazuki and I ask simultaneously.

"You saw her on the footage, and obviously, only a Feral like Mixie would be able to get in and out of someone's locker like that. What if someone put her up to it?"

Kazuki's eyes widen. "Like—"

"Landon," I say.

Gwen nods. "It's a theory."

"We can't count him out of this," I say. "Landon is one of the only students who has openly expressed how much he loathes Yalamba."

Kazuki adjusts his glasses, and his eyes bounce between Gwen and me. Something tells me he's trying to process both of our thoughts at once.

"We have to talk with Mixie," I say. "Then we might have a chance of figuring out what's going on."

"How are we going to do that?" Kazuki asks. "After getting caught on camera, she's sure to have been suspended, if not expelled. I don't think we'll be seeing much more of her from now on."

"We might if she lives close by," I say.

"She does," Gwen says.

Kazuki and I turn to Gwen, dumbfounded.

"Don't look at me like I'm crazy," Gwen says. "Addresses are easy to come by. Besides, Mixie and I used to share the same shuttle bus before I got my flyer's permit."

"Do you know which housing complex she's in?" I ask.

"Of course. Complex G009. It's behind the factories. I'm not sure which specific unit she's in, but it shouldn't be hard to find once we're there."

We're? Does this mean we're officially on the same team?

Kazuki smiles widely. "It most certainly does." He places a hand on my shoulder and another on Gwen's.

"My body, my space," Gwen says in a threatening tone.

Kazuki's hand drops to his side in less than a second.

"How are we supposed to get into the housing unit?" I ask.

Gwen gazes at me with her amazonite eyes and grins.

"Don't worry, Alé. I've got a plan."

I close my eyes and squeeze the ridge of my nose. Whatever Gwen's plan is, I'm sure it's bound to involve violence and life-threatening action. Just what I've always wanted.

"Sounds about right to me," Kazuki says, reading my mind.

I never thought I'd be doing this in a million years, but Yalamba is still missing. The details aren't adding up, and it doesn't seem like the academy is any closer to finding answers than we are.

We don't have any time to waste. I may be a Deficient, but that doesn't mean I won't do everything I can to help Yalamba no matter the cost.

"I'm ready when you are," I say.

CHAPTER TWELVE
OPERATION GWEN

We leave the Achewon Green and head to the factories not by shuttle bus or on foot but by Gwen. She holds on to us tightly, me with her left arm and Kazuki with her right.

Sky Gliders make flying seem so easy, but it is probably the scariest thing I've ever done in my life. Gwen doesn't prepare us for it. There are no demonstrations, instructions, or warnings in the case of an emergency. We're just up and zooming. Everything below us shrinks so fast it makes my stomach churn. I press my eyes shut and hope I won't slip from Gwen's grip.

"Don't worry, Alé!" Kazuki shouts. His voice carries over the cold rush of sky-high wind. "It's gonna be okay!"

Okay, my culo. One wrong move and I'll fall for miles until I splatter into an unrecognizable puddle.

"Take a deep breath!" Kazuki yells. "That's right. In and out. In and out."

"I can't breathe, Kazuki!"

"Yes, you can!"

"From the diaphragm," Gwen chimes in.

I grunt at her instruction, but I have no choice. I suck in the air and hold it until it feels like my lungs might burst.

When I finally let go of my breath, my heartbeat slows, and the clamminess disappears from my hands. I open my eyes slightly to peek at the world around me.

"Look straight ahead," Kazuki says.

I open my eyes fully and see a beautiful, pre-dusk sky. The sun is only a few inches above the hilly horizon. The blue of the sky is darkening as evening creeps upon Achewon.

I know I'm not supposed to look down, but I've never seen the hills and fields at this angle before. I'm seeing all kinds of things in a completely new way. The narrow highways look like blue lines full of tiny moving specks instead of vehicles. The farms are shaped into perfect quadrilaterals. I see the dense woods and the dark, towering form of the abandoned chapel. I can even see the academy. It looks so small nestled next to the massive Achewon Lake. I love how minuscule it is from up here. A mere blip on the landscape.

Now that I've risen above a fear I didn't know I had, the sensation of flying through the sky without limits transforms into a total rush. This is what it must feel like to soar like an eagle. I spread my arms out, pretending they're wings, and laugh. And laugh. I can't stop. Tears slide from the corners of my eyes across my temples. This is the sensation of undiluted freedom.

I haven't had so much fun in a long time, yet I feel guilty. For each laugh. For each wave of exhilaration rushing through me. For each second I stare at the multicolored sky, the setting sun, and the green hills.

I don't deserve any of this. Not when Yalamba is gone.

The flight ends all too soon. Our descent is smooth and gradual as we pass behind the factories to the ring of high-rise housing complexes. Gwen slows down and lands softly, so Kazuki and I can catch our footing on the grass. My legs feel clumsy as they readapt to walking.

As we approach Mixie's housing complex, I realize we have a problem. The fact that we know which housing complex is hers is little consolation. Her building is about twenty stories high with five housing units on each face. We could try having Gwen fly to each window until she happens upon Mixie's unit, but a Sky Glider peeking into people's homes would likely result in a complaint to the prefectural authorities. We've got to be more strategic.

Kazuki and I debate the best way to enter while Gwen applies a dark shade of maroon lipstick to her lips.

"Follow me," she commands.

Kazuki and I exchange a confused look and trail after Gwen as she struts toward the housing complex.

"See that?" Gwen points to the side of the building. Most of the first floor is open, and it's lined by a row of landscaped bushes. "Go over there. Watch, listen, and don't let anyone see you. Wait for my cue."

Kazuki and I obey wordlessly. We sneak through the bushes and find a place to perch near the side of the building. We peer over the plants and see a security guard at the complex's front desk.

Kazuki and I remain as quiet as we can while Gwen enters the building. She's still wearing her red dance costume and silver heels, which makes her look older than her sixteen years.

I have no idea what her plan is. Kazuki is smiling like he's about to watch a movie. I wonder if he has read her mind or if he's as clueless as I am.

Gwen steps into the lobby and immediately catches the attention of the middle-aged security guard. His eyes widen, and he fidgets with the collar of his uniform.

"Haven't seen you around these parts before." He speaks with a nasal drawl.

"I've never been around these parts before, silly." Gwen plays along with a falsified accent of her own. She sounds like a twenty-five-year-old woman who's oozing sensuality.

"She's good," Kazuki whispers.

"How can I help you this afternoon, ma'am?" the guard asks.

The corners of Gwen's mouth lift into a coy smirk.

"As you can see, I'm an entertainer. I've been sent by the prefecture to settle down in Achewon. I'm looking for a suitable housing unit."

"We could use some more entertaining around here, if you know what I mean." The guard makes a noise that's a mixture between a laugh and a grunt. "But everyone knows you've got to go through the Housing Registrar to get a housing unit under your name."

"Of course. I love this area and want to put in for a special request. I was hoping I could see one of the empty units." Gwen leans on the low counter, drawing closer to the guard. "You know, so I could see if it suits my…tastes."

I cover my mouth. I can't believe she's doing this!

Again, the guard pulls at the collar of his uniform. "You'd fit in here, real good. Imagine yourself, wearing whatever you like and doing whatever it is you do, all while overlooking the cityscape."

"Oh, you've got me so excited already. If you show me one, I'm sure I could find a way to repay you for your kindness."

"I'm a big believer in favors. I do a couple for you, and you do a couple for me. We all end up happy."

This conversation is the creepiest thing ever, but Gwen keeps going.

"Sounds like a plan to me, stallion. By the way, do you know the Trait family? I recently met Ms. Trait, and she's the one who referred me to this complex."

"The Traits, of course. They live in unit 1312."

"Would it be possible for me to drop by unit 1312 to surprise them?"

"Ms. Trait isn't back from nursing at the hospital yet. Maybe you can message her to let her know you're here?"

"That sounds like a fabulous idea. Let me give it a try."

The man nods. "I'll be in the back getting the key cards, sweet thing."

The guard moves out of sight. Gwen motions at us and points to the stairwell. That's our cue to move.

Kazuki and I climb over the wall and land in the lobby. We keep moving, not even stopping to acknowledge Gwen as we bolt past. We climb the stairs, leaping up two at a time. I'm already tired by the time we make it to the fourth floor, but we can't stop. We don't know how long Gwen can keep the guard distracted from the security cameras.

When we reach the thirteenth floor, Kazuki and I are huffing, puffing, and sweating, but there's no time to lose. We race down the hall, following the signs to unit 1312. When we turn the corner, we stop abruptly. Gwen and the security guard are standing in front of one of the units. They must have taken the elevator. The guard is searching through a collection of key cards.

Gwen spots us right away. She shakes her head and gestures for us to turn around.

We're not fast enough.

"Hey, you!" the security guard shouts. "What do you kids think you're doing? Get back here!"

He runs after us, but luckily, he isn't a Racer. It doesn't take long for Gwen to outrun him. Kazuki and I watch as Gwen grabs him by his shoulders. She spins him around like a spider would its prey.

"What's all the fuss about, sweet thing?" she asks.

"Let me go!" The guard struggles against her grip. "You're their accomplice, aren't you?"

"Accomplice in what? Housing unit hunting?"

"Get out of my way, you stupid streetwalker!"

Immediately, Gwen's eyes shrink into slits.

"What did you just call me?" Her voice is barely audible.

"A streetwalker! Look at how you're dressed. You're asking for all sorts of trouble."

Oh no, he didn't.

The guard flies back like a rag doll and slams into the wall. He squeals in pain, and his limbs don't move. Gwen must be using her Mind Mover ability to pin him down.

"I don't like that word very much, sweet thing," Gwen says. "And I dislike it even more coming from your disgusting mouth. Now tell me, have you ever been lucky enough to kiss a streetwalker?"

Gwen leans in and plants a long kiss on the guard's lips. As she kisses him, the man's body seems to go taut.

When Gwen pulls away, there's a sparkle in her eyes.

"What…did you do…to me?" the guard asks, his speech slurred. His eyes roll into their sockets, and he collapses to the floor with a thud. Gwen does nothing to ease his fall and looks without pity at his unconscious body.

"Just a bit of chemically enhanced lipstick I thought you might like." She puckers her lips.

The guard is out cold. His chest rises and falls with each breath. I'm glad he's not dead, but there's no telling how long he'll stay knocked out. We've got to get inside Mixie's housing unit fast.

Gwen knocks on the door. No one answers. She waits a few more seconds before knocking again, but still, no one responds.

"We have to break in," Gwen says.

"Have to or want to?" Kazuki asks. He's kneeling down next to the unconscious guard, holding a link of key cards. He tosses them to Gwen with a grin.

"When there's a problem, there's always a solution," Kazuki says.

Gwen grunts at Kazuki's optimism and catches the key cards. She flips through them until she finds the one we need, and she swipes it across the door's sensor. The indicator light glows green, and the door slides open.

We're in.

The housing unit is unlit, but there's still enough light coming through the windows to guide us. No one seems to be home. There are a few boots and sandals scattered near the entrance. The small kitchen is clean and has an untouched feel to it. I hear nothing, and the silence suggests absence.

"I hear something," Kazuki says, "on the balcony."

We step over the paneled floor into the common area, and I notice the sliding glass door that leads outside to the balcony is open. I follow Kazuki through the light curtains.

Then I see Mixie. She's standing on the edge of the balcony—thirteen stories above ground level.

"What's she doing?" Gwen's tone is atypically urgent.

"She wants to jump," Kazuki whispers.

Gwen and Kazuki turn to me as if I miraculously hold the solution for getting Mixie to step back and change her mind. I've only talked to her once. I don't know what I could possibly say to her, but one of us has to try.

Mixie must not have heard us. It's windy on the thirteenth floor, and her flame red dreadlocks blow behind her while she stands on the ledge. She faces the seductive purple sky that bathes the buildings of the city center and the distant hills with a coat of glowing orange.

"Mixie, we know what you're going through," I say.

Mixie looks over her shoulder. She nearly loses her balance when she sees me but recovers it.

"What are you doing here?"

"We…I need to talk to you, Mixie. I know something weird is going on at the academy. Something really strange is happening, and I don't think you can take all the blame."

"How can anyone think that?" Mixie's knuckles have gone completely white as she grips the railing. "They recorded me. They showed me using my ability to get inside Yalamba's locker."

"I don't always trust videos. They only show one side of a story."

This is it—now or never. It's time to ask the golden question.

"Did someone put you up to it, Mixie?"

Mixie's eyes widen into small, glossy plates. She closes her mouth, and her lips quiver. Her stare doesn't shift from mine, even as tears stream down her cheeks.

She nods.

"Who was it?" I ask.

Mixie shakes her head and digs her fingers into her fiery hair. Her balance is shaky on the other side of the railing. "I don't know. I honestly don't know."

"Was it Landon?"

Mixie's face wrinkles, and she begins to sob. "I said I don't know! How many times do I have to tell you people that I don't know?"

How can she not know?

"Mixie, if you know anything, and I mean *anything*, you have to tell me. I'm trying to figure this out for Yalamba. If we don't make some sort of breakthrough soon, she might—"

I can't finish the sentence. Anything I say will sound too final.

"Please, Mixie. We need you. *Yalamba* needs you."

Mixie stops sobbing and swallows. A few silent seconds pass before I hear a woman calling Mixie's name from inside the unit.

"It's Mixie's mom," Kazuki whispers. "She just got home."

I don't budge. I keep my attention fixed on Mixie alone.

"I don't even know if this is my voice anymore," Mixie whispers. "It feels like there's something inside my brain. I'm so scared."

I hear footsteps behind me on the balcony and a voice I don't recognize says, "Mixie, where are you? Something happened to the guard."

"Mom," Mixie says. She breaks eye contact with me and looks over my shoulder.

"Mixie, what on earth are you doing?" her mom yells. "Get down from there!"

"That's what Alé's been trying to get her to do," Gwen says.

"Mixie, your family loves you." I look into her eyes. "Your friends love you, including Yalamba."

"You don't know that!" Mixie cries. "How could you possibly know that?"

"I just do!" I say. "We wouldn't be here right now trying to get you off that ledge if we didn't care about you. We believe in you and want you to do the right thing. And right now, that thing is helping us figure out what the hell is going on so we can save Yalamba's life."

Mixie's tears stop. I know she heard me, but she remains on the ledge.

"If you're not interested in helping Yalamba, that's fine," I say. "You can change what is happening if you want to, but if you'd rather let it consume you, then go right ahead. Leave the world the same as it's always been."

Mixie stands there with her brown eyes squinting and her mouth partially open. She's completely still except for her wind-rustled dreadlocks. She looks like she might tip over any second. The only thing I'm not sure about is what direction she'll fall.

Mixie bends her knee and lifts her leg. We all watch in silence as she brings one leg over, and then the other. Finally, both of her boots land on the balcony's surface. Once there, her knees give way, and she collapses.

"Oh, Mixie!" Ms. Trait weeps as she throws her arms around her daughter. She rocks Mixie back and forth.

"Thank you," Ms. Trait says to me. Her face is moist with tears. "You have no idea how grateful I am. You saved my daughter's life."

I lower my head. I can't help but think about what might have happened if we hadn't come.

"Um, Alé?" Kazuki pokes my arm. "The guard is awake. I can hear him, and he sounds angry."

"That's our cue," Gwen says.

"We might reach out later, Ms. Trait," I say, "if that's all right with you."

Mixie's mom nods and tells us she owes us the world.

This time, Gwen, Kazuki, and I are the ones who assume places near the balcony's edge. Ready to bring Operation Gwen to a close, Gwen wraps one arm around Kazuki's waist and the other around mine. Together we leap over the railing and freefall with no hesitation. I press my eyes shut. My body tingles as my internal organs sink from the inertia.

When I open my eyes, we're soaring toward the bright orange sun that is just a sliver above the horizon of silhouetted hills.

I keep my eyes open for the rest of the ride. How can I not? As the sky blackens, the scattering of evening stars twinkle like thousands of tiny diamonds. How many there are is impossible to know. I lose count by the time I finally remember to blink.

CHAPTER THIRTEEN
A BIG DAY OF FIRSTS

Everyone is exhausted, but we need to debrief. People rarely use the courtyard of my housing unit at night, so I suggest we head there. It shouldn't draw any unwanted attention. Kazuki and Gwen decide it's a good plan, so off we fly.

A part of me wants to invite them inside, so I can prove to my brothers and parents that I finally have friends, but it's not worth it. It might satisfy my ego in the short-term, but it would raise too many eyebrows. Plus, introducing new friends to my family now would feel like I'm abandoning the old.

I'm not. No one, not even two fantastic Legions, can ever replace Yalamba.

Once we're in the courtyard, Kazuki plops himself on a stone bench with a sigh. Between breaking into the headmaster's meeting room, escaping the prefectural authorities, and sneaking into Mixie's housing unit, it's been a long day for him to say the least.

There's plenty of room beside him, but Gwen remains standing with her arms crossed. It amazes me that nothing about the day seems to show itself in her appearance. Not a single strand of her golden hair is loose, and her smoky eye shadow and maroon lipstick haven't faded.

They look to me, just as they had when we were at Mixie's. Their eyes are hungry for direction.

"I have no clue what we're supposed to do now," I admit, defeated.

"That attitude will get us nowhere fast," Gwen says.

She's right. There's got to be a way forward. We're in the middle of a puzzle, but even the hardest puzzles have solutions.

"Then let's assess what happened at Mixie's," I say. "Kazuki, what could you tell from her thoughts?"

Kazuki shrugs. "I think she's gone crazy. And not just regular crazy, but *crazy* crazy."

"Has she always been like this?" Gwen asks.

"I don't know," Kazuki says. "I've never read Mixie's mind before today. She was convinced she had nothing to do with what happened even though she saw herself in the footage. And she wasn't lying when she said someone put her up to this."

"Did she think anything about who that someone was?" I ask.

Kazuki shakes his head. "Nope. Nothing came to mind even when you asked about Landon. She doesn't know."

How could she not know who made her leave a death threat? *None of this makes sense.*

"Let's not rule Landon out just yet." Gwen punches a fist into her palm to emphasize her point. "I've dealt with him before. If he's the one behind this, then putting an end to it will be easy."

I can't help but smile at the thought of Gwen beating up Landon for a third time. "I don't think we have to resort to violence right away. What we need to do is to catch him in the act."

"Then can we bash his face in?" Gwen asks.

"If he's the one behind it, bash away," I say.

Gwen says, "Good. I'll put myself in charge of this one then. I'll track Landon's every move."

"Maybe someone should contact Mixie tomorrow after school to see how she's doing," Kazuki says.

"Good idea," I say. "Any takers?"

Kazuki and Gwen look at me as though I've asked the stupidest question in the world.

"I think that's all you, Alé," Kazuki says.

"Why all me?"

"I could have forced Mixie to come down with my abilities, but you actually convinced her to step off that ledge by her own volition," Gwen says. "You're connected to her now, whether you realize it or not."

That's one way to make someone feel responsible for the well-being of another, but I see their point.

"Fine, I'll do it," I say. "It'll be good to make sure she's okay."

With our plans somewhat set, there isn't much else for us to do. I bid Kazuki farewell with a hand slap and fist bump. Gwen does the same, pounding my fist with knuckle-cracking force.

Kazuki grins and assumes a piggyback position on Gwen. Gwen doesn't have her headlight on, which is compulsory for Sky Gliders when they fly at nighttime. She levitates anyway, unbothered by the rules, and they take off. They shrink into the distance, blending perfectly with the ocean of blackness that is the night sky.

❋ ❋ ❋

Sleep doesn't come. I don't know how it can, when Yalamba's still out there. *Missing.*

Eventually, I must slip into unconsciousness, because suddenly, I'm back in Yalamba's room. We're kids again, playing on the hard floor.

Butterflies of different colors and sizes flutter around the room. There's a small rabbit hopping in circles in one corner. In another, there's a birdcage with a beautiful red, blue, and yellow parrot. A tiny white fluff of a dog rolls around on Yalamba's sleeping mat.

"Your parents let you have all of these pets?" I ask.

Yalamba shrugs. "They don't know about them yet. I just made them."

Yalamba giggles and takes out one of her sketchpads. She opens it to a beautifully drawn, pastel sketch of a bunny with light brown fur. My eyes shift back and forth between the rabbit and the sketch. The rabbit stops hopping. Its nose twitches up and down and it appears to scrutinize me with its unflinching, peripheral gaze. *Does it realize I'm watching it?*

"Not all of my drawings come to life for some reason, but animals almost always do." Yalamba's nose twitches like the bunny's.

I flip the page to see the next drawing—a caged parrot whose feathers are a splattering of primary colors. The image is so realistic that I feel like the bird is practically begging for me to pet its masterfully textured feathers.

Immediately, I reach out to touch them.

"Don't!" Yalamba says.

The warning breaks my trance. I pull my hand away and apologize.

"Don't worry, Alé. It's just that every time the drawing is touched, it changes. Here, let me show you."

Yalamba grabs a forest green pastel from her collection of materials. She goes straight for the parrot's wing, recoloring the tips of its long blue feathers.

"Watch," she says upon finishing.

I look at the image and then at the bird in the birdcage, chewing at its feathers. The strips of blue at the tips of its wings gradually become the exact shade of forest green Yalamba had added to the drawing.

"And check this out."

Yalamba flips to another page where she had drawn a bright yellow tulip. I hadn't noticed the flower before, but the exact replica is sitting on her desk in a small terra-cotta pot.

Without warning, Yalamba tears the page from her sketchbook in half.

"Yalamba!" I extend my hand as if to stop the irreversible. "Why would you do that?"

Yalamba grins. "Look."

I stare at the potted tulip as its colors fade. It becomes so light that I can see through it. It eventually disappears completely, leaving no trace of its existence.

"That's crazy," I say.

Yalamba giggles. "I know. I wonder what else I can do with my ability."

"I think you can do almost anything. Why don't you— Wait, Yalamba, what's happening?"

Yalamba's eyes widen as she stares at her hands. They have gone translucent, just like the potted plant.

"Something is wrong, Alé!"

She continues to lighten, as though she's being erased. I reach for her, but my hands pass through her shoulders, as if she's made of air.

"Yalamba, stop! Come back! Please, don't leave me!"

She tries to speak, but the words don't make it out of her mouth. Tears slide down her cheeks. I watch one fall to the floor, splashing on impact.

When I look up from the tiny droplet, my best friend is gone, and so are all her animals.

My heart is racing and my jaw is locked when I wake up. My hands are clammy, and sweat drips from my scalp. I pant as though I've been sprinting for miles.

The dream felt so real because all of it happened shortly after Yalamba got her ability.

Everything except for the end.

Yalamba didn't fade away. It was just a nightmare. Only a nightmare.

Yet the realization brings no relief. Even here, safe from the terrible realm of dreams, Yalamba is still gone.

✹ ✹ ✹

I arrive at the academy in the morning with a headache and dark circles under my eyes. My exhaustion won't stop me. I head immediately to Yalamba's locker to wait for her—a daily ritual I've committed myself to until I find her. But of course, she doesn't show.

I had hoped with all my heart she'd turn up. That maybe, just maybe, whoever had taken her had decided this whole thing was pointless.

My head snaps to the side when something warm and gooey splatters against my face.

Wonderful. The ever-familiar glob of spit.

"That's right, Feral-killer! Get the hell out of Achewon!"

My shoulders tense up the second I recognize Jeong's idiotic voice. I wipe the saliva out of my eyes with the sleeve of my jacket. I want to see who spit and jeered at me. If they want a killer, I'll give them one.

The group is already walking away down the hall. They're a bunch of third-year culos who are tough enough to spit in my face but duck out before I have the chance to react.

But I'm already reacting.

I run up behind them and kick the back of Jeong's knee to trip him. He falls to the ground with an embarrassing smack. I pull my fist back and let it fly into the cheek of one of the Racers, who lets out a high-pitched cry.

My attack comes to an abrupt end when an Atlas grabs me by the shoulder and forces me into a headlock. I struggle to escape, but I feel like a mouse trying to move a mountain. He's at least ten times stronger than I will ever be.

"Looks like the worthless defect got angry," he says.

My heart is fluttering and I'm breathing heavily—from exhilaration instead of fear. I finally stood up for myself to these stupid arseholes, like Yalamba had always wanted me to. The way I should have done from the start.

Jeong is back on his feet and in my face. He raises his fist and scowls.

"I've wanted to kick the scheisse out of you ever since you cost me that dodgeball game, defect."

I close my eyes and prepare for the powerhouse punch. Yeah, it'll hurt, but I don't regret what I did. Not one bit.

The punch doesn't come. I'm reluctant to open my eyes, thinking that maybe Jeong is waiting for me to do that. Maybe he wants to give me the joy of watching his fist as it plunges into my face.

After a few unbearable seconds, I peek one eye open. When I do, Jeong has barely budged. In fact, his hand is exactly where it had been before I closed my eyes. The only difference is that now his fist is trapped inside Gwen Manghi's palm.

"I'm going to give you a five-second head start, you pathetic little toad," Gwen says. "Then I'm going to squish you under my boot like the filthy piece of scheisse you are."

Jeong's entire body quivers.

"I'm sorry, Gwen. I didn't mean to! He's the one who—"

"One," Gwen says coldly.

"No, Gwen! I swear! It's not my fault! He—"

"Two."

Jeong squeaks and sprints down the hall. He's around the corner before Gwen reaches three. The other guys are gone too. I guess they ran away when Gwen made her appearance.

"How are you doing today, Alé?" Gwen asks as though nothing has happened.

I'm relieved beyond belief. "Fine, until I got spat on and all. Thanks, Gwen."

"Anytime. It's usually ill-advised to piss off a group of idiots like that."

"I know. I must not have been think—"

"I like that you don't always do what's advisable. It's refreshing and brave. People are rewarded for their bravery. You'll see."

Her eyes shift to Yalamba's locker. "So, she didn't come in today?"

I shake my head.

"No matter," Gwen says. "We'll continue with the plan like we decided last night, right?"

"I think that's our only option at the moment."

"Good. I'll see you later. Until then, try not to pick too many fights. It's getting hard to keep track of you."

Gwen winks and struts away. She only makes it a few steps before turning around.

"Alé, save me a seat at lunch, will you?"

My jaw drops, and I feel my eyes practically bulge from their sockets.

"Don't look so surprised," she says.

"I'm…not surprised," I fib. "It's just… What if my table gets too crowded? I might have to kick someone out."

"You're a good kicker, it seems. Just ask Jeong." She flashes her perfectly straight teeth and struts down the hall.

I know I'm not Gwen's best friend—I barely know her—but something seems different about her. I can't put my finger on it though.

No one bothers me for the rest of the day. I wonder if word has gotten out that every time someone threatens me, Gwen Manghi shows up to bring things to an embarrassing and painful end. I guess some of them probably look down on me even more because I have a Legion saving my butt all the time, but I don't care. Gwen is like a guardian with the way she seems to be watching over me to help make things right. I like being on her team and that she seems to like being on mine.

Even though Gwen had told me to save her a seat at lunch, it surprises me when she sits across from me. The act inspires stares and whispers throughout the cafeteria.

"These people need to get a time-consuming hobby," Gwen says, "and soon."

She tosses her nutrition pack on the table, and the dried cubes land with a thud. Her eyes scan what I'm eating—a triangle of forest-green seaweed filled with wheat rice and brown bean paste.

"You brought your lunch from home?" Gwen asks.

I nod. "I never acquired a taste for cubed things."

"Neither have I, unfortunately. I prefer the red bean paste though."

"Me too, but I take what I can get."

Gwen sighs and looks at her nutrition pack. "Don't we all?"

She takes a reluctant bite from one of her cubes and stares at the crowd of chatty students.

"Do you like the academy?" Gwen asks.

"Who...me?"

"No, the other person at the table."

I scratch my head. "I...I don't really know how to answer that."

"Yes, you do. Use your vocal cords."

It's clear Gwen isn't going to let me off the hook with this one. I take a big bite of my juicy seaweed wrap to buy myself time to think.

"I like some of my modules," I eventually say while chewing on the moist rice. "If that's what you're getting at."

"That's not what I'm getting at."

Time to lift the barrier, the way I've only ever done with Yalamba.

"Then I don't think I do. In fact, I might hate it with the blazing passion of all the stars in ten trillion galaxies."

Gwen laughs at the comment. It's a monotone *heh heh heh*, but I'll take it. Another first.

"Why do you hate it?"

"The people. I can't stand them, because for some stupid reason, they can't stand me."

Gwen nods. "A commonality we share. Human beings suck."

"I guess I don't understand why they can't get over it. I'm not like them, and I'm never going to be. Does having an accelerated ability force you to interpret the world in terms of hierarchies and status? Does it mean you have to believe that certain people aren't worth speaking to—or aren't worth educating—just because they're different? I can't see how it makes sense, but that's the world we live in. That's the world *I* live in each and every day at this stupid academy."

Gwen stops chewing and crosses her arms. She doesn't respond right away, and the pause makes me nervous. Have I offended her?

"Do you mind if I tell you a story?" she finally asks.

"Go for it," I say.

"Once upon a time, there was a little girl named Gwen. Gwen had two mothers who were entertainers and a little sister named Willow, who was six years younger than Gwen to the day."

I'm already captivated by the story, not to mention surprised that Gwen is sharing something so personal. Everyone in Achewon knows who Gwen's mothers are since they're famous Legions who sing, dance, and act in movies. I've never heard anything about Gwen having a sister.

"When Gwen realized she could fly, she decided to share the gift with Willow, who didn't have an ability yet. Gwen was good at keeping secrets and only flew with her sister when she was sure that her mothers wouldn't notice. Willow would laugh the entire time, screaming for Gwen to go higher and higher. She said she wanted to touch the sun." Gwen's eyes twinkle when she says that.

"When Gwen was nine, she took Willow on one of their usual rides through the clouds. They weren't too high up when Gwen noticed they were being followed by a Sky Glider. She recognized him from their housing complex—a strange man with an unhealthy fascination with her mothers. Gwen tried to get to the ground to protect Willow, but the Sky Glider caught up with them and grabbed Gwen by the arm. Gwen struggled, but she was unable to defend herself while holding her sister. The man didn't give up. He pulled and pulled, and as he did, Gwen felt Willow's grip slipping."

My breath catches in my throat, and I realize Gwen is staring past me, focused on something far, far away.

"Willow fell from Gwen's arms while she struggled against the man." Her eyes well with tears. "Gwen broke free from him but not fast enough to save her sister from the fall. He even had the nerve to follow her to the ground where Willow was lying, unconscious. Enraged, Gwen turned on him, punching him so hard he lost consciousness. That didn't stop Gwen though. She wrapped her fingers around the man's pale neck and squeezed. She would have choked the life out of him had adults not interfered and pulled her away."

Gwen closes her eyes and takes a deep breath. She's a Legion with four abilities, but even she can't stop the single tear from falling down her cheek.

"After the incident, Gwen was taken in for observation and psychological support. She went for months until she was declared healed. Willow, on the other hand, was never the same. The head trauma stunted her development, reducing her mental capacity, and robbing her of her ability to speak. Willow never developed an ability either, which left her classified as a Deficient."

Gwen wipes away the tear and reestablishes eye contact with me. Her irises swirl with anger and pain.

"I live in it too," Gwen says. "Every day I see my sister, I think about it. How messed up it is that someone could cause that to happen. How messed up it is that other people treat her like she's less than human. And how messed up it is that I could develop four abilities, while my sister can't even brush her own hair or put on a pair of boots."

A lump builds in my throat. I never imagined Gwen going through something like that, and I never knew that she, of all people, was related to a Deficient.

"The difference is that most people are content with the status quo," Gwen says. "A rare few want to change it. You're one of those few. I've sensed it for a while now."

"How? Don't tell me you have another ability."

"Nope—just the four. I guess I figured that you'd want to change it with what they've put you through. With what you let them put you through."

"*Let* them put me through?"

"Just because you don't have an accelerated ability doesn't mean you're helpless, Alé. What I like about you is that you seem to be realizing that. Each day I see you, you're stronger than you were the day before."

I'm silent. I have no idea what else to say.

"It's people like the bullies you got into trouble with this morning. The stupid Atlases and Racers and—"

Gwen's amazonite eyes shift over my shoulder and lock onto something in the distance.

"Landon," she whispers.

I turn in the direction Gwen is looking to see Landon as he's exiting the cafeteria's sliding door.

"Now is our chance," Gwen says. "Are you ready?"

I nod. We wrap up the rest of our lunches and stuff them into our backpacks. Then Gwen and I are out of our seats and into the hall.

Gwen takes off at a sprint. I try my best to keep up with her at my pathetic, unaccelerated pace. Not bothering to wait for me at the end of the hallway, she flies up the steps with her Sky Glider ability. I propel myself up the stairs as fast as I can. For the billionth time, I wish had an ability so I could keep up.

Gwen is already halfway down the second-story hall by the time I make it out of the stairwell. She's walking, so it's somewhat easier to catch up with her. When I reach her, she silences my panting by bringing a finger to her lips. She's looking at her wrist comm like she's waiting for a message. She smirks lightly when one finally arrives. "Kazuki is on his way," she says. "We could use a Know-it-All."

I don't have a clue what Gwen is scheming, but as I learned yesterday, she's worth trusting even when she confuses you beyond belief.

It only takes a couple of minutes for Kazuki to reach us.

"Can we try to make this quick?" He's out of breath. "I'm supposed to be in the bathroom, and I don't want the other Know-it-Alls to think I was taking a scheisse."

Gwen rolls her eyes before walking to the arched doorway that leads to the balcony of the academy's auditorium. It's a door that can only be opened with a code that's programmed into its keypad.

Gwen lifts her hand to the keypad and types in several numbers. When she's finished, the door slides open.

"It's all four corners of the keypad," Gwen says. "The janitors are lazy with their codes."

"How did you get the code in the first place?" I ask.

"That's a story for another day."

"That's one way to lie to us," Kazuki says with a huff.

"I'm not lying. I'm simply postponing the truth."

"Which is the same as lying," Kazuki says.

"No, it's the same as postponing the truth."

"Which is as good as saying something false."

Gwen grins. "How easily I underestimate the little man's perseverance. Fine, let it be known. I used to have a thing with one of the janitors. Are you happy now?"

Kazuki crosses his arms. "Yes, in fact, I am!"

I wonder if Kazuki is the one who's lying now. I've never seen his face go so red before.

Gwen leads Kazuki and me into the dark balcony. The door slides shut behind us, blocking out the light from the hallway. The pathway is dark—so dark that I feel around with my hands before each step.

"I could use a little light over here," Kazuki says.

Gwen silences Kazuki with a sharp *shh*. I move cautiously, hoping I won't trip and tumble over the balcony's edge.

The balcony brightens slightly when I round the corner of the walkway to the seating area. The auditorium is dark, but a faint glow comes from the crack beneath the rear room's door.

I gulp. Unless a janitor accidentally left the lights on, someone is inside that room.

Gwen steps into the semidarkness. Kazuki and I follow until we're in front of the rear room. It has an old door that uses a lock and key.

"Is someone inside?" Gwen whispers.

Kazuki nods. "Two people."

"Can you hear what they're thinking?" I ask.

Kazuki squints for a few moments before a grin brightens his face.

"Sexy thoughts. Maybe we should turn around?"

"Turn around, my culo," Gwen says.

Gwen brings her hand to the knob and turns it as gently as she can. She bites at her lip the moment the knob stops. It's locked.

I'm shocked when she tugs at the knob with all her might, tearing it away from the door. She pushes the door forward, and it slams against the wall of the rear room with a bang.

If it were possible for my jaw to dislocate completely from my skull and collapse to the floor, that's what would be happening right now. I never thought I'd see *this* in a million years.

Landon Waters is sitting on the ground with his bare torso exposed—dark, smooth, and toned. Next to him is an equally shirtless Ivan Rahman. Landon turns away from Ivan with his arms raised. I only get a glimpse of Ivan's coal-colored eyes before he panics and goes invisible. His pants back up against the wall.

"Landon Waters," Gwen says with a grin. "Who would have guessed you've got a soft spot for Unseens?"

"I don't have a soft spot for anyone," he says with a growl as he bares his teeth.

What I assume are Ivan's hands snatch a black academy jacket from the floor. The legs of the pants stand up and bolt for the door. Ivan brushes against me as he passes.

"We were exercising," Landon says.

"Is that what they're calling it these days?" Gwen asks.

I'm silent, embarrassed, and surprised beyond belief. My mind can't seem to process what I saw. I never thought Landon was emotionally capable of doing anything other than causing pain.

Landon looks lost and vulnerable in a way I never knew he could be. I almost feel pity for him. For the first time, I wonder if there might be a human inside of him after all.

"What are you staring at, defect?" Landon asks.

So much for the human theory. "I dunno. I just—"

"You don't know anything, got it?" Landon says. His thick bottom lip quivers. Though I never thought it possible, it looks like he's about to cry.

"There's nothing wrong, Landon," I say. "I think you and Ivan make a really handsome couple if that's what you both want. If not, then it's really none of my business."

Landon grits his teeth. His chest puffs with each infuriated breath, and his muscles are thick and taut.

To my surprise, he remains silent. It's one of the few times he has failed to retaliate.

Suddenly, Kazuki gasps and covers his mouth.

"Read my mind and I'll strangle you, Know-it-All," Landon says, seething.

"Enough with the threats, Landon," Gwen says. "Unlike the last two times we met, I'm not here to kick the scheisse out of you. We want to know once and for all what you know about Yalamba's disappearance."

"Did you come here to accuse me too? The headmaster put me through an hour-long inquisition this morning to see if I knew anything about Yalamba. I don't like the girl, but I didn't do anything to her. Stop treating me like it's my fault!"

Kazuki nods to indicate that Landon is telling the truth.

"What about Mixie?" Gwen asks. "Do you know anything about her involvement with the locker incident?"

"Other than that's why she was expelled?" Landon asks. He slips his white shirt over his built torso. "Nope, not at all."

"What about the '*DIE FERAL*' message written in Yalamba's locker?" Gwen asks.

Landon shakes his head, and the silver arrowhead in his ear dances with the movement. "I'm telling you, Legion, I had *nothing* to do with it."

Landon might implode if we ask him another question, but I can't help it. There's one more that needs answering.

"Do you have something against Ferals, Landon?" I ask.

"I don't have anything against anyone," Landon retorts.

Gwen laughs. "Says the person who's been tormenting Alé since primary school."

"I don't have anything against him!" Landon says, practically shouting. "I don't!"

"Then why have you been so terrible to me all these years?"

I'm shocked that I ask the question, half expecting to be ripped to pieces for doing so. I'm even more shocked when Landon doesn't lash out. Instead, he lowers his head, and his posture sinks.

"Want me to tell you what he's thinking?" Kazuki blurts out, trampling on the moment.

"I said stay out of my mind, stupid Know-it-All!" Landon jumps to his feet.

"Don't mind him," Kazuki says. "When he gets angry, he reverts to criticizing people based on their accelerated status. He's probably criticized Alé more than most people, but that's because—"

"Kazuki, you little runt!" Landon yells. "I'll kill you!"

"Landon, I honestly don't care about what's happened in the past," I say. "The only thing I care about right now is Yalamba. If you can't help us find her, let us know and we'll move on. If you can, then I really wish you'd tell us something."

"This is the last time I'm gonna say it." Landon is seething. "I had nothing to do with this. Yeah, maybe I wanted to get back at Yalamba after she broke my nose and all, but I got over it. It healed. Life went on."

Kazuki nods to confirm the sincerity of Landon's words.

There's nothing more we can do. If Landon is telling the truth, then we're out of leads.

Gwen places her hands on her hips. "We'll let you get back to your *exercising*. For your sake and ours, let's pretend this conversation never happened. Got it?"

"How generous of you," Landon grumbles.

Gwen smirks. There's no need to say more.

* * *

I can't pay attention in my modules for the rest of the day. It feels like everything we're doing is for naught. Someone has done something to Yalamba, but I still have no idea who that someone is. On such a big day of firsts, I'm back at square one.

We've hit a wall. A *big* wall. Though I know I shouldn't be doing it, I'm questioning everything and everyone, myself included. Even Kazuki and Gwen are on the table. Kazuki was working for Landon in the beginning, my brain reminds me. What if he wasn't telling the whole truth when he read Landon's mind on the balcony? And Gwen has been appearing at odd moments, saving me right before I'm beaten up or tortured. Why has she taken such a special interest in me? How does she always seem to know where I am?

No, Alé. Don't push them away. Kazuki and Gwen are the only people who have had the courage to stand up and take a risk to help me and Yalamba. They're good people. As difficult as it is for me to trust them—to trust anybody—something inside tells me that I need to. That I can.

I think about it on the shuttle bus ride home. I'm mesmerized by the trees flicking past my window. Maybe I'm too late. Maybe saving Yalamba really is out of my hands. All the other students have this perpetual edge over me that I'll never be able to overcome. It makes this challenge so much more difficult. I don't have any abilities. I just have me.

But giving up on Yalamba isn't an option.

All I need is one hint. A single clue that Yalamba is okay and that there's still something I can do to find her. One handout to help me figure out what happened. Something that will help me save my best friend's life.

* * *

They say that if you want something bad enough, the universe will conspire in your favor. I don't know how it happens, but that something finally comes to me as I open my journal to write about breaking into the balcony and finding Landon.

The journal's cover feels off like it does when I close it with the pen inside. When I open it, I expect a pen to roll out and into my hand.

But I'm wrong. I do a double take to make sure what I'm seeing is truly what I'm seeing.

Lying there in the crevice at the center of my journal is a white identity band. It's a replica of the one that's on my wrist, but with an unmistakable difference. This one has two small charms dangling from it—a pair of black dice with white dots on their surfaces. The charms are unmistakable, since I was the one who gave them as a birthday gift a couple of years ago.

The identity band is Yalamba's.

CHAPTER FOURTEEN
UNGRATEFUL LITTLE DEFECT

My hands shake as I examine every minute detail of the identity band in my fingers. How the feck did this get here?

No one can know I have Yalamba's identity band. If anyone at the academy finds out, I might as well hand myself over to Prefectural Security. It's so incriminating that even Kazuki and Gwen might think I was guilty. Of course, Kazuki could read my mind and know I'm not lying, but I have no way of explaining how I have this. Yalamba's identity band should be with the person who kidnapped her, but here it is in my possession.

Am I being framed? The Deficient is the easiest person to blame. Even if another inquisition reveals that I'm not guilty, it will only slow us down and buy more time for Yalamba's kidnapper.

As much as I want to tell Kazuki and Gwen, I know I can't. At least not right now. I need to figure out what to do with this on my own.

I inspect the deactivated identity band several times, trying to identify some hint that might explain why it's now in my possession. After a painfully long dinner with my family, I spend the next few hours looking for additional clues, searching for some sign lying around my room or in my drawers. When that results in nothing, I spend hours poring through every page of my journal, looking for a hidden message. Nothing.

I read so late into the night my eyes start to cross. I lay my head on top of the journal, resting for a minute... two minutes...three minutes...

Suddenly, I'm floating in the air on the bed of bubbles. I drift higher and higher with no control over where I go. It's fun at first, but soon I'm too high up. I don't want to rise anymore. Concern turns to dread when I remember what happens next.

Pop! Pop! Pop! One by one I can feel them give way underneath me, exploding and falling as droplets of water, victims of gravity's incessant pull. Then they're gone, and I'm plummeting in a frightening free fall that tugs at my organs. I try to scream, but it feels like there's a cork lodged in my throat. Nothing comes out.

I slam into a hard surface and spring from my bed, gasping for breath. I look at the glowing digits above my door. It's 05:27—three minutes before my alarm goes off. The dream leaves me completely shaken.

While getting my things together, I hide Yalamba's identity band in the bottom of my backpack. Though the band can no longer be tracked, the chip inside should still open her locker. Maybe there's a clue inside that the prefectural authorities missed. It's as good a place to start as any.

None of this brings me any closer to understanding how the identity band ended up in my journal. I can assume Yalamba didn't sneak into my room and place it there, so that leaves my family members as suspects. My brothers have never liked Yalamba. Could one of them have done it to mess with me?

I decide to broach the topic at breakfast. My dad is still getting ready, and my mother has prepared daily portions of porridge, nuts, and berries. We normally eat in silence, but today, silence isn't an option.

"Has anyone been going through my things lately?" I skip straight to the point.

My brothers carry on eating as though they haven't heard me.

"What do you mean?" Mom asks while scooping porridge into an empty bowl.

I answer her, but I keep looking at my brothers. "What I mean is what I said. Has someone been going through my things in my room?" Their expressions remain unchanged.

"I've thought about going in there to help you clean it up, but that's your job," Mom says. "Why do you ask?"

"Because someone has been tampering with my stuff. I want to know who it was."

Diego puts down his spoon and offers me his critical brown stare.

"If I gave a piece of scheisse about anything that belonged to you, I would have taken it by now."

"I appreciate your honesty, Diego." I don't bother trying to hide my sarcasm. "What about you, Rigo?"

Rigo is in the middle of chewing. He shakes his head.

"Neither of you had anyone over who went into my room?" I ask.

"Diego had some friends over earlier this week," Mom says. "Diego, did any of them go into Alé's room?"

Diego rolls his eyes. "What kind of question is that, Mom? Alé is a Deficient, lest we all forget. No one in their right mind would want to set foot in his room, even if it were filled to the ceiling with bars of gold."

If only. At least I'd have plenty of heavy objects to hurl at my brother's empty skull.

Mom snaps at Diego and tells him to show me respect, but it goes nowhere. Their discussion pauses when my father enters the kitchen, dressed in his navy blue prefectural uniform. My dad is big and bulky, and his work clothes make him look like a puffed-up action figure.

"What's all the noise for?" His voice booms throughout the room.

"It's none of your concern." Mom uses her mind to make his bowl of porridge float over to his place on the table.

Unfortunately, the offering does nothing to distract my dad.

"If it's none of my concern, then why did I hear yelling?" Dad asks.

"We were yelling because our Deficient brother accused Rigo and me of going through his things," Diego says.

"Did you go through his things?" Dad asks.

"No."

"Then it's settled."

I slam my fist onto the table, causing the plates to rattle. "No, it's not!"

My dad acknowledges me for the first time that morning. His brown eyes darken with anger.

"Watch your tone, boy."

As long as you watch yours with me. I clench my teeth to keep the words from spilling out. "I know for a fact someone has been going through my things. Logically, I figured it had to be someone in this housing unit."

"What did they take?" Dad asks coldly.

"They didn't take anything. Someone put something in my room that wasn't there before."

Dad says, "Then I don't see what you're complaining about. It sounds like someone gave you a gift."

A gift, my culo.

"It was *not* a gift," I say.

My dad lets out a heavy puff of breath and reaches for his bowl of porridge. He likes it extra clumpy. He lifts a thick spoonful into his mouth and chews, every gooey bite audible.

"What was it, Alé?" Mom asks.

I want to explain, but that's impossible. I can't tell them what I've discovered. They might think I'm the one responsible for what happened to Yalamba.

"It's nothing," I say. "Forget it."

"So you brought it up for no reason?" Dad asks.

"All you need to know is that it's an object that leads me to believe someone linked to Yalamba's disappearance was in my room."

"Whoa, whoa, whoa. Back up," Diego says. "Now he's accusing us of kidnapping his Feral friend?"

"Her name is *Yalamba*," I say.

"Whatever," Diego says. "A Feral is a Feral."

And an idiot is an idiot. "She's a person who disappeared. What if she's gone forever? You wouldn't care at all?"

Diego shrugs. "Why should I? She's not my friend."

Mom shudders. "Diego, if you could only hear yourself."

"He has a point, Paquita," Dad says. "Diego and Rodrigo have never associated with her."

"We never even liked her," Diego says. "I have been very vocal about that."

"Same here," Rigo finally chimes in.

I turn to my little brother with disappointment. I had always hoped he'd become something different—someone better.

"Thank you for that constructive offering of scheisse, Rigo. I truly appreciate it."

"I'm not going to tell you again!" My father's voice booms around the room. "Watch your mouth!"

"Then get me a fecking mirror and I'll watch away!"

My dad throws his bowl of porridge to the floor. It shatters, and my heart leaps inside my chest. Clumpy white oats splatter across the tiles.

"I don't know who you think you are, but you're living in my housing unit under my rules!"

"Your rules? At least now I know who's to blame for this dysfunctional mess."

My father's face crinkles like tissue paper, and a vein around his eye throbs. If he could kill me with his stare, he would.

"The only reason it's dysfunctional is because of you," he says with a growl.

"Los!" Mom yells. "That's enough!"

"Don't try to silence me, Paquita!" Dad yells. "He and that girl have always been freaks. She's a bad influence and you know it."

"You might not have to worry about that ever again," I say bitterly. "Yalamba might be dead."

My dad shrugs off the possibility. "Then good riddance."

It's official—I have never hated this man more than I do right now.

"You know what? I don't give a scheisse about what you or anyone else thinks. Yalamba is my best friend. You and my stupid brothers have never treated her with the respect she deserves for being one of the most—no, *the most*—important person in my life. She's been nothing but kind to all of you, but you always gave her the same scheisse the Atlases gave her at the academy. It's not right. It never has been, and it never will be."

"You have the same problem she does," Dad says. "Or did. You don't know when to shut up."

Oh no, you didn't.

My mom glances at me with frightened eyes. Her expression seems to be pleading with me.

But it's too late.

I lift my uneaten bowl of oatmeal and hurl the contents in my dad's direction. He tries to block the hot, white slop with his arm, but it doesn't help. The oatmeal splashes across his face and ruins his uniform.

"Alé!" Mom screams.

"Dammit, it's in my eyes!" Dad yells. "I'll kill the little fecker!"

I don't wait for that to happen. I run as fast as I can out of the kitchen and to our front door. I'm nearly out when someone yanks at the collar of my shirt. Of course, it's Diego.

Suddenly, I'm transported back to when we were little, and he was watching on the sidelines of the dodgeball court, waiting for me to be manhandled.

"You're not getting away with that." Diego tightens his hand into a fist.

My body whips backward, and I fall to the floor. I'm shocked as Diego flies away from me, his back banging into the wall. He remains pinned there alongside my behemoth-like dad.

Mom is standing a few feet away from me. Her green eyes are focused on me, but I can tell she's using her telekinetic energy to restrain Diego and my father.

"Everyone, stop!" she yells. "I won't take any more fighting in this housing unit!"

"You're lucky you were born the way you were," Dad yells as he strains against Mom's energy. His face is red and clumps of oatmeal have dribbled down his cheeks. "If you had an ability to defend yourself with, I would have smacked the scheisse out of you long ago."

Thanks, Dad. Good to know.

I look back at Mom. She remains silent, but her eyes are urging me to run while I still can.

I decide it's not worth it anymore. Yalamba used to tell me that I've got to know which battles to pick. Right now, it seems like I've picked this one to its end.

I swing my backpack over my shoulder. If I'm lucky, I'll never see this place again.

"That's it, you ungrateful little defect," my father says with a roar. "Once you walk away, there's no coming back!"

"Wasn't planning on it." What's left for me here anyway? This isn't a family despite all appearances. I've known it for years. Why bother clinging to it any longer? I'm done pretending it's something that it will never be.

I take a deep breath and walk toward my shuttle bus stop. The door slides behind me, closing a terrible chapter of my life.

I have a missing friend out there who has been more of a family to me than my father and brothers combined. I'm going to find her, no matter the cost.

CHAPTER FIFTEEN
DEAD AND ON DISPLAY

By the time I make it to the academy, I have a more pressing urge than normal to see Yalamba. I want to know once and for all if she's okay. I want to tell her everything that's happening in my life. I want her to know how hard I'm trying to find her and what the process has cost me—my home and my family. Most of all, I want her to know I don't care about any of the things I've lost if it means she's safe.

I lose myself in these thoughts while the other students chat and joke with one another before first module like nothing is wrong. They don't even notice Yalamba is still gone.

The first bell beeps and the hallway clears. I'm frozen in place in front of Yalamba's locker. The straps of my backpack feel heavy as I remember the object that can open it is in my possession. Not that opening it will do much. I doubt there will be anything inside. Yalamba's parents have probably cleared it out already. Since I have no other ideas, I try my luck. I make sure no one is coming before pulling the identity band from my backpack. I take a deep breath and lift it to the locker's sensor. Something clicks, and the sensor's green light shines.

My heart flutters. I want to jump up and shout. I can't believe it worked!

I examine my surroundings before opening the door. The inside is bare, practically sparkling. The janitor must have washed it after the rabbit incident. There isn't a trace of blood anywhere.

The sight is disheartening though. As predicted, it seems that whoever had cleared out the locker had taken everything.

The realization is a knife to the gut. How can I have come this far to find an empty locker?

My hands pass over the flat surfaces inside, but there's nothing. I'm too short to see the top shelf even on tiptoes. I stand as high as I can and reach my hand over the shelf, hoping against hope that I'll stumble upon something.

And stumble upon something I do. When it feels like my shoulder is about to dislocate, my fingers brush against a rough surface. I pull the object toward me as gravity brings me back to the floor. The object falls. I catch it with both hands.

When I realize what it is, I'm hardly surprised. Of course, the only item I'd find in Yalamba's locker is one of her sketchbooks. The janitor must have missed it.

I close the locker and lift the sketchbook with its hard black cover to my nose. It smells of cinnamon incense. Like Yalamba's room.

I don't know how much time passes while I stand there, hugging Yalamba's last notebook. The object and familiar scent cast me into a strange trance. Even though my eyes are open, I see flashing memories of my friend. Rolled dice and adventures in the woods during primary school. Sleepovers at my housing unit when we got older and talking until sunrise.

"May I ask what you are doing in the hallway after the start of first module, Student Aragon?"

I spin around to find Headmaster Slaughter standing a few feet away from me. He's so tall that I have to bend my neck back to see his face.

"Please do not make me repeat myself," the headmaster says. When he speaks, his breath forms a cool wave that hits me with a fresh and minty scent. It reminds me of my dentist's office, eerie and sterile.

"I…well… I was just…"

I'm stuttering. Or stammering. Or stumbling. Pick any one of those unflattering *S* words, and I'm doing it. I can only imagine what the headmaster is thinking as I stand before him, bumbling like a guilty person.

"I…wanted to see if she'd come back," I finally say.

It's an honest answer.

Headmaster Slaughter nods. "I can assure you the authorities are investigating Student Koroma's disappearance to the best of their ability. There's no need to revisit her locker every morning."

I try my best to keep my expression as fixed as possible. How does the headmaster know I've been visiting Yalamba's locker every day? Am I being watched?

"I know. I'll stop doing it eventually." *When I'm dead.*

"I am glad we have that covered." The headmaster looks over my head before returning his focus to me. "Student Aragon, I come with a request for information. I do not suppose you would happen to know anything about Student Kerrain?"

"You mean Kaylee? I haven't seen her since…well…since what happened to her aunt and uncle."

The headmaster clears his throat. "I thought…I thought that maybe you…"

For the first time in my memory, Headmaster Slaughter is fumbling over his words. For a second, he sounds nearly as inarticulate as me.

"Oh bother," the headmaster says with a sigh. "It is clear from our meeting with the Truth and Justice officers that you had nothing to do with this, but we need answers. Unfortunately, Student Kerrain has also been reported missing."

"Oh no," I whisper, bringing my hand to my heart. It's the only answer I can offer as the headmaster inspects me with his smoky eyes.

"I imagine a formal alert from Prefectural Security will go out soon. I don't know who is responsible for what is going on, but this is a very serious development. Please keep your eyes wide and your mind open. As Student Koroma's closest friend, you must inform me if you notice anything suspicious at the academy."

"Of course, Headmaster Slaughter."

I remain where I am, hoping he'll go away. He doesn't, so we stand there, nodding at each other for a few seconds.

"What is that you are holding?" Headmaster Slaughter asks.

"Oh, it's just a sketchbook."

"Are you an artist?"

I bite my bottom lip. "I'm more of a doodler, really."

"May I see?" The headmaster extends his hand for the sketchbook.

"No!" I respond quickly and with more volume than I'd like. "I can't!"

"You cannot what?"

"I can't show you." I hug the sketchbook to my chest. "The drawings are awful."

The headmaster crosses his arms and sighs. "I understand. It is important for an artist to reveal their talents when the moment is right. I believe it is time that you report to your module, is it not?"

"I'm on my way, Headmaster Slaughter."

The headmaster bows. I respond in kind and speed walk to my class. I'm convinced I've given myself away with my awkward behavior. Luckily, there were no Truth and Justice officers around.

I'm so on edge that I find myself counting down the seconds of each module until lunch. That's when I finally get the chance to open the sketchbook in the privacy of a bathroom stall.

I examine the book's contents, and I'm disappointed to find only two sketches inside. For some reason, I'd thought there'd be more. A note or something. But no, only two pictures.

The first one was done in graphite. It's an image of what looks like a crystal heart hitting the ground, and shattering into thousands of tiny fragments. It doesn't take too long to understand what it means. Looking at the date, Yalamba drew it the day after we kissed.

The second picture is a mixture of charcoal and graphite. Two hands are reaching for each other in the rain. The fingers are barely clinging to one another, as though they're about to release. Though it's a still drawing, the movement of the rain and the tension between the two hands is palpable.

I'm confused. The first picture captures Yalamba's sadness, and the second represents what I think must be our bond after the night she visited me in the rain. Our connection—despite the rift, despite the distance—is still holding.

I know Yalamba's artwork well enough to know what can and can't come into existence. These images are too abstract to materialize into reality. Yalamba needs to draw concrete things for her ability to go into effect, and even then, her ability has its limits. It can't change the past or transport people through space and time, but it can affect the present and by doing so, rewrite the future.

I wish I knew how I could do the same.

I don't know what to do with the sketchbook. I had hoped for a message that would bring clarity to what happened to Yalamba. If anything, the sketches only make things more ambiguous.

It's impossible to pay attention to anything else after lunch, and time seems to float by. I'm walking through the crowded hall to eighth module when, all of the sudden, the headmaster makes an announcement over the sound system. The students go silent as he requests for everyone to report to their next module as quickly as possible and to remain there until further notice. A second later, I get a message on my wrist comm telling me to do the same.

The headmaster's message doesn't seem to bother the other students. They obey his orders without question. But with everything that's been going on, I know it can't be mere routine. The headmaster never makes announcements like this between modules. Why would he start now unless it were for some sort of emergency?

I'm sure the situation is serious when I see Prefectural Security officers rushing through the academy's lobby and into the main entrance of the auditorium. Officers guard the entrance, turning curious students away.

I try to get closer to see what's going on, but an officer spots me and commands me to move on to my next module.

I'm not about to pick a fight with her, but I know something is in the auditorium.

Fortunately, I acquired some experience in stealth the previous day when Kazuki, Gwen, and I broke into the balcony. If I did it once, then I can do it again.

By the time I make it to the balcony's entrance on the second floor, the bell has already beeped for our next module. I'm late, but I don't care. If there's any chance I'll find something that could help Yalamba, it's worth it. Even if it means risking expulsion.

The only problem is I never asked Gwen about the code to the balcony entrance. I try contacting her with my wrist comm, but she doesn't pick up. She's probably in class. I send a few voice recordings but receive no reply.

I smack my head and think some more. I remember Gwen saying something about how the combination was all four corners. Assuming that's still the case, maybe I can guess the code.

I type 1397, hoping it will activate something. It does—a red light and a message that reads: *Code invalid. Please try again.*

I give it another shot. This time I try 3971. *Code invalid. Please try again.*

I wipe the sweat off my palms and try a third time, entering 7139. The code is wrong, and this time the error message changes. *Code invalid. A fourth failed attempt will activate the security alarm.*

Scheisse. I had planned on guessing until I had the right code, but that's clearly not going to work. I try calling Gwen again, but she doesn't answer.

It occurs to me that I've been going from right to left when I could just as easily have gone from left to right or diagonally. If my math is correct, then I have a total of twenty-four possibilities. I've incorrectly guessed three, leaving me with twenty-one choices remaining.

That's only a 4 percent chance of getting this right.

What should I do?

Gwen said the janitors were lazy. The laziest code I can think of is 1379. It's a Z shape, not a square as I had initially tried, but after the codes I've already used, it seems like the simplest variation to remember.

My hands shake as I enter the code. I press my finger to the one, then the three, and then the seven. I move slowly, knowing one wrong button will mean I'm done for.

When I press the nine, I hold my breath and wait. I fully expect the light to turn red, the alarm to sound, and for me to be apprehended by academy security.

The sensor light turns green, and the door slides open.

I let out a tremendous sigh. I'm in.

I tiptoe through the small passage that leads to the balcony. It's not as dark as it was the day before since the lights on the first floor are on. Though I can't see anything below the balcony, I can hear deep, reverberating voices. It's impossible to tell what they're saying, but it sounds like one with a particularly low baritone is issuing a series of commands.

Something tells me that these people have information about what's happened. I suspect Kaylee's sudden disappearance has something to do with Yalamba's. I've got to get closer to hear what they're saying.

As quietly as possible, I inch toward the edge of the crescent-shaped balcony. I keep low to the ground, crawling on my hands and knees so no one from the stage below will see me.

I remain as still as I can while I listen.

"How are we going to explain this to the prefecture?" a man asks.

"She was undergoing counseling after her aunt and uncle were found dead." I recognize the low hum of the headmaster's voice. "I wonder if it was all too much."

"So what are we going to do with…her?" a woman asks.

"The investigation must be completed," says a different man. "We mustn't taint any evidence of foul play."

Foul play? This can't be good.

I lift my head ever so slightly, doing my best not to make any sudden movements that might draw the attention of anyone below. Soon my eyes are level with the balcony's ledge. Just a few more millimeters and I'll get to see what everyone else in the auditorium can already see.

When I finally look, I wish I hadn't. Positioned in the middle of the stage is Kaylee Kerrain, dangling from a ceiling wire like an ornament. Her thin form is limp and hunched over. Her chin has dropped to her chest, and her long black hair falls over the front of her face. The balcony's spotlights shine down on her, granting her figure a graceful, almost angelic quality.

Kaylee doesn't move as her body spins slowly. She's stuck there, unwavering in a state of constant pause.

I nearly puke. This is the first time I've ever seen a dead person, but I know straight away that's what she is.

Dead and on display.

CHAPTER SIXTEEN
EVEN MORE DISGUSTING THAN MOTHS

I bite my arm to keep from screaming.

This can't be real.

This. Can. Not. Be. Real.

But it is. Death is staring me in the face. A body hangs from the stage. An ornament, dangling.

She's dead. Kaylee Kerrain is *dead*.

How could this happen? How could the academy *let* this happen? Someone here wants Ferals dead. The academy has wasted time. There are no answers. They still know *nothing*.

She's dead. Kaylee Kerrain is dead.

That makes three bodies now. Nearly four, if Mixie had jumped from the balcony.

All Ferals.

Ferals.

Ferals.

Why Ferals?

Where the hell is Yalamba?

Not Yalamba.

I'm coming for you. Hang on. Wait for me.

Call me. Tell me where you are.

I run. As fast as my legs can carry me. Like a Racer.

The war drum is back.

Bum. Bum.

Bum. Bum.

Blood is pumping through my veins.

It's pumping through my veins in a way the blood will never pump through Kaylee Kerrain again.

The volume rises.

BUM. BUM.

BUM. BUM.

I close my eyes. What's going on?

When I open them, the room is pitch black. I try to walk, but I stumble. I sink.

And fall…

Fall…

Fall.

✸ ✸ ✸

I open my eyes to a fuzzy yellow world. I blink a few times before the yellow divides into other colors and my vision clears.

Even with my sight back, it takes a while for me to realize I'm lying on one of the stiff beds in the nursing unit. Nurse Miranda rushes over to me. She shoves a metal bottle into my hand and demands that I drink.

I'm parched, like a desert flower that has never known rain. The sweet drink fills me with energy, and I chug gratefully, not caring about the droplets trickling down my chin.

"You've been out cold for nearly half an hour," Nurse Miranda says. "You were found unconscious on the second floor. Student Aragon, have you been experimenting with intoxicants lately?"

Even if I had been doing drugs, I wouldn't be stupid enough to admit that to a school nurse.

"No, Nurse Miranda. I was feeling dizzy."

"Why were you on the second floor when you were supposed to be in your eighth module?"

"I don't remember. I wasn't feeling well."

"Why didn't you come to my office then?"

"I don't know. It all happened so...suddenly."

Nurse Miranda glowers. Her wrinkled expression screams skeptical.

"What module is it now?" I ask.

"There are no more modules, Student Aragon. The academy has been closed indefinitely. All students were supposed to report to their shuttle buses fifteen minutes ago."

Normally, I would have cursed myself for missing my shuttle bus...again, but my mind flashes back to the image of Kaylee Kerrain's dangling body. It starts to make sense. Of course, the academy was closed.

I must look sick again, because Nurse Miranda zaps my forehead to retake my temperature.

Little does she know that there's no cure for how I feel, no undoing what can't be undone.

"The academy will be informing all students and families of its current situation," she says, undoubtedly sticking to a previously hatched sound bite. "The most important thing now is getting home."

"How am I supposed to get home if the shuttle buses left fifteen minutes ago?"

Nurse Miranda shrugs. "Do you have a parent you can call?"

I sigh. It hits me on top of everything else—I'm technically homeless.

A voice on the intercom interrupts my thoughts. It says there are visitors waiting to see me.

"Visitors?" Nurse Miranda sounds as surprised as I feel. She asks if I'm in a condition to receive visitors. I nod, though I'm not sure who would visit me.

Nurse Miranda presses a button, and the door slides open.

Kazuki and Gwen.

I smile when I see them. They haven't given up on me...yet.

"How did you know Student Aragon was here?" Nurse Miranda asks.

"Word travels quickly," Kazuki says.

The nurse crosses her arms. "Of course. A Know-it-All."

"A Legion, actually. M-2 to be precise," Kazuki says. "I forgive you for the common misperception."

Nurse Miranda proceeds to do what most people do in the presence of a mind reader. She scuttles away as quickly as possible.

Kazuki and Gwen present their usual contrast. The tiny Kazuki gives me a wide-eyed look of pity as if I'm on my deathbed, while the towering Gwen offers her typical emotionless stare.

"Are you okay, Alé?" Kazuki asks.

I nod. "I'll be fine. I just passed out in the hallway."

"Right outside of the balcony entrance shortly after contacting me for the code," Gwen says in her disinterested monotone. She doesn't sound pleased.

"That's about right," I say.

"What were you doing out of eighth module anyway?" Kazuki asks.

"You could have at least passed out a few meters away from where we were yesterday," Gwen says.

I don't want to think about it, but I can't block out the image of Kaylee.

"Oh." Kazuki covers his mouth with his hands.

"He saw her from the balcony, didn't he?" Gwen asks.

"That would be a yes," Kazuki says.

"Was she really dead?" Gwen asks.

I nod, shocked by the nonchalance with which Gwen delivers the question. "She was hanging there. I've never seen anything like it before."

"So what I've been hearing is true," Kazuki says. "The academy is closed until further notice because Kaylee Kerrain killed herself on academy grounds."

"We don't know if it was suicide," I say, "but that's another Feral down. Now we've got Kaylee, whose aunt and uncle were just killed. Mixie nearly took her own life. Then there's—"

I can't bear to say her name. I lower my head and pinch the ridge of my nose to stunt the flow of tears. *What if it's too late?*

A small hand touches my shoulder.

"It'll be okay, Alé," Kazuki says. "It's not too late. We can still figure this out. When there's a problem, there's always a—"

"Is there?" My vision is blurry with tears. "Do you really think we can solve this problem and save her life without any leads?"

"I…I don't know." Kazuki lowers his head.

"Of course, we can," Gwen says. "Don't tell me you're thinking of giving up now, Alé. After what happened today, it's more critical than ever that you believe in yourself and do something to save Yalamba's life."

"That sounds good and all, Gwen, but what if Yalamba doesn't have a life left to save?" I ask.

Gwen snorts and looks away. I'm two-for-two at shutting up my new friends.

Suddenly, Kazuki's hand shoots into the air. "I've got an idea! A really, really good one."

I resist the urge to roll my eyes. "Spit it out then."

"We've got to get creative. What if we reach out to others who might be able to help? Maybe people who have more of an idea about what's going on around us than we do. You know…people who can hear things others can't."

"You mean Know-it-Alls?" I ask.

A large smile stretches across Kazuki's face. "I mean the Know-it-All of Know-it-Alls."

"You mean the one in the hoverchair?" Gwen asks.

"Gwen!" Kazuki says.

"What?"

"You can't just say 'the one in the hoverchair.' That's politically incorrect," Kazuki says.

"I don't subscribe to politics," says Gwen.

Kazuki shakes his head. "What our tactless, four-powered friend meant to say was that we should ask Simon Polk if he's heard anything."

That's a brilliant idea. After all, Simon is the only Know-it-All who can read a roomful of minds at once. He might have heard something today that could give us a lead on Yalamba. Plus, he had offered to help me out before.

"Thanks for the compliment, Alé." Kazuki grins smugly. "The occasional act of kindness suits you well."

"I think it's a brilliant idea," I say out loud for Gwen's benefit. "Let's ask Simon what he knows."

"That's the spirit!" Kazuki pats me on the back.

I close my eyes and try to suppress all the cynicism inside until I'm left with one semi-hopeful thought. This better lead to something, otherwise I really will have nothing else to turn to.

❋ ❋ ❋

Unlike when we went to Mixie's housing unit, there's no sneaking involved at Simon's. We ring in at the front desk of his complex and hear Simon's soft voice respond on the intercom. When the security guard informs Simon that he has guests, he sounds surprised. We give our names. After a few seconds of silence, we're invited upstairs.

I'm lost in thought, wondering what we'll find, as we walk up to Simon's unit. Simon was paralyzed in a vehicle accident when he was a small child. His father died in the accident, but Aileen, his mother, survived. She was stuck in a coma for weeks due to her injuries. When she finally woke up, she was completely mute. Rumor has it that no one, including Simon, has heard her speak since. I wonder if she might be here.

We buzz the doorbell once when we're in front of Simon's dark blue door.

"May I ask who it is?" Simon says from inside the unit. "Just as another security check since I can't see through the peephole."

It strikes me as odd that the prefecture hasn't given Simon a door to accommodate his needs.

"It's us, Simon," I say. "Gwen, Kazuki, and Alé."

The door slides open, and there's Simon seated in his chair.

"I was just kidding about the peephole." Simon taps his head. "I can read your minds, remember?"

Kazuki and I laugh awkwardly—the way one does after missing the punch line of a joke. Gwen doesn't react, standing with perfect posture and her hands on her hips.

Simon is wearing a white shirt and gray pants. It's always weird seeing people from the academy wearing something other than their uniforms. With Simon it's particularly shocking, since his clothes reveal the contours of his surprisingly athletic body. I continue to study Simon as he takes a moment to clean his glasses before setting them back onto the ridge of his prominent nose.

I can only imagine what he must be thinking as he examines us—a ragtag group of misfits who have banded together under a common cause.

"I'm as much of a misfit as you are, I assure you," Simon says. "Of course, I'll help you out. Come on in."

Simon reverses and we follow him into his common room. It's decorated sparsely with only a square marble table in the center of the wooden floor. Gwen, Kazuki, and I sit down on the gray pillows surrounding the table, while Simon remains in his hoverchair.

"Can I get you tea or water?" Simon asks.

"We're fine," Gwen says. "We're only here for one thing."

"Of course." Simon nods. He pauses a moment, taking in our thoughts about Kaylee and our worries about Yalamba. It's nice not to have to repeat everything out loud.

"Allow me to apologize in advance." Simon directs his gaze more at Kazuki and Gwen than me. "I know there are certain rumors about my ability, but the truth is I don't have total control of it."

"I suppose even prodigies have something to learn at the academy," I say.

Simon lets out a light laugh. "We're all students for life as far as I'm concerned. So, it seems you want to know who caused this chain of hate crimes against Ferals, and if I overheard anything suspicious at the academy. Am I right?"

"He's good." Kazuki is practically drooling.

Gwen rolls her eyes. "You could do the same thing if you put your mind to it."

"Not like that!" says Kazuki.

"Yes, that's exactly what we're after, Simon," I say, steering the conversation back to where it needs to go. "It seems like someone is deliberately targeting Ferals. They started with Kaylee's aunt and uncle, then Yalamba, Mixie, and now Kaylee. I don't know who's next. I suppose it could be anyone. We want to stop any other bad things from happening and save Yalamba by whatever means possible."

"You're a good friend, Alé." For the first time today, Simon looks me straight in the eyes. Something about his ocean blue irises forces me to wonder how Simon's life might have changed had he never lost the ability to walk.

"I'm trying," I say. "We need to find Yalamba, but I'm worried that it might be too—"

I close my eyes and take a deep breath.

"Don't worry," Simon says. "The headmaster brought me in for questioning too, and I told him and the Truth and Justice officers what I knew. I said that you had nothing to do with it, and that Landon was especially angry at Yalamba after the dodgeball game. Since then, I've kept my mind open. Though I've heard several people say and think things that aren't too favorable about Ferals, Landon has been the most outspoken by far."

"Been there, done that," Gwen says. "We've ruled Landon out already."

"I know," Simon says, "but he's an interesting case. Lately, his mind hasn't been focused on hating Yalamba, Mixie, Kaylee, or even Alé. Though he says he doesn't like Ferals or Deficients, his thoughts seem to prove otherwise."

"I disagree on the Deficient front," I say.

"I think his motives for bothering you might come as a surprise to you, Alé," says Simon.

I raise an eyebrow. "What do you mean?"

"People sometimes treat those they admire in very odd ways," answers Simon.

A laugh bursts from my lips. "If you're implying that Landon admires me, I'm going to have to beg to differ."

"You might have to beg to concur instead," Kazuki says.

"Come on, Kazuki," I say. "Landon has treated me like absolute scheisse for all the years I've known him. He hates Deficients."

"Some people take longer to reach a state of emotional maturity than others," Simon says. "Give Landon time. He might surprise you one day."

"Why are we wasting our time on Landon anyway?" Gwen asks as blunt as ever. "We already said he didn't have anything to do with this. What we need to know is who made Mixie put the jar with the rabbit's head in Yalamba's locker."

Simon nods. "Mixie is a strange case indeed. There was no motive there. She's very fond of Yalamba almost to the extreme. There's no doubt that Mixie committed the act, but she feels as though it was out of her control. As if some third party made her do it unwillingly."

Simon goes quiet and stares at me through his black-framed glasses. "You did the right thing by saving her. She wasn't well, and she needed help. In fact, she probably still does."

"What about Kaylee?" I ask. "Did you hear anything about who could have done that to her?"

"Absolutely nothing. I had read Kaylee's thoughts before today, and it seemed like she was grappling with a lot of issues. No one could blame her for that, not after what happened to her aunt and uncle. But whether this is a case of suicide or murder, I have no idea," Simon replies.

"Did she ever think about taking her own life?" I ask.

"I can't tell you how many negative thoughts I hear on a daily basis," Simon says. "They come in droves, especially at the academy. It's how people think. You'd be surprised how many suicidal ones I hear, but thankfully, they're rarely entertained. Most Know-it-Alls don't have much of a desire to listen when the thoughts are that dark."

Simon readjusts his glasses. "I wish I could tell you something different. I still don't know why Kaylee died or where Yalamba could possibly be. I'm so sorry, Alé."

I lower my head. Of course, Simon doesn't know. No one in this whole fecking world seems to know.

A sudden scream interrupts my thoughts. It sounds like an irate cat that's being stepped on repeatedly. The piercing shriek comes from behind a door near the entrance.

"Simon! Simon, help! Get them off me!"

Simon's cerulean eyes widen at the source of the sound. His face goes even paler than normal.

"Mom," Simon whispers. There's a sense of urgency in his tone, but he doesn't go to her straight away.

The woman bangs loudly against the door. "Get them off me! The moths, they're everywhere! Simon, help me get rid of them!"

"I'm so sorry." Simon isn't looking at us anymore. His voice is shaky and distraught, and his expression is unreadable. "She usually sleeps until dinner. This isn't like her."

He moves into the hall, accidentally bumping into the edge of the table with the front of his hoverchair.

"Moths, Simon! Moths!"

"Mother, calm down," he says, pleading. "I'll get them off you. Just calm down."

"Come now, come now! They're everywhere, Simon. *Everywhere!*" Simon presses a button to open the door. His mother splatters onto the floor. She is a frail woman with noticeable strands of gray in her frizzy brown hair. Her nightgown rises high, revealing two sticks for legs that are bumpy and discolored with varicose veins.

"I thought they would never go away." Tears stream from her bloodshot eyes. "I hate the moths."

It's a terrible sight. I know I shouldn't look, but I can't bring myself to look away. Ms. Polk isn't right—on that the rumors were true—but she's far from mute.

Simon presses another button, and his hoverchair lowers. It adjusts automatically to the floor's surface, and the straps binding him release. Using his upper body strength, Simon pushes himself to the ground. He scoots forward and wraps his sickly mother in his arms. She thrashes violently, but Simon holds her still with a tight hug until she calms down.

"It will be okay, Mother," Simon says. His voice trembles as he rocks her back and forth. "Please relax. We have guests."

"Guests?" Ms. Polk whips her head toward us, suddenly alert. "*They* are our guests?"

Simon nods. "Please go back to sleep, Mother. We don't want them to feel uncomfortable."

A little late for that.

The woman's blue eyes narrow. Her stare burrows straight into me.

"Why on earth would you bring the likes of that *thing* into our home?"

The dagger sinks into me the way it always does. Ms. Polk must be a Know-it-All too. How else would she know a Deficient was in her housing unit?

"Mother, don't—"

"Get him out of here. He's even more disgusting than moths! Get him out. Get that *thing* out!"

I turn to Kazuki and Gwen. Kazuki's squinting has gotten out of control, while Gwen remains focused on Ms. Polk.

"Simon, I can't help but notice that your mother is in need of care," Gwen says coldly. "But if she refers to Alé as a *thing* again, I'll smack her so hard she might turn sane."

My breath catches. How can Gwen be so fearless in confrontation? She has absolutely no filter whatsoever.

I love her for it.

"A bold statement to make in a housing unit that isn't yours," Simon says.

"Where people say things is of no concern to me," Gwen responds. "What they say and how they say it is a different story."

Simon fixes his attention on his mother.

"Mother, I really think you should—"

"Don't tell me to calm down, foolish child!"

"Mother, please."

Foamy saliva sprays from Ms. Polk's mouth. "You calm yourself down!"

She smacks Simon with a terrible force. The sound makes me gasp. Simon's eyes are closed, and his cheek is pink from the impact.

"Her mind is all over the place," Kazuki whispers at my side. "I've never heard anything like it."

"Calm down and go to your room!" Ms. Polk yells. "Go to your room, I say! How dare you defy the rules of this housing unit. You aren't the head of this place. You never were. The king of our home died a long time ago. You may have thought yourself to be the worthy heir, but you aren't! You are simply space. Space! Nothing more."

Simon's eyes go glossy, and his chin sinks to his chest.

"I think we should go," Kazuki whispers.

"Agreed," Gwen says. "We've heard and seen enough."

"The time has expired!" Simon's mother directs her scream toward the ceiling.

"Let's get out of here," I say.

Simon uses his arms to place himself back in his hoverchair. He moves the chair out of the hallway so Gwen, Kazuki, and I have space to exit. He refuses to look at any of us. Who could blame him?

My heart is racing, and my palms are moist with sweat. I'm terrified about having to walk past the crazed woman. It's like walking by a vicious dog, not knowing if it will attack or cower.

But we've got to leave the housing unit. There's no other choice.

I'm the first to pass. I draw closer to Simon's mother. Her chewed and bloody fingernails scratch the wooden floor. She huffs loudly as she remains there, crouched with her chest against the floor, staring with those wild blue eyes. I shuffle past as quickly as possible, trying not to make eye contact.

I yell the moment Ms. Polk springs at me. She's stronger than I imagined, and she presses me against the wall. Her skeletal fingers clutch at the fabric of my academy jacket.

"I told you that you were unwelcome in my home, disgusting creature!" she says between gritted teeth. Her words are vile in sound, and her breath smells as if she hasn't brushed her teeth in years.

"Back off!" Gwen shouts.

In less than a second, Ms. Polk's body is flung away from me and hits the door of the housing unit. She falls to the floor like a broken scarecrow, silent and still.

I look at Gwen. Her hand is extended, her expression determined. She's protected me yet again.

"Why did you do that?" Simon asks with a growl.

"Because someone had to," Gwen says. "Your mother was incapable of heeding my warning."

"You had no right to harm her!" Simon exclaims.

"She had no right to attack Alé despite her condition. The prefecture should be taking care of her, Simon, not you. There are facilities for people with her needs," says Gwen.

"I know what those facilities are like," Simon says. "I'm all the care she needs."

I examine Simon's mother. She hasn't moved, but she's mumbling words I can't discern.

I'm so embarrassed that I can't bear looking at Simon. I feel mortified by everything. By everyone.

"I'm sorry, Simon," I say.

"Just go," he commands.

"But, Simon—"

"I said *go!*" Simon yells. "I have to take care of my mother!"

He's angry. Beyond angry. I don't think there's anything we can do that won't make things worse.

Gwen, Kazuki, and I let ourselves out of Simon's housing unit. We step over the crumpled body of the sickly Aileen Polk, a woman who has proven to be far more ill than the rumors implied.

We're back at square one. Except this time, square one feels about ten thousand times worse than it did before.

CHAPTER SEVENTEEN
CLUELESS

After we leave Simon's housing unit, Gwen flies Kazuki and me to the northern side of the Achewon Lake. The lake is lit at night, but no one is there at this hour. Just us, the still body of black water, the mountain-shaped academy on the other side, and the wind rustling through the collection of tall deciduous trees.

The solace of the lake is welcome after what just happened. We seem no closer to figuring out the truth, but I want to believe that the visit to Simon's hasn't been an absolute waste. It's definitely raised a lot of questions. For instance, if Simon hasn't heard anything at the academy, maybe the true culprit is an outsider. But how could they have gotten inside the academy so easily if they weren't a student or a member of the faculty or administration?

Maybe that's it. Maybe it's someone working at the school. Someone with such well-trained accelerated abilities that they could block out the thoughts of a student as gifted as Simon.

If that's the case, it will be even more difficult to stop them. We still have to figure out who the culprit is first.

"What do we do now?" Kazuki readjusts his glasses.

"Can't you read my mind?" My question has an angry bite to it that I can no longer hide.

"You're clueless," he says, "and sleep-deprived."

I offer an annoyed sigh, but it's true. I have no idea what to do, and it seems like I haven't slept in ages. Having a brain that feels like it's made of porridge won't do much for my strategic thinking.

"You've been hiding something from us," Kazuki adds.

"What?" I ask.

"There's no hiding it, Mr. Denial." Kazuki taps a finger to his head. "I could hear you thinking about it on the way over—a certain sketchbook you might have found?"

I can feel my face flushing. Of course he'd heard my thoughts.

For Gwen's sake, I verbally open up about Yalamba's identity band and the sketchbook I found in her locker.

"Normally, I'd give Kazuki a smackdown for intruding into your thoughts," Gwen says, "but he was right to do it. We haven't come this far to be withholding information from one another. There's too much at stake."

"Besides, we're friends, right?" Kazuki asks. "You can trust us, Alé."

"I'm sorry, guys. I thought telling you what I'd found would only make you question me and slow us down. I do trust you, but my mind has been running in circles, questioning everyone and everything. I'd be lying if I said I haven't questioned you along the way—why you're risking yourselves to help me and Yalamba and how you keep turning up right on time to save me from a beating. I know they're crazy thoughts, but I can't figure out how to push them away. Every time we have a lead, we only seem to move backward."

"We're the last shot Yalamba has," Gwen says. "If we aren't honest with one another, we might as well give up now."

"Hear! Hear!" Kazuki adds.

"You're right," I say, "but the sketchbook isn't going to help us with much. It only has two pictures that Yalamba drew before she disappeared."

"I hope you don't plan on making me ask to see it," Gwen says in her unfazed monotone. "Hand it over. Now."

The hairs on my arm stand up in response to the command.

"Don't worry, she'd never hurt you," Kazuki says. "Deep down she's a big softy. Plus, she likes you a lot."

Gwen yanks Kazuki by his jacket and pulls his face to hers.

"Share my thoughts again without my permission, and I'll pummel your face into bloody mush."

Kazuki laughs. "No, you won't."

Gwen grunts and releases Kazuki. "Can I just see the sketchbook already?"

I let my backpack slide down my arm. I reach in and remove the book.

"I'm telling you"—I hand it over to Gwen—"the pictures don't provide any help at all."

Gwen flips through several pages.

"Funny. I count four pictures."

"What?" I'm shocked. "What do you mean?"

Gwen lowers the sketchbook so I can see.

"Here's one with a shattered heart. How romantic." She flips the page. "One with hands grasping each other in the rain. Better than poetry. And here's number three."

I stare at the third page of the notebook—a page that I'm absolutely certain had been blank before. The picture is of a woman and a baby boy. It reminds me of one of those Madonna portraits from the Middle Ages with the baby straddling his mother's thigh and reaching up to touch her face like it's the only thing he'll ever need.

I do a double take when I realize that there's something odd about the mother. Her torso is reclined at a slight angle, and her neck is tilted at a diagonal. Her eyes are rolled back into her head—the whites visible through the tiny slits between her eyelids. Her mouth is partially open. The muscles of her face and body appear stiff and lifeless.

I'm convinced that the Madonna is either dead or dying. It's disturbingly dark, but I recognize the cross-hatchings and shadings as Yalamba's.

"Why would she draw that?" Gwen asks.

"Yalamba draws all sorts of things." I still can't believe I hadn't seen the picture earlier. I could have sworn there were only two.

"Can that image come true?" Kazuki asks.

"I don't know." I hope not. "If they aren't real people, it won't happen in real life."

"This is number four." Gwen turns the page.

There's a surprising degree of difference between this picture and the last. It's a pleasant scene I recognize even though it took place many years ago. For some reason, seeing it on paper makes it feel like it only happened yesterday.

In the picture, a little boy is kneeling across from a girl who wears her hair in two big puffs. They're playing with large, wooden dice that have letters on each face. The boy's and girl's mouths have wide grins as they stare down at the dice.

"*SUNNOT*," I whisper. My eyes are watering. The tears start to fall, and I can no longer make out the details of the picture.

"What's that?" Gwen asks.

"It's a memory," Kazuki says, reading my mind. "That's how Alé and Yalamba first met when they were in primary school. They were spelling out funny words with the dice."

I wipe at my tears so I can see. "It's an image from the past, so it won't be able to manifest."

"Did you honestly not see these pictures before?" Gwen asks.

I nod. "Maybe the pages were stuck together or something. I swear I only saw the other two."

Gwen sighs. "That's settled then. We have four pictures in a sketchbook and no information from Simon."

"Except that his mom is in desperate need of therapy," Kazuki says.

"It isn't much to go on," Gwen says. "Our investigation doesn't seem to be going anywhere. I wonder if I should try beating up Landon again."

"You wouldn't want to interrupt another one of his exercise sessions, would you?" Kazuki asks.

Gwen chuckles, but the sound transforms into a terrible ringing in my head. My fingers shoot to my temples. Suddenly, my head is throbbing. My brain is beating like a heart.

The migraine is petrifying. It's as though my skull has been pierced by a thousand needles. I blink repeatedly, but I can't tell if my eyes are closed or open. I can no longer see Gwen or Kazuki. The inside of my head is burning up, like it's been lit by a torch.

"Something is wrong." Kazuki's voice seems quiet. Distant.

My knees give way. I expect to slam into the ground, but the impact never comes. I simply drop, descending into a dark abyss until it almost feels like I'm floating. This must be what it would feel like to be a feather—almost as weightless as air.

Or just as weightless as air. I am the air.

Is this what it feels like? To fly alone. To be a Sky Glider.

I open my eyes and am lying on my back. I'm on a floating bed of bubbles. Moist, round, perfect bubbles.

I brush my hand down. My fingers pass through some of the bubbles' liquid surfaces, inadvertently popping several of them.

Of course, I know what comes next. The bubbles pop beneath me, and my body sinks with each tiny rupture. The bed of bubbles self-destructs, one layer at a time, until there's nothing left to hold me.

The sky welcomes me into its embrace. I soar downward, dropping through the great shadow that surrounds me.

What am I supposed to do before the earth meets me? Should I bother making a wish? Think about the ones I love? There are so few…

I wince as I prepare for impact. *BOOM!* I slam into the ground like a space rock plummeting from the atmosphere. The vibration overwhelms my battered body.

But I'm still here. My chest heaves as I try to catch my breath from the fall. I somehow survived despite the distance.

This time, the dream continues. After a few moments, I decide to get up so I can see where this dream will take me next, but I can't. No matter how hard I try, I can't lift my arms from the ground. I try to move my legs, but they aren't listening either. I've lost command of everything from my neck down. My body is still.

Great. As if things couldn't get any worse, now I'm paralyzed.

Paralyzed.

Paralyzed.

Paralyzed.

I repeat the word in my mind. This isn't how it feels to be a Deficient. This is how it feels to be...

I gasp at the realization. Suddenly, the puzzle pieces shift, interlocking until they form the image I've been looking for all this time.

I try to shake myself out of my immobile state, but I can't. The more effort I put into moving, the more frozen my arms become. My body is entirely disconnected from my mind, and there's nothing I can do about it but scream.

So that's what I do. I scream. I scream and scream until my throat goes dry, hoping that someone, anyone will hear me. Someone has to find me so I can share what I've learned. Someone has to help me reveal my discovery.

I shake without warning. A harsh seizure. I'm conscious of everything around me as my body jerks. My head rises and falls, slamming against the hard ground. I know the rest of me is shaking as well, but I'm still too numb to feel it.

I nearly choke on my inhalation when my eyes open to see the golden Gwen with her arms extended. She's grabbing my shoulders, trying to force me awake with her Atlas strength.

"I think you're hurting him," I hear Kazuki say.

"He needed it." Gwen lets go of my shoulders.

I fall back, gasping for air. It feels like someone punched me in the gut and took all my breath away. I breathe slowly. In and out. In and out. I need to relax and collect myself. I need to remember what happened in the nightmare I just experienced.

But I can't. I can't remember for the life of me what I had been thinking while I was asleep.

"You fell from a bed of bubbles in the sky," Kazuki says casually. "When you reached the ground, you couldn't move and kept repeating the word 'paralyzed' over and over in your head. Then everything went fuzzy."

My jaw drops.

"Kazuki…you're brilliant!"

He smiles. "Above average really, but I'll take the compliment."

I don't respond. I lie motionless on the ground. My mind is perfectly at ease for a few soft seconds.

Kazuki shakes my arm. "Say something! Think something! Let me know you're alive."

I push myself up with my arms and look out at the lake. Its surface sparkles with thousands of silver highlights from the full moon above.

"The sketchbook," I say. "Give me the sketchbook!"

"Someone has found his inner authoritarian." Gwen hands me the black sketchbook. I flip past the first two drawings to the third and fourth ones. I investigate the pictures, hunting for details.

It doesn't take long. The first clues I find are located below Yalamba's bubbly initials. The new drawings have dates.

"November 18," I say. "She drew both of these on November 18!"

"Today?" Gwen asks. "How can that be?"

The discovery is good, but the others are better. I find them spelled out in the fourth picture.

It's hard to make out the letters on the faces of the dice given their angle, but not impossible. After squinting and shifting the angle of the drawing, I figure out that the boy's three dice read *H*, *A*, and *P* and the girl's read *L*, *C*, and *E*.

Immediately I start rearranging the letters.

LEAPCH.
LACEHP.
PLACEH.
PEACHL.
CHLPEA.
CHAPLE.
CHAPEL.

Of course! I smack myself on the forehead. *How did I miss this?*

"What is going on?" Kazuki asks. "Why are you playing with the letters?"

"Does anyone have a holo-screen I can use?" I ask, ignoring Kazuki.

"For what?" Gwen asks.

"Doesn't matter. Somebody get me a holo-screen now!"

"He gets bossy like this sometimes," Kazuki whispers to Gwen. "Yes, sir! One holo-screen coming right up."

Kazuki pulls his holo-screen from his backpack and hands it to me. I perform the search, putting in the right names and words until I find exactly what I'm looking for. I scan the article's text until I'm sure of my discovery.

"What is it?" Kazuki asks.

I shake my head. I can't believe it. All the pieces are finally lining up, just like they did in my dream. It's brilliant. *She's* brilliant. I can't believe it's taken me so long to see.

"I know I'm not supposed to be reading Alé's mind right now," Kazuki says, "but I have a strange, non-telepathically related suspicion that he's just figured out something important."

Gwen huffs. "I'm getting bored. Does someone plan on telling me what's going on?"

"We need to search for a few more records," I say. "Then we'll need to make some calls."

"To whom?" Kazuki asks.

I don't say anything. There's no need. Kazuki's dark eyes widen, and he covers his mouth with his hands.

"Have you gone bonkers?" he asks. His words come out muffled, escaping through the cracks between his fingers.

"Maybe," I say. "But if we're going to get to the bottom of this, we'll need to talk with Mixie Trait and—"

I swallow before saying the words.

"Landon Waters."

CHAPTER EIGHTEEN
MOONLIGHT AND CRUMBLING CUPOLAS

The chapel is surrounded by a dense wall of trees and bushes—a product of seasonal rains and neglect. The sky has gone dark with a screen of tempestuous clouds. It isn't a matter of if it will downpour, but when.

It would have taken me a couple of hours to get to the chapel by foot. With Gwen flying us, it takes only minutes—time that may end up being the difference between Yalamba's life and death.

My mind spins. I'm not sure if it's the adjustment to being back on the ground or my nerves. Through the flora we can make out the form of the chapel. The tall, prism-shaped building is made of dark gray stone that reflects the light of the full moon. We climb a small hill and sneak through the chapel's overgrown property until we're standing before the dilapidated stone building. With its crumbling exterior, the structure is a relic from a time when people still had organized religions. It's easy to believe no one has worshipped here in centuries.

Which is why this is the perfect place to hide someone.

The minutes pass as I wait for my plan to take shape. I bite my nails, suddenly conscious of the threat this wasted time poses.

"Are they coming?" Gwen whispers.

"It's up to them," I say.

"Unless they've turned into Unseens, I think they've stood you up."

Gwen is probably right. We have no more time to waste.

"Let's go," I say.

The chapel's doors are stronger than they appear, despite the moisture and jagged cracks in the old wood. I push several times, but they're locked from the inside.

"Let me." Gwen nudges me aside.

She spins in a quick circle, and her leg juts out, bashing straight through the wooden doors. They break from their rusted hinges and slam to the ground. A plume of light brown filth rises, causing us to cough.

So much for a quiet entrance.

Gwen doesn't hesitate. She struts into the abandoned chapel, looking like a fearless model in her red, cropped jacket, low-cut top, and black tights. She moves with total confidence, walking with one leather boot in front of the other.

Kazuki and I tiptoe behind Gwen down the main hall with its dark walls and broken columns. Tree roots spring from the uneven stones, and vines wind around the pillars and across wooden pews that have been devoured by termites. I don't see anyone, but that brings me no relief.

He must be here. Somewhere.

The back of the chapel is partially lit by the moonlight streaming through a glittering, rainbow-colored masterpiece of stained glass. The light reflects the rusted pipes of a large organ that looks exhausted and unplayable.

There's no sign of Yalamba.

We walk further down the main aisle. Silver rays of moonlight shine through the chapel's crumbling cupolas, but the stained-glass window that's built into the chapel's main dome is still intact. Colorful slices of glass form the wings of an angel whose features are unapologetically androgynous, with long hair, a square jaw, and a curvy yet muscular form.

With so much destroyed, it seems like a miracle that this glass angel has survived the scourge of time.

I bring my focus back to ground level. No one is at the end of the chapel, and no one is in the pews. For a second, I start doubting my theory about Yalamba's sketchbook. I was sure there was a hidden message, that we'd found something, but maybe I was only seeing things.

I take a few more steps forward when I notice something odd to my side. Several rows of wooden pews are missing. In their place is a large, open hole leading into the earth below. I can't see into the darkness, but I imagine the space is filled with mud and millipedes.

It looks like the perfect place to hide someone. A corpse, certainly. A living person, hopefully.

"You've finally made it, I see."

I spin around the second I hear the soft voice. I search the chapel in vain, but the sound hasn't come from inside the building. The voice resonated within the walls of my mind.

"Idiots," the voice says with a mocking laugh. "Look up."

As I lift my head, my entire body reacts to an unexpected roaring of thunder, and I start to shake. A flash of lightning illuminates the chapel's crumbled balcony.

That's when I see his form, hovering up and down ever so slightly in his chair. I clench my hands into fists.

"Simon Polk," I say between gritted teeth.

"Alejandro Aragon." Simon's voice reverberates through the chapel. "It appears you've found me. It took you longer than I expected."

"We figured out your little game," Gwen says, "and now we're here to put an end to it."

"End?" Simon asks. "This isn't going to end today, dear Gwen. We've only just begun."

I wince at the comment. Simon must have something up his sleeve.

"It seems I've underestimated the tenacity of my prisoner," Simon says. "How foolish of me."

Prisoner. Does that mean Yalamba is still alive?

"Where is she, Simon?" The question echoes within the chapel, as if ghosts are whispering behind the columns.

"You're closer than you've ever been, don't worry."

"Give Yalamba back and we'll go. We don't even have to know what kinds of crazy things you've been doing here."

"And then what?" Simon laughs. "You'll leave me in peace? Yalamba will simply waltz back into the academy as if nothing ever happened. As if she had never been kidnapped, Mixie had never been expelled, and Kaylee and her family had never been murdered."

Murdered. The admission sounds terribly casual, like some off-hand remark about the weather. The rage inside me goes nuclear.

"Did I make you angry, Deficient?" Simon asks. "My apologies if understanding is beyond your defective mind's capacities."

Simon has never insulted me like that before. It must be something else he was hiding.

"Alé's mind isn't defective at all," Kazuki says. "He's the one who figured out why you did what you did when no one else could."

Simon crosses his arms and smirks. "Oh, really? Do enlighten me then. Why did I do what I did?"

"Your family suffered a car accident ten years ago," Kazuki says. "You were only six at the time, but it's one of the first memories you can recall. Your father was driving, and your mother was in the passenger seat. A megastorm was passing over the highway. It caused the malfunctioning of the magnetized fields that normally prevent vehicles from crashing into each other. A vehicle veered onto your side of the road and took everyone by surprise. Your father tried to turn, but it was too late. The collision was head on. Your father didn't survive, and your mother was badly injured. She remained comatose for a few weeks. She finally woke up, but she was never the same."

My eyes shift between Kazuki and Simon. The longer Kazuki speaks, the stiller Simon becomes. His eyes appear glassy even from a distance. Something about them sends chills up my spine.

"You were secured in the back," Kazuki continues, "but when your father's seat snapped, your legs were caught beneath it. They were crushed by the pressure of the seat, his body, and the other vehicle that had landed on top of yours. The rest of you was fine—unburned and unscarred—but your paralysis is something you carry with you to this day. It's the scar that constantly reminds you of what happened that night."

Gwen takes a step forward and places her hand on Kazuki's shoulder. "The doctors said you would never walk again. You were devastated and confused, and your mother wasn't there to comfort you. She was unresponsive even after the coma. No one showed you pity or love. No one understood what you were going through."

I watch as Simon's grin transforms into something gnarled and monstrous. The shadows on his neck shift as he clenches his jaw.

"Since you had no other family, you were raised under prefectural care while your mother received specialized support for her condition," Gwen continues. "When you were old enough, you left prefectural care to share a housing unit with her."

"You committed yourself to learning who destroyed your family," Kazuki says. "It wasn't until years later that you discovered whose vehicle had driven into yours. The vehicle had belonged to David and Kendra Kerrain—both only thirty-three years old at the time and the parents of a girl named Kaylee. Both David and Kendra died on impact."

"You still didn't know everything that had happened," I say. "You didn't know what was going on in the Kerrains' minds or on their side of the highway, but that didn't matter. You knew their names. And you knew they had been Ferals."

"Is this the part where you tell me I killed Kaylee Kerrain and her family, because her parents killed my father and destroyed my mother's life?" Simon asks.

Kazuki nods. "That's what we were thinking, yeah."

Simon's head falls back, and he laughs. It's a haunting, ghoulish sound that no sixteen-year-old should make.

Then Simon goes eerily silent, and his blue eyes narrow behind his glasses.

"Looks like you've figured it out then, dream team. You've cracked the case. You've uncovered the villain. And guess what?"

Something about the question—its maniacal tone mixed with several pitches of insanity—makes me not want to know the answer.

"You're about to catch me red-handed," he says.

Simon shifts to his side and extends one of his legs. He does the same with the other and bends his knees before hopping free from the hoverchair. He stands with both feet planted on the balcony's surface.

I take in a breath so deep I nearly choke. I can't believe it. Simon—who is *paralyzed*—has miraculously learned how to walk.

Simon steps toward the balcony's broken edge. His legs seem much sturdier than I imagine they should be after years of paralysis.

"You feel so free just before you fall," he says as his toes dangle over the side.

Simon's face, now fully illuminated by the moonlight, appears as tranquil as can be. His eyes are closed, and he lifts one of his feet.

"Simon!" I shout instinctively. "Don't!"

But he does it anyway. He walks over the edge of the twenty-foot-high balcony and drops.

I gasp and close my eyes.

But there's no thud. There's no slam, no crack, no shout, no groan. When I open my eyes again, Simon is floating above the surface of the chapel floor, doing what only Sky Gliders can do.

Simon is flying.

"I've learned a few new tricks this semester." Simon levitates even higher. "Do you like them?"

"What have you done?" Gwen asks.

"Let's just say your Feral friend has been very useful."

My mouth drops. *Yalamba*. Of course, I don't know why I hadn't thought of it earlier. Why would Simon have wanted to kidnap Yalamba out of all the Ferals at the academy? He wanted her ability. She could make seemingly impossible scenarios real, if only temporarily. It's a power that can be used to create tremendous things.

But as I look at the twisted Simon, I see how he's been using Yalamba's gift to fulfill his own destructive purposes. Now he can walk and fly. I can only guess how many other abilities he's acquired by forcing Yalamba to draw them into existence.

As Simon floats before us without the slightest hint of fear on his face, it's clear this former Know-it-All can do much more than read minds.

"You're not the only ones who've done their research," Simon says. "Don't forget that I know more about you than you'd ever imagine."

Simon's focus lands on Gwen.

"You've set up so many barriers. They might help you block out everyone else, but none of them are strong enough for me."

Gwen growls. "Stay out of my mind, you sadistic piece of scheisse."

"As you wish," Simon says with a vile laugh. "I only wanted you to know that I'm planning on picking up your little friends and dropping them from the sky. Just like you did to your Deficient sister back when you were stupid little girls."

I gasp. Simon has pressed Gwen's most sensitive button on purpose. There must be a reason why he'd do something so insane.

"It's a trap," I say, but I'm too late.

Gwen launches at Simon, screaming like a banshee. Soon the two are in the air, zipping through the open space in a series of flashes. Gwen strikes like a scorpion targeting its prey. Simon dodges and counters with punches and kicks. They are fast. Too fast for a normal person. Simon has also acquired the power of a Racer.

Suddenly, Gwen's body flings back. She crashes into the wall of the chapel, and a web of cracks forms in the stone. Bits of rock fall from the ceiling and wall, but Gwen remains where she is. She won't give in to gravity.

There's no way Simon could have done that with normal strength. It seems he's obtained the power of an Atlas too.

Gwen springs from the wall and flies at Simon again. She attacks with a combination of punches that are impossible for me to see, but Simon is just as quick. He shifts from side to side, his body appearing in one spot of the chapel, disappearing, and then reappearing in another.

From what I can tell, Simon has acquired the abilities of an Atlas, Racer, and Sky Glider. I have no idea what other abilities he has, but I wouldn't be surprised if he has them all. If he does, he'd be even more gifted than Gwen since Simon has the one power Gwen doesn't—the ability to read minds. If Simon's thoughts are as quick as his body, he'll be able to foresee every one of her attacks before she strikes.

Gwen stands no chance. Even as powerful as she is, the fight will be pointless if every move she makes is predictable.

I turn to Kazuki, but I don't see him anywhere. *Where did he go?*

"Alé, she's down below," someone whispers in my ear. "I can hear her thoughts."

"What?" I ask.

"Quiet. He can hear everything."

I find Kazuki's black robe on the floor. He's gone invisible.

When I look up, Gwen and Simon are still at it, their bodies dancing through the air in haphazard blurs. Gwen shrieks as she fights—a contrast to Simon's laughter.

Then Simon's head and hands vanish. All that's left is his academy uniform, floating in the air. The realization that Simon can turn invisible must startle Gwen, because he is able to give her a kick that sends her flying straight into one of the large columns. The column cracks, and I watch as the crack grows until it wraps around the entire column. The collision shakes the ceiling and causes a shower of pebbles to fall from above.

Gwen winces as she slides down the column. Her cheek leaves a trail of blood along the stone.

Lightning flashes, and Simon's blue eyes seem to blaze, visible once again. He grabs his collar and rips his academy uniform down the middle with his enhanced strength. His lean, muscular body is so pale it practically glows beneath the moonlight. He almost looks holy, like a dark angel without wings.

Then he's gone. It takes less than a second for his body to fade. His pants and shoes slide off and fall to the ground. Suddenly, he's an Unseen.

Gwen's amazonite eyes shift around the chapel. She shoots forward and pummels the air with her fists, fighting nothing. She must realize the strategy isn't working because she stops. She's breathing heavily and sweat-darkened strands of hair stick to her face.

Out of nowhere, Gwen takes a hit that sends her shooting to the ground like a falling asteroid. She plummets into the pews with a crash, stirring up a cloud of dust.

When the dust clears, I see Kazuki's small form leaning over Gwen. She's covered in bloody scratches. Her eyes are pressed shut, and her teeth are clenched. She moans with pain. Somehow, she's still conscious.

"Gwen!" Kazuki yells. "You have to get up!"

Gwen turns onto her side with a grunt and rises to her hands and knees. I've never seen her arms tremble like that before.

"Get away from me, Kazuki," she says.

Kazuki's eyes widen. "What?"

"I said get away from me." She sits on her heels and digs her fingers into her hair. "He's in my mind!"

Kazuki seems flustered as he searches the space around him. Simon is still nowhere to be found.

"What do you mean?"

Gwen lets out a ferocious roar before she clutches Kazuki's neck. Kazuki tries to say something, but he can only choke.

"Gwen!" I shout.

"I can't stop!" Gwen yells. "Simon is making me do it, Alé! He's in my head!"

Kazuki's face turns a deep shade of purple. His eyes look like they might pop from their sockets, and his legs thrash.

I search for something, anything to make what's happening stop.

My gaze falls upon one of the planks of wood that broke during Gwen's fall. I pick up the plank, lift it as high as I can, and bring it crashing down onto Gwen's head.

Kazuki falls to the floor. His face is still purple, and he isn't moving.

Gwen collapses to her knees, holding the back of her head.

"Hit me again, Alé." Her words sound slurred.

"What?" I ask.

She stares at me with clouded eyes.

"Hit me again…or he'll make me kill you both."

Not knowing what else to do, I lift the plank and swing it down for a second time against Gwen's skull. The wood splits when it makes contact, and Gwen falls next to Kazuki's body. Her arm lands on his bare side. She is silent and still.

I can't believe what I've just done. Now I'm alone—a Deficient fighting against the impossibly powerful Simon.

That won't stop me though. I need to see Yalamba, even if it's the last time.

I run from Gwen and Kazuki and sprint to the pit in the chapel's floor. I'm not sure how deep it is, but there's only one way to find out. I leap over the edge, ready to be consumed by the darkness.

But I freeze in midair. I try to move my arms and legs, but it isn't possible. I feel the telekinetic energy tugging at me, the same way my mom's did whenever she'd controlled my movements as a child. Slowly, it pulls me back to the chapel floor and spins me around. I can't see Simon until Kazuki's black robe rises from the ground and wraps itself into the shape of a human torso. Once it's tied, Simon's face and limbs brighten into visibility. His eyes are angry orbs of ice.

"Where do you think you're going?"

"She's down there, isn't she?" I'd look down at the pit, but Simon's Mind Mover energy has my head and neck locked in place.

Simon nods. "She is, and she's not taking visitors."

"What did you do to her, Simon?"

"I haven't done anything to the Feral. Not yet anyway."

If Simon is being honest, then Yalamba is still alive. Kazuki said he could hear her thoughts. I need to know if it's true. I need to see her with my own eyes.

"Why can't you let her go? I know the Kerrains were involved in your family's accident, but that's no reason to blame Yalamba."

"Ferals killed my father. Ferals took away my mother's ability to think. Her ability to raise her only son."

I close my eyes and imagine Yalamba's sketch of the lifeless Madonna and her child. It was a symbolic image—not one that would ever come true, but one that represented Simon and his mother's relationship.

"Ferals are useless people," Simon continues. "Their powers, their existence. There's nothing beneficial about them. They aren't meant to be with the other accelerated groups. Just as Deficients aren't either."

It's obvious my death is on the horizon, but I don't care. I'm not going to hold back anymore. Not if I have even the slightest chance of reaching Yalamba.

"You might be a genius, but you sound like a complete idiot."

Simon raises a single eyebrow. "It seems like the defective has finally found his courage."

I ignore the insult. "You read people's minds, but you can control them too, can't you? It all makes perfect sense. You made Mixie put the jar in Yalamba's locker against her will. Once she was caught on camera, she stood no chance of explaining her way out of that and was expelled from the academy. You single-handedly ruined her life. And because that wasn't enough, you nearly made her jump from a building."

"It looks like I gave the Deficient less credit than was due," Simon says, his blue eyes unblinking. "Go on. Tell me what else you've learned."

The anger inside is so intense I'm nearly boiling. "You entered the Kerrains' minds and forced them to kill each other. You nearly made Mixie jump to her death. You made Kaylee hang herself. And just now you controlled Gwen's thoughts, turning her against Kazuki."

"Rather poetic, don't you think?" Simon examines Gwen and Kazuki's fallen bodies. "The tragedy of star-crossed lovers."

"They're not dead," I say, although I'm not entirely sure.

"Yet."

"You've never used it to control me though, despite the fact that I was piecing this all together."

"Control *your* mind?" He scoffs. "Why would I even bother?"

It's official. I despise Simon more than I've ever despised anyone on the planet.

"You've always had this gift, haven't you?" I am barely able to keep my voice steady. "The gift of reading, entering, and controlling people's minds simultaneously."

Simon grins. "As long as I can remember. It makes me the most evolved of the Know-it-Alls."

"Know-it-All?" I laugh. "That's not what a Know-it-All does, Simon, and you know it."

Simon's eyes turn to slits, and his smirk disappears.

"How would a Deficient know what a Know-it-All does or doesn't do?"

The insult slides off me. "Your ability doesn't conform. You might be able to read people's thoughts, but you can also insert your own thoughts into their minds to control them. That doesn't make you a Know-it-All. It makes you a—"

"A what?" Simon's voice is a cold and cutting whisper.

"A *Feral*."

Simon's punch is so fast I don't have a chance to react. The power behind it makes my brain ricochet against the inside of my skull. I fall backward as my world spins in dark circles.

I wait a few seconds for my vision to refocus. Once it does, I realize Simon is holding me by my collar. His grip is tight, and I can barely breathe.

"I am not a Feral, you stupid Deficient! Take it back! Say I'm not a Feral! I want to hear you say it!"

I can't say anything because I'm being choked. But I can think.

You aren't a Know-it-All. You purposefully hid your mind-control ability to avoid having your classification changed. I spent enough time being tested for abilities growing up that I know there isn't another explanation. As far as I'm concerned, you're a Legion with Know-it-All and Feral abilities.

"You fool!" he exclaims. "You'll die for your thoughts!"

So be it.

I hear another loud bang and feel tiny fragments of wood flick against my face. Simon lets go. I fall to the ground and gasp for breath.

I see Landon Waters standing above me, holding a broken plank of wood. His cheekbones are defined by shadows and moonlight. Mixie Trait stands behind him, and her eyes are wide with concern.

My attention shifts to Simon. He has fallen too, but only to his knees.

"Impressive," Landon says to Simon. "But the next time I do that, you won't be moving."

"You'll pay for what you've done, Simon," Mixie says. "For all that you've destroyed."

Simon spits. "I'll take pleasure in killing you myself, Feral. You should have jumped to your death when you had the chance!"

Simon growls before rushing at Mixie. Landon intercepts the attack, and the two tumble on the chapel's stone floor. It doesn't take long for Landon to pin Simon in a wrestling hold. Landon's muscular legs are wrapped around Simon's torso, and he's pressing a hand against Simon's head, holding him in place.

I can't believe what I'm seeing. For the first time, it looks like we have an edge.

"I've got this, Alé!" Landon says. "Go find Yalamba!"

I want to stay and watch. I want to know that Simon will be taken care of, and it will all be over soon. I want to believe Landon will be okay, and nothing bad will happen to him.

I feel a hand on my shoulder. It's Mixie.

"Let's go get her."

I nod. It's time.

I don't look back as I scramble away with Mixie to the pit. All I can think is down, down, down. I allow my legs to fall over the edge while my hands cling to the surface. As the last of my strength leaves me, I drop helplessly. I land on my feet but collapse, sinking into a moist and muddy surface. Mixie falls at my side.

I turn on the light on my wrist comm to illuminate the space. The floor is made of earth and broken stone tiles. The granite walls, by comparison, are well-preserved, and both sides are lined with cells with rusted, iron bars. I shine my wrist comm into the empty cells and wonder who could have possibly been held here and what they could have done to deserve this place.

It isn't until I aim my light at the farthest cell that I see her, amidst the darkness. Her face is pressed between the iron bars.

"Yalamba!" I shout.

"Alé?" Yalamba asks, her voice a hoarse scratch.

My legs propel me forward. I forget how tired they are. Something inside me ignites the moment our fingers interlock. I nearly collapse when I recognize their familiar shape. Yalamba's dark eyes come alive the second we make contact.

"You came!" Yalamba is crying. "I knew you'd figure it out!"

"Yals…is it really you?" There's enough space through the bars to make out her ragged hair and tired expression. Shadows lurk beneath her eyes.

Yalamba nods, and tears stream down her cheeks. "I didn't know how to get the message to you without Simon finding out. But once I realized what I needed to do, I sent you my identity band. I knew you'd put the pieces together."

"I'm sorry it took me so long." I don't bother wiping away my tears. "But I never gave up."

"I knew you wouldn't." Yalamba tightens her grip on my fingers. Her eyes zigzag, inspecting my wounds. "He's hurt you."

Her face is gaunt. She looks like she hasn't eaten in days, yet she's worried about me.

"I guess this is what happens when you finally stand up for yourself," I say.

We lean our foreheads against the bars and close our eyes. I want to stay here forever, to bask in this moment. Yalamba is alive, and I've finally found her.

But we're far from finished.

Yalamba and I pull away slowly. Mixie is standing next to me with her hand extended.

"We're getting you out of here, Yalamba," Mixie says. "For good."

Mixie takes my hand in hers, and I close my eyes. Suddenly, I'm consumed by a tingling warmth that spreads from my fingertips to the rest of my body. The energy spirals across my skin and deep into my core. Eventually, the warmth reaches my brow.

This is what it feels like to fade.

I open my eyes and watch as my hands and arms pass through the bars. It tickles when I sink into them at first, but then it feels cold, like my insides are freezing. I take a deep breath before letting my head, neck, and shoulders pass through the metal, which only intensifies the sensations.

Once I'm in the cell, Yalamba and I sink into one another, tears flooding from our eyes.

I can barely believe it's true. She's here. She's alive. By some miracle, I made it in time.

I can't help but notice how much smaller and more fragile she feels in my arms. Looking around, there isn't even a place on the rocky floor for Yalamba to sleep. No wonder she looks so tired. She probably hasn't slept this entire time.

"You never got that application in, did you?" she whispers.

I can't help but laugh. Of course, she hasn't forgotten.

"Yalamba," I say. "Simon's powers... What happened?"

Yalamba's chin drops to her chest, and she twitches her nose.

"I drew them into existence, Alé. He's no longer paralyzed, and he has all of the abilities. I'm so sorry. He said he would torture me if I didn't cooperate. I resisted at first, and he...he did awful things to me. I decided I had to do his drawings to gain access to the pencils and paper I needed. It was the only way to send you my identity band and those pictures."

"Where are the drawings now? We need to destroy them."

"He keeps everything in a chest outside, but it's locked. He stopped letting me draw after he saw my latest pictures. He knew what I'd done, of course, but he underestimated you. I don't think he believed you'd figure it out."

"Mixie, you'll need to do the honors."

"The pleasure is mine," Mixie says.

I smile from ear to ear. "We couldn't have done any of this without you."

She smiles back. "It's the least I can do."

I hear a horrible scream from above. It's Landon, and it sounds like he's in terrible pain. It's followed by a deafening crash of thunder and the noisy splattering of raindrops.

"I have to get back up there," I say.

"Simon keeps a ladder near where you came in," Yalamba says. "He used to use it before he learned how to fly."

Mixie holds hands with Yalamba and me and guides us through the iron bars. Once we're on the other side, I run to the ladder. It's heavy, but Mixie helps me lift it up and set it against the wall. Once I'm sure the base is sturdy enough, I glance over at Yalamba. Though she looks worn, she hasn't lost the determined expression she's had since we were kids.

"Let's kick his fecking arse," Yalamba says.

"Not with lollipops and bunnies," I say. She laughs, and tears slide down her dirt-covered cheeks.

I don't waste any more time. Landon has risked his life to save mine. I can't leave him up there alone with Simon any longer.

I climb the ladder with shaky limbs. The rain is pouring in buckets. My feet slip on the wet rungs, but I hold steady. There's no going back.

When I'm out of the pit, Simon is standing over Landon. Soaked from head to toe, Landon has his back against one of the broken pillars. His right eye is swollen and purple, and his lip is bleeding from a large gash. I can't tell if he's breathing, but he's not opening his eyes.

I want to collapse. Landon can't be dead, not after all that's happened.

I pick up a sharpened piece of wood from the destroyed pews and charge at Simon. He spins around just before I can stab it through his back. He catches my wrist and laughs.

"Think you're being sneaky, defective?"

"You're sick, Simon. You need help."

Simon grins. "So do you."

Before I can respond, Simon twists my wrist until the bones snap. The wooden stake falls from my fingers, clattering against the stone, and my ears fill with dense pressure. That, combined with the rain, makes it impossible for me to hear myself scream.

"Aw, does the poor Deficient have an ouchy?" Simon asks.

"The entire prefecture will know!" I yell against the pain. "You can kill us all, but they'll still find out what you are!"

"I always thought you were stupid, but I didn't know you were brain-dead."

Simon tightens his grip on my shattered wrist. The pain is so extreme that my entire arm goes numb.

"Can a Feral do this, Deficient?"

My body rises several feet until I'm suspended in the air and incapable of breath. Without warning, Simon uses his Mind Mover ability to thrust me back to the ground.

I slam against the stone. My temples feel like they're imploding. I blink several times to fight off the darkness.

"I asked if a Feral could do that!" Simon yells.

The taste of copper fills my mouth. Warm blood coats my lips and drips down my chin.

"A Feral just did," I mutter. My words slur, but they're clear enough for Simon to get the point.

Simon's growl crescendos until it turns into an all-out roar.

"You're wrong, stupid defective! I'll show you what a truly accelerated being can do!"

I moan as Simon grabs my forearm and drags me against the chapel's wet and jagged floor. The rain is pouring even harder through the cracks and exposed spaces in the ceiling.

Simon tightens his grip, then we're airborne.

Up and up we go, flying higher and higher toward the circular display of stained glass set in the top of the chapel. Simon flies faster, and I'm afraid he isn't holding back.

I close my eyes when Simon's fist bursts through the colorful dome. The beautiful angel shatters into a puzzle of glass shards. I cover my face to protect against the pieces, but I'm unable to tell if I've been cut.

Thunder booms, and the sky flashes blue with a spidery display of lightning. The rain hits me so hard I can barely open my eyes. The air grows frigid the higher we fly. I shiver and squint against the pelting raindrops. We're headed straight for the moon that appears to rest on the outer edge of the black storm cloud.

I look down, allowing my eyes to follow the trajectory of the falling raindrops. The chapel shrinks with each passing second. My insides feel hollow.

"What are you doing, Simon?" As I ask the question, the sky flashes with another bolt of blue lightning.

"I'm teaching you a lesson, defective! Never mess with business that isn't yours. You were never meant to be a part of this. You weren't worth the time."

If there has ever been a moment I've wished to have an accelerated ability, it's now. If I were an Atlas, I'd knock Simon out. If I were a Sky Glider, I'd fly to safety.

Simon must read my thoughts. "Who knows, Deficient? Maybe in your next lifetime you'll be born with an ability. Your death will be my gift to you. You'll finally be free from your sorry, unaccelerated existence."

I want to tell Simon that I don't want to die. That I'm not ready for it to happen, because I have a whole life ahead of me outside of Achewon. That it's not fair to take my life from me, because before this, I never would have thought of taking his away from him. I'm not like that. People—good people—aren't supposed to be like that.

I don't express any of that out loud though. I don't have to. I close my eyes and allow the combination of wind and rain to rush against my face. I think about the new friends I made who risked their lives for me and Yalamba and showed me I wasn't alone in all of this. I think about my family—my lovely mom and even my father and brothers who couldn't find it in their hearts to accept me for who I am. This will make life easier for them. For everyone.

Simon and I suddenly start free-falling toward the ground. I gasp. We fall for who knows how long until we pause in the middle of the sky. Simon has stopped our descent, but his grip on my forearm loosens until he's only holding me by my broken wrist.

"What the hell is going on? What are you doing, defective?"

"Nothing." I try to swallow my fear. Of course, I know what's happening. Mixie and Yalamba must have found the drawings, and they're destroying them—starting with the one that had granted Simon the power of an Atlas.

"My legs!" Simon yells. "My arms! What's happening?"

Simon tries flying higher, but his acceleration has slowed. His Racer ability is gone.

We drop again, guided by the rain. I feel like I've left my insides somewhere in the clouds. I can no longer breathe. Simon's grip slips from my wrist to my palm as he holds me with his regular, unaccelerated strength.

It's happening. It's really happening. But I don't want to die. I'm not ready. I've got to stop this.

"Go down, Simon! They're taking away your abilities!"

"Shut up, Deficient!"

"No, listen to me! You can't fly any higher! If you do, we're both going to die!"

"I *can* fly higher! I won't stop until I prove it to you all!"

Then it happens. Simon's body shakes and putters like a faulty engine. We drop for several more seconds. He stabilizes and putters some more, resisting gravity, before we drop further. Simon keeps fighting against the pull and squeezes out a few more inches.

All the while, Simon's fingers slip. From palm to knuckles. Knuckles to fingers.

And fingers to air.

I'm falling, and Simon is falling too.

It all happens in slow motion. Simon screams. His blue eyes bulge and his ghostly face contorts with fear. I observe the individual raindrops as they fall, tiny watery comets pelting from the blackened sky. I follow their pathway down. The chapel is closer than I expect, but still too far. I only have a few seconds to learn how to fly before I meet my end.

But I'm never going to fly. As much as I had hoped when I was little that I'd grow up to have an ability, it's not going to happen. That window shut long ago.

I am Alejandro Aragon, the Deficient of Achewon. I don't have any special abilities, and I never will. For all my life, that has been something I've held against myself. Defective. Lacking. Undesired. Untouchable. An error among *Homo sapiens*. A blemish in the tapestry of our supposedly advanced society.

Suddenly, however, I'm fine with that. I'm all right with the person I am and what I lack. I lived my life the best I could. Now it's time to move on. To change. Like the raindrops that guide me, losing themselves in the puddles below.

My body does the opposite of what I expect as death approaches. It relaxes. It reminds me of those soft few seconds before the mind slips into sleep and the spirit enters a world of nonsensical dreams.

I close my eyes and take one last breath before the stone floor greets me. I am gone.

CHAPTER NINETEEN
HEAVENS ABOVE ACHEWON

Tingling.

Heat.

Pain.

Release.

I can't see the waves, but I know they're bright red and untainted. They snap and flow, snap and flow, dancing through me like fiery ribbons.

Heat gathers at my crown, its energy condensing the longer it glows. Soon there's a halo of light above my head that spins in rapid circles before cracking. Heat streams from the halo, pouring through the rest of my body. Warmth floods my face and limbs. It gushes to the tips of my fingers and toes.

I don't want to open my eyes. It's like the perfect dream you never want to end. I want to remain here forever, enjoying the sensation of absolute peace.

But I hear the voices. They pull me toward somewhere far yet near, someplace strange yet familiar.

"What's going on?"

"I don't know. I don't know."

Something warm and moist hits my face. The drop is followed by another and another.

I hear commotion all around me. One person asks if she should call someone. Someone else says we have to calm down. Another tells them all to be quiet. He says he can finally hear me again.

Gradually, I open my eyes. I'm shocked to see a face staring at me. Dark skin. Wide but tired eyes. Ruffled black hair.

"Yalamba?" I ask.

"Alé!" Yalamba screams. "He's awake! He's really awake!"

I shake my head and sit up. My hands splash in something wet and warm. Too warm.

Red. Pure red. I'm in another puddle of blood. A recently spilled one, judging by its temperature.

"What's this?" I crawl away from the puddle, but the blood is everywhere, already seeping through my clothes.

Yalamba is still on her knees, and tears are falling from her sunken eyes. She stares at me as though I've sprouted seven heads.

"What did you do, Alé?"

I scratch my scalp, forgetting that my fingers have blood all over them.

"He doesn't know," Kazuki says. He's draped in a dark blanket. I have no idea where he got it. When we came to the chapel, he had been wearing his robe.

I examine the chapel's interior. It's illuminated with silver moonlight pouring in through the broken ceiling. Water droplets fall, but the rain has stopped.

Gwen and Mixie are here too. Mixie's clothes are covered in mud, and Gwen is injured and bloodied. She has two huge reddish-purple bruises—one on her forehead and one on her cheek. There's a bloody gash on one side of her face and red splotches on her neck and clothes.

Simon. Suddenly, I remember his power. Omniscience combined with almost every physical and mental ability one could fathom.

"Where is he?" I choke the words out.

The others lower their heads in near perfect synchrony. No one says anything. I'm not sure why they're speechless and still.

Yalamba is the first to move. She shuffles to the side, and her black boots splash in the blood. She points.

Simon's pale body lies broken on the chapel floor. His head is turned toward me, but I can't make out his features. It's not for lack of light—the moon is oddly bright. It's the blood. Simon's nose and mouth are covered entirely. There are more spatters on his ears, neck, and shoulders. His arms are completely red. Only a few patches of his skin are visible, white to the point of translucence.

Simon is surrounded by a puddle of his own blood just like me. But he's not moving.

I don't need to get any closer to know it's over. Simon Polk will never move again.

More memories rush back to me. Simon grabbing me and flying higher and higher. Breaking through the dome of stained glass. Soaring against the rain and wind as we drew closer to the inflated moon.

I wonder if he had been clearheaded enough to read my mind and realize it was all coming to an end. That we couldn't fly through the heavens above Achewon forever.

The moon casts a halo of light over Simon's dark hair. I've heard bodies are supposed to appear peaceful, but his face is frozen with the horror of his final moments.

"I can't believe it," Yalamba says. "I truly can't believe it."

"What don't you believe?" I ask.

"*You.* You're alive. But you were just…you were just…"

"I was just what?"

Yalamba swallows and her lower lip quivers.

"Dead."

Dead? The word sounds so odd. So final.

I turn once again to Simon's body. Then I re-examine the blood all around me, mixed with shards of glass from the shattered dome.

Is this really mine?

All of a sudden, I can feel my heart beating inside my chest.

Bum. Bum.

Bum. Bum.

It's the impossible beat of an organ that shouldn't be working, a rhythm that can only be felt by the living.

Yalamba crawls toward me, her hands and knees splashing in my blood. She takes my hand in hers and brings it to her heart. She laughs and cries, alternating between the two until I can't tell the difference between them. She wraps her arms around me and squeezes as tightly as she can.

"You're a miracle, Alé," she whispers.

I close my eyes. It's her. It's really and truly her. The friend I'd thought I had lost forever.

Yalamba squeezes my shoulders and pulls back so she can look at me.

"Do you know what this means?"

I shake my head. Of course, I don't. I've forgotten how to think.

"He really doesn't," Kazuki says.

Standing at his side, Gwen pokes her elbow into Kazuki's stomach. Kazuki bends forward and groans.

"Oh, be quiet," Gwen says. "I know that didn't hurt."

"I know," Kazuki says, "but I was expecting it to."

"Next time it will if you don't stop butting into people's minds."

I want to laugh, but I've forgotten how.

"I know what it means," someone else says.

Landon. I hadn't realized he was here too. His lip and eye are terribly swollen, and blood runs from his temple.

The sight crushes me. He sacrificed himself so I could reach Yalamba. He nearly died for that cause. My cause.

"You came back to life," Landon says. "People don't do that. Defect—"

I lower my head. To Landon's credit, he catches himself before finishing.

"People who don't have accelerated abilities don't do that," Landon says.

"What are you implying?" I ask.

"Maybe you're not a Deficient after all," Landon says softly. "This entire time we were wrong about you. I was wrong about you... Alejandro."

My jaw drops. I stare at Landon as though he's gone crazy.

"I think you're a Feral like me." Yalamba smiles. "There's no other explanation. You healed before our eyes. Even after you lost everything—your blood, your consciousness, your pulse. Alé, we thought you were gone forever."

Yalamba hugs me again. I still don't know what to do. I think about my body defying death as some sort of bizarre act—some strange ability I still can't be sure I have.

The tingling warmth stirs inside me once again. This time it's concentrated entirely in my heart.

Tears pour freely from my eyes as I embrace Yalamba. I don't care about what I have or haven't done. She's here. We saved her life, and that's all that matters. Who or what I am can wait until we have her back home, safe in the company of her family.

Flying is out of the question, so we decide to call our families. I'm reluctant to do that at first, given our recent blowup, but I think my mom would want to know that her son who died is okay. Plus, I'd been wrong to blame my brothers for Yalamba's disappearance. As hard as it is to admit, I owe them an apology in this situation, though I doubt they'd ever offer me one in return for all they've done to me over the years.

Yalamba's family is the first to pull up to the dirt road behind the trees. Following them are several Prefectural Security vehicles with their glowing blue-and-white lights. None of us called the authorities, but I assume the Koromas decided it was necessary.

The Koromas' vehicle hasn't even landed when Yalamba's mom exits. She sprints through the trees and straight to her daughter. They run toward one another and burst into tears the moment they embrace. Mr. Koroma emerges from the trees soon after and wraps his arms around his wife and daughter. They're all crying.

The sight makes me choke up. After all these years, I've never seen Yalamba's parents display this kind of affection toward their daughter.

It's not long before more people start coming through the woods. First, there's a stunning couple that must be Gwen's parents. Quinn, her biological mother, is practically glowing. I've never seen her appear this distraught though, not even in the movies she has starred in. Sparrow Williams, Gwen's other mother, is just as radiant with her dark, flawless complexion and caring eyes.

I see Kazuki's mother in a snow-white dress and matching sandals. She's accompanied by a short, modest-seeming man with glasses who looks like an older version of Kazuki.

Mixie's mom follows Kazuki's parents through the woods. She smiles when she sees me and runs over to give me a hug.

"You helped save another life it seems," Ms. Trait says. "You're getting very good at this, Alé."

I thank Ms. Trait, and she goes to find her daughter. My eyes water as I watch the displays of love playing out around me.

There's no sign of my family yet, but my mother answered my call right away. She told me she was worried sick about me and couldn't sleep. I know she'll be here soon. I wonder if my dad will come with her. Maybe now there's a way for us to put everything in the past and move on.

Nearly everyone has met up with their parents, but I'm not sure what to do with myself. I look to see if Landon's family has come, but I don't see them or Landon anywhere. I wonder where he went. Maybe he's speaking with Prefectural Security.

"Alé!" Yalamba calls.

She waves her hand, gesturing for me to join her and her parents.

Suddenly, I'm conscious of how disgusting I must look. I know I'm covered in dried blood and have scratches and bruises all over. I'm not in Yalamba's family's good books even when I'm sparkling clean. Bloody pulp isn't exactly the impression I'm hoping to give.

"Alé is the one who saved me," Yalamba says as I approach. "He used my identity band to find my sketchbook. He figured out the clues I drew and found out where Simon took me."

Ms. Koroma's face has gone glossy with tears. Meanwhile, Mr. Koroma looks at me with his cold, beady-eyed stare. His expression is blank. I can't tell if his mind has gone entirely void of thought from the shock of seeing his missing daughter or if he's furious that I took so long to figure out the mystery.

Mr. Koroma lifts his hand to me, and I flinch, expecting a strike. But he doesn't. Instead, he places it gently on my shoulder and speaks in the calmest tone I've ever heard him use.

"I could do a thousand favors for you each day from now until the end of time, and it would still never be enough to repay you," he says. "I am so terribly sorry for everything I did and said to you, Alejandro."

I have no idea what to do. I've never heard Mr. Koroma apologize to anyone, let alone me—someone I was sure he hated.

"He wants to shake your hand," Kazuki whispers in my ear.

I don't know when Kazuki managed to sneak up on me and started listening to my jumble of confused thoughts, but here he is.

I nod and raise my hand to Mr. Koroma's. Instead of merely shaking it, he grabs it tightly and pulls me into his embrace. Yalamba wraps an arm around me. I'm welcomed into the fold that is the Koroma family for the very first time.

"Can we give you a ride home?" Mr. Koroma asks.

I'm not sure what to tell him. I thought my mom was coming, but she should have been here by now.

Lights flashing through the trees catch my attention. My family's silver pod vehicle hovers in a few moments later. I consider running to greet them, but instead, I walk casually away from the Koromas and wait for them to come to me.

But it's not *them*. My mother has come alone.

"What on earth happened, Alé?" she asks as she runs from the trees. She wraps her arms around me, and I press my face into her shoulder. A part of me wants to melt into a puddle, but I know I've got to hold it together just a little longer.

Over my mom's shoulder, I see Kazuki speaking with his parents who look concerned. Mixie is in serious story-telling mode as she and her mom speak with the prefectural officers. Gwen's supermodel mothers inspect her wounds and apply ointments to their daughter's unflinching face. Landon is still nowhere to be seen.

And then there is Yalamba. She and her parents still haven't let go. Her parents' arms are wrapped tightly around the gift that is their daughter—a gift they never realized was so special until she was taken away.

I take a deep breath and remind myself that everything here is done. What happened to Yalamba, Simon, and all of us is over, and there's no going back.

"It's a long story, Mom," I finally say.

✷ ✷ ✷

The story of what happened at the chapel evolves over the course of several days. At first, the local newscasters sell me as the Deficient who saved the life of a Feral and solved the mystery behind a chain of hate crimes. Then it gets a twist. I am the Deficient who saved a Feral, solved the mystery behind a chain of hate crimes, and died and came back to life.

What pushes the story over the edge and into worldwide renown is the next twist. I wasn't just a Deficient who died and came back to life, saved a Feral, and solved a chain of hate crimes. Now I'm not even a Deficient at all. I'm a Feral who lived his entire life oblivious to that fact.

It's all ridiculous, but it has people talking on a very large scale. I've had to do countless netvision interviews, often in the company of Kazuki, Gwen, Mixie, Yalamba, and even Landon. The journalists hail us as heroes, and they can't get over the fact that I have an ability that enables me to come back from the dead. They ask me things like, "Can't you just hold your breath for a really long time to show us what happens?" Then they laugh it off as if it's the funniest thing ever. Some get all quiet and serious, looking at me as if they're waiting for me to go kill myself for them right then and there.

I take all sorts of exams and go through even more interviews with what seems like an endless number of wide-eyed scientists. They only confirm what I already know. My ability went undetected because, by nature, it's latent. For some reason, it didn't appear in my genetic makeup the way an active ability would in a normally accelerated person. My ability has never been documented before, and the scientists have labeled it as Renaissance, meaning rebirth.

I think the scientists were frustrated they couldn't do much to test my ability. They tried seeing if my body healed at a faster pace than others when it was injured, but that didn't seem to be the case. Paper cuts and pricks bled the way they always had, and they took just as long to heal as they would for anyone else. Beyond that, there wasn't much else they could do. I started having nightmares of mad scientists abducting and killing me as part of some top secret experiment, but fortunately, those never came true. Not yet anyway.

The scientists currently have no way to figure out the specifics of my ability or how it works when I die. But that's fine. I don't need to know more about it, nor do I want to. I still don't know if it's a onetime sort of thing or if I'm like a cat with nine or more lives to spare. I'm already down one, but I might have more to go if I'm lucky.

It seems like nearly everyone recognizes me at the academy and on the street. Their attention is completely foreign to me. Suddenly, I feel more visible than I ever have in over fifteen years of existence. People wave to me and introduce themselves at random. Some even offer me gifts or try to get their photos taken with me. For someone who grew up as a scourge to society, this new kind of spotlight is as overwhelming as it is unsettling.

I have no idea what this all means for me, my education, and my career. I never did make the deadline to influence my prefectural assignation. I'm not particularly drawn to working with the Truth and Justice Division now anyway, not after the way they fumbled the investigation. Instead, I'm leaving my path open. The future will fall into place when it needs to.

My mom has taken all the publicity and run with it. She's initiated a popular campaign to convince the Supreme Chancellorship that new laws have to be codified specifically for the Deficiently Accelerated, guaranteeing them equal rights—including the right to an education at all academic institutions. She's also demanding an end to the ability-based classification system if there's no way to guarantee someone's classification is 100 percent certain before the age of eight. She refers to Simon a lot. I'm not the only one who wonders if all of this could have been avoided had he been correctly classified long ago.

My father and brothers haven't helped out with the campaign, but with the newfound visibility and fame we're all getting, they have no choice but to take me back. That said, the welcome home isn't all that welcoming. My brothers listen to my apology, but they don't really respond to it. My dad and my brothers keep quiet around me now that I'm a Feral with a strange and cryptic ability. My mom tells me not to worry about them. They just need time. I'm not sure what they need time for exactly, but I guess I'll give it to them.

My feelings about my near daily netvision interviews are mixed. I know I'm not the greatest speaker. It would be one thing if I could write my words down and read them out loud, but people who watch netvision aren't patient enough for that kind of thing. They want spontaneity. Improvision. Pizzazz. Reading would also conflict with the show hosts' and journalists' proclivity for putting me on the spot with their invasive questions. They probe into things like my relationship with my family, how people treated me at the academy, and the worst stories I have from when I was a Deficient. It's all really personal, but they're thirsty for entertainment. I guess they figure I'll eventually spill something juicy if asked enough times.

The world seems to respond particularly well to Gwen. Of course, none of the attention affects her in the slightest since she still doesn't give a scheisse what anyone else thinks. More than one journalist tells her that she's the most beautiful woman in Region I if not the world. When that happens, Gwen resists the urge to knock out their teeth. Instead, she makes statements about the superficiality of our patriarchal culture before abandoning the interview and flying away, oftentimes with an especially lovesick Kazuki on her back.

Kazuki is still my second friend of all time. He's been unwavering, as he was when Yalamba was gone. He can still get on my nerves with his relentless mind reading and unsolicited psychological evaluations, but that's who he is. Many more people want to be friends with him now that he's so well-known, but with his Know-it-All ability, he can spot their motivations right away. He has me over to his housing unit every so often to see his dad's latest creations and share delicious meals. His mother even apologized for that time she didn't give me a ride home from the academy. Kazuki never lets her live that one down.

Headmaster Slaughter invited Mixie back to the academy, offering profuse apologies for the misunderstanding. After seeing everything Mixie went through and was able to overcome, not to mention what she did for us at the chapel, I can't think of many people who have earned their place at the academy more than she has.

Landon isn't the same after everything that has happened. He doesn't seem to like the limelight, and he isn't very vocal during interviews with journalists. He's distanced himself from his former group of Atlas friends, and whenever I see him walking around the Academy, he's usually alone.

He takes Yalamba, Gwen, Mixie, and me by surprise the day he sets his lunch down at our table and sits. I nearly choke on a bite of my seaweed wrap.

I don't know what to say, or even what I should do in his presence. Should I put my arms here or there? Should I sit up straight or sink into my chair, feigning relaxation?

He takes a bite of a toasted empanada doused in red sauce and peers at me with his umber gaze. I can't possibly hold eye contact with him, so I focus on my food.

I listen to the girls talk, like everything is normal, until I feel Landon tapping his foot on mine.

"Want to go for a walk in the courtyard?" he asks.

"Sure." Some privacy would do me well. I get up from the table and say bye to the others. I can't help but notice the slight grin playing on Gwen's lips. Yalamba winks at me and carries on with her conversation.

Once we're outside, Landon's demeanor shifts, and he communicates more openly.

"Look, Alé. I think I've owed you an apology for a very long time."

I have no idea what to say. I'm about as stunned as I was when I found out I had come back from the dead.

"I never meant to hurt you," Landon continues. "Well, maybe I did on one…or several occasions, but I'm not happy about it. Those feelings came from a terrible place. I want to say that I'm sorry, and I hope you'll be able to forgive me one day."

My attention is focused on the blades of grass. My mind goes blank. These are words I never thought I'd hear.

"You've really been horrible to me, Landon, but you came through for me and Yalamba, even before you knew I had an ability. Something has changed in you. It's a change for the better."

I want to keep my head lowered, but I remember what Kazuki and I had once agreed to about making eye contact. I bring my focus to Landon's brown eyes, but now he's the one having trouble looking at me.

"It's a work in progress. I can never take back all the terrible things I did, and I have to live with that. If I could turn back time and undo it all, I'd do it in a heartbeat."

Landon clears his throat. I can tell he wants to say something else, but he's having trouble finding his words.

"I think you're a good person," Landon says. "You always have been, even when we were little. I guess I thought if I could break you, then you'd turn out like me and all the other people who only cared about themselves. But you never broke. You never even came close. Now I know that the one who needed breaking was never you. It was me. It was all of us."

I smile. At the end of the day, Landon is still an Atlas, which means that he still has a very strong ego. But he's done something I've never heard another Atlas do, my father and brothers included. He has accepted his fault.

"Thanks, Landon. That means a lot."

Landon smiles, and we share a moment—a prolonged, mutual stare that I can't make myself break away from. For some reason, I feel like I'm looking at somebody new. Someone mature, changed, and in the strangest way, beautiful.

Landon takes a step forward. My eyes widen as he swoops in and places his lips on mine.

The only way I could be more shocked is if I ran into an electric fence. I try pulling away, but Landon pushes forward, keeping contact for a few more seconds.

Then he just stays there, waiting. His warm lips blanket mine, gentle and unforced. I close my eyes and listen. My mind is a white screen, but my heart beats in a way it never has before. Sensations surge through me I thought I couldn't possibly feel.

What they are, I don't know. But I know I like them. A lot.

It goes blurry after that. I kiss Landon back. We touch each other and laugh. The bell for next module beeps, and neither of us cares.

The kiss ends like a dream that I don't want to finish. When I open my eyes, Landon turns away. I can't help but notice the dimples in his cheeks as he fails to hide his grin.

"Sorry. I've been wanting to do that for a while," he says.

I don't know what to say. All I know is that something inside me has sparked, igniting a fire I have no desire to extinguish.

"Are you okay?" Landon asks.

I nod. "Confused…just confused."

"I'm not. I think we'll have time to sort it out."

"I think I'd like that."

Landon scratches at his hair twists and a few awkward seconds pass. "So have you been working on your dodgeball game lately?"

I laugh at the change in subject and shake my head.

"No, not really."

"You could practice with me after PE if you want. I can show you a few tricks that might help. You wouldn't be so bad if you made an effort, you know."

"Me…bad at dodgeball? That's news to me."

Landon laughs, his lips parting to reveal his straight teeth.

"How about Wednesday?" He raises his chin. Suddenly, it seems like his usual self-confidence is back. This time it feels different though. Authentic. Pure. Warm.

"Sounds great, Landon."

❋ ❋ ❋

After school I update Yalamba on what happened during lunch.

"It comes as no surprise to me, Alé. You know that. You're a beautiful person, inside and out. I'm glad Landon can see that too."

It feels strange to hear those words, even from someone as close to me as Yalamba is. Beautiful was the last thing I ever believed I could be.

She grins. "Besides, after everything that's happened, it's good that Landon is trying to make things a little more normal around here and less…crazy."

"I think we've had enough crazy to last a lifetime."

Yalamba's grin slips as she ponders for a moment.

"Enough *bad* crazy." Her face brightens. "There's plenty of time for good crazy."

Yalamba slides her backpack over her shoulder and pulls out her latest sketchbook. She opens it to a vivid sketch of her and me flying over the landscape of Achewon.

When I look up from the picture, I see the same mischievous glimmer in Yalamba's natural brown eyes that I remember from when we were kids. She takes my hand in hers and gives me a light tug. As my arm lifts into the air, I realize she's levitating.

"Yals." I pull back, and my heartbeat quickens. "What are you doing?"

"Don't be afraid, Alé. We're going for a ride."

I close my eyes. We both know what happened the last time I did that.

"Trust me," Yalamba whispers. "You have nothing to fear anymore. Just make a wish and fly."

I can't help but laugh. Yalamba, like me, knows what it feels like to teeter on the edge between life and death. She is absolutely mad, but I've always loved that about her.

I think about my wish, but it's hard to come up with anything when my biggest wish has already come true. Yalamba is still with me. I can see her smile and hear her laugh—simple things that were nearly gone for good. I didn't need some miraculous ability to make that happen. The universe has a weird way of orchestrating those kinds of things. If we know what we want—a clear, unambiguous, and heartfelt wish—then unseen forces will work their magic, doing their best to give those dreams form.

They have to. What else can explain the liberating sensation I feel when my toes rise from the earth and I fly through the air next to my best friend? I squint against the wind and light as we soar toward the sun with invisible wings.

Looking from on high at Achewon's vast, green expanses below, there's nothing more I can ask for. At least not from this existence. The pieces of my reality have arranged themselves into a completed puzzle that I'd never change—not even if someone handed me a box of brand-new pieces for the exact same scene. I find value in the old ones with their wrinkles and those places where the stickers have lifted from the cardboard. Those are the pieces that make history—a legend that contains value in each and every detail.

ACKNOWLEDGMENTS

I wrote the first draft of *Deficient* from 2011 to 2012 when I was working for the Organization for Youth Empowerment (OYE Adelante Jovenes) in El Progreso, Honduras. My time with OYE was life-changing professionally and personally, and working with youth on a variety of issues, including creative writing, gave me the inspiration—and audacity—I needed to write a young adult, sci-fi book like *Deficient*.

I loved El Progreso, but it presented challenges to the young people who called it home. It sat in the shadow of a city that was then called the murder capital of the world. During the day, the markets were bustling, colorful places with *baleada* stands on most corners and where fruit sellers would greet me on a first name basis. As soon as the sun set, though, the scene took a haunting turn. The streets went cryptically dark, without a person to be seen or a whisper to be heard. Gang violence was common, poverty levels were high, and a shocking number of youth were classified as *ni-ni*—neither studying nor working. The solution for many was to take the perilous journey north to the United States in search of an often-elusive American dream. An unknown number would never make it there, with several returning with lost limbs from their train journeys or, in the worst cases, losing their lives along the way.

The sensation of powerlessness in the face of such extraordinarily difficult circumstances was very real, but so was the determination to persevere and overcome. Many of the youth I met possessed a sense of resilience that seemed supernatural. That resilience is what I believe we must all tap into if we're to survive the tumultuous years of adolescence, though we require it in different measures given the size and scope of the challenges we face. My desire to capture this quality in a futuristic setting is what sparked *Deficient*. I wanted Alejandro to channel exactly what the young people of El Progreso embodied. I also wanted him to represent anyone struggling to make sense of growing up in a world that can be cruel and unfair—someone who looks everywhere but inside for the answers until inside becomes the only place left for discovery.

So thank you, Honduras. Thank you, El Progreso. And thank you to everyone I met at OYE, including Justin Eldridge Otero, Ana Luisa Ahern, and Patrick and Trish Ahern.

Muchas gracias to my favorite renaissance man and Catracho, the legendary Guillermo Mahchi, for housing me in *La Mansión* in El Progreso, where the first draft of this book was born. That little plaza with its vibrant, Mayan/Buddhist inspired paintings, apothecary with meticulously arranged potions, and open-air design that welcomed the moon and stars, was the best writing space I've ever had. Thanks to mi madre hondureña, Yvonne Delgado, for introducing me to several inspiring Honduran artists and for being a wonderful yoga partner. And thank you to my favorite dragon lady, Jenny Zuñiga, for your tough love and giving my butt the kick it needed.

Thanks to various readers who have read and commented on the book, with a big hug to Patriece Nelson, who always carves out time to read my work and provide critical and honest feedback. Thanks also to Dan Gwinnell for hunting me down until I shared my manuscript and for reflecting on it so thoughtfully, Cassie Farrelly for your energy, ideas, and enthusiasm, and Quinton Sloan for sharing your views on *Deficient* from a hammock in Lamu.

My initial attempts at publishing were rocky, probably because the book wasn't ready yet, and I found myself editing it over the course of a decade. Thanks to the publishers and editors who read versions of the manuscript and, even when rejecting it, gave thoughtful advice for how it could be strengthened.

While living in Sierra Leone, a few years went by when life and work became so intense that writing took a back seat. As I neared the end of my sixth year there, Patriece Nelson checked in and asked: "Are you still writing?" Double thanks to you Patriece. I had nearly lost hope at that stage but decided to give publication another go, with a lot of encouragement from Lucy Timmons, the best coach on Earth. I returned to my manuscript, giving it the time and attention it needed, refining it, strengthening it, and filling it with new life.

After going through the literary agency experience once, I decided to try my hand with independent publishers, and that was where the magic happened. Thanks to BHC Press for being the publisher who stood up for *Deficient*. As Lady Gaga once said (on numerous occasions), "There can be one hundred people in a room and ninety-nine of them don't believe in you, but all it takes is one." In my case, I had two. Joni and Vern Firestone believed in me and *Deficient* and helped bring this book into the light, and for that I will be forever grateful. Thank you also for promoting the voices and perspectives of LGBTQI+ authors. Our voices matter. Special thanks to the book's professional editors, Stephanie Bennett, Chris Frentzen, and Grace Nehls—I loved working with you and appreciate all you did to help me make *Deficient* shine.

Family and friends, thank you. Thanks to my parents, Leah and Merced, for your unwavering support throughout my life. Mark and Alisa, thanks for checking in on my writing every so often—it means a lot. It has been a gift to get to see you grow on my periodic visits home, Lucas, Sophia, and Caiden, and I hope you can find some meaning and magic in this book when you read it. To Joanne Robinett and Dagmar Oette, thanks for gifting me a writing journal after I graduated from college, and thanks Darcey Lund for asking about my writing every time we met.

Thanks to Tara Lyons, my first Yalamba, for telling me the first draft of the accelerated dodgeball match was way too long. I dedicated this book to you, because you gave me several of the childhood memories that filled its pages. (And yes, for the record, SUNNOT was an actual thing!) I hope Dylan and Tyler enjoy the story too.

And thanks to Yalamba Koroma for being you. You are a star and were such a rock for me in Sierra Leone that I knew you needed to be Alé's bestie in Achewon. I hope Kamal can read *Deficient* one day and see how awesome his mother has always been, even in fiction. (Who runs the world? YALAMBA!)

Thanks to Jackie Hehir and Katy O'Donnell—Jackie for being another Yalamba in my adolescence and life and for connecting me to Katy, who gave several helpful insights along the publication journey.

And thanks for the friends who let me couch surf in your homes during my younger years and who created space for me to get my creativity on—Lauren and Jon Parnell Marino and Rebekah Emanuel, to name a few. Thanks to Trina Vargo and Mary Lou Hartman for helping me meet these wonderful spirits through the US-Ireland Alliance and connecting me to a volunteer experience with Fighting Words in Dublin, which inspired me to pursue work in youth empowerment in Honduras. Thanks to Ryan Dick for always being a fan of my fantasy and sci-fi, even in its rawest forms. A big thanks to Mohsin Ali for being my communications and publicity guru, and Sorcha Fennell for encouraging my passion and linking me with your brilliant sister, Natasha Fennell. And thank you to other dear friends like Danny Arnold, Angela Lytle, Johar Singh, Carol Wrenn, Emma Newbury, Emma Warwick and the Irish mafia, Janieke Drent, Kelly Brady, Morgan Kennedy, Tatum Lenahan, and many others for being so supportive of my creative endeavors and this project. Thanks to the Campbell-Coelho clan (Heather, Nelson, Calvin, and Liam) and Kobi Bentley for our sci-fi/fantasy + Booker Prize winner writing group (may it rest in peace), and for helping me get through Covid with my mental health intact.

And arigato gozaimasu to Mary "Mez" Trait, you artist extraordinaire you! I love absolutely everything about how you have captured my characters over the years. And thanks to BHC Press for *Deficient's* killer book cover.

And of course, thanks to the supernatural readers of *Deficient* for giving it your time and attention. I fought to bring *Deficient* to a broader audience because I felt it was a story with characters and messages worth sharing. I hope you found something special in it. If you didn't but managed to make it this far, then wow. Your perseverance is extraordinary. You might just be a Feral...

ABOUT THE AUTHOR

Michael Solis is from New Jersey and currently lives in Nairobi, Kenya. He has spent most of the past fifteen years working in development and humanitarianism in Sierra Leone and Latin America. A Princeton graduate, he has master's degrees in human rights law and gender studies. While traveling, he fell in love with telling thought-provoking stories based on his personal experiences. *Deficient* is his debut novel.